SCUDDER'S GORGE

Geoffrey Craig

Acknowledgements: I would like to thank my friends and family for their support and encouragement over the years, and especially those who critiqued the manuscript. Special appreciation is extended to Nick and Anita Danigelis, whose invaluable research contributions enhanced this novel. I would also like to express my appreciation to everyone else who assisted in various ways, through research, brainstorming, or just plain listening to me while I was on this journey. The responsibility for any factual errors is, of course, entirely my own. Finally, I want to express my appreciation to Glenn Lyvers and April Zipser, Publisher and Editors at Prolific Press, for their encouragement and dedication to bringing this novel to market. Their edits, advice, and friendship have challenged and enhanced my experience as a writer, and greatly improved the finished product.

Scudder's Gorge
Geoffrey Craig
©2016 Geoffrey Craig

ISBN: 978-1-63275-055-6
Edited by Glenn Lyvers and April Zipser
Published by Prolific Press Inc.
Harborton, VA
Printed in the USA

For Danielle, Barbara, and Stacey
with love and many thanks.

Table of Contents:

Prologue

ETSUKO HAYATO

(1877 – 1945)

August 6, 1945

Etsuko Hayato had not slept well. Sirens sounded throughout the night, and he tossed and turned on his thin futon. It was still dark when he sighed and carefully folded the cotton mattress, placing it in a lacquered chest. He re-read the war stories in yesterday's newspaper.

When his wife died, Etsuko moved in with his older son and daughter-in-law, both of whom worked in munitions plants in the city. Etsuko's second son was in the navy, and his wife also lived with Etsuko's older son who was at sea early in the war but was now at the nearby Kure Naval Base. It was a comfort to Etsuko to live with his family, even if the wooden house was rather small. It did have a vegetable garden and shrine in the back. Etsuko spent a lot of time in the garden.

He had three grandchildren, two boys and a girl. One grandson had been killed at Okinawa. The last letter from his other grandson was dated three months earlier. It said nothing about his situation, except that he had been promoted to captain. His granddaughter, a schoolteacher, had been evacuated from Hiroshima, along with her pupils, to a rural temple.

Etsuko knew he was fortunate to have both sons alive, and to be living with one while seeing the other several times a month. His daughters-in-law were pearls. He grieved for his grandson, but other families had suffered more. His friend, Mitsuo, had lost all three of his sons.

Hiroshima had not been hit hard by the allies, despite its military facilities. Fortunately, its government hadn't demolished the houses in his neighborhood to create a fire lane. Etsuko murmured a prayer of gratitude as he knelt on a tatami while his daughter-in-law served him a

1

cup of tea and a small bowl of rice topped with pickled vegetables. At seven, the radio broadcast an air raid alert. Everyone froze - utensils in mid-air. They all rushed from the house and searched the clear sky. Would this be the day when terror and destruction rained down on Hiroshima? They started for the shelter, but no huge B-29s droned overhead. Instead, a lone plane – clearly not a bomber – circled the city.

They waited outside the shelter, talking to neighbors, still anxiously scanning the skies. At seven-thirty, his son, Jotaro, decided that the danger was past. He and his wife took a tram to work. Etsuko's other daughter-in-law returned to clean up the breakfast dishes before going downtown to her job in a government office.

After inviting the neighbors to come over that evening for a glass of precious sake, Etsuko took a walk. He did not have to report to his fire warden's station until ten. Perhaps he would find some fruit in a shop. With the disappearance of so many commodities, their diet had become bland and meager. He walked through narrow lanes crowded with small houses. After his restless night, it felt good to use his legs. The morning sun was warm on his face.

Having lost one grandson, he wondered, as he did frequently, if the rest of his family would survive the war. He revered the Emperor, and initially supported the war as vital to Japan's interests, but the loss of lives, the physical destruction, and the rending of the fabric of Japanese society had been overwhelming. Etsuko sadly concluded that the time for surrender might have arrived.

Japan's sun would rise from the ashes and shine more brightly than ever, but it was far too dangerous to utter such thoughts. He prayed, instead, that the Emperor, the living God, would seek an honorable peace. Otherwise, they must fight on. Japan must never abandon the 'Divine One' who ruled over the sacred homeland.

He saw a few yellow flowers growing in a scrap of yard, and smiled. He wished he could identify the flowers. He had worked as a mid-level manager in one of the big zaibatsu for forty-four years. Now that he was retired, he would devote some time to studying nature. His wife, Shizue, had worked miracles with flower arrangements.

He stopped briefly at a small temple with curved, red beams protruding over the lane. He prayed in memory of Shizue, and for the safety of his family. It would be a clear, hot day. Through an open window, he heard the radio blare another air raid warning. He glanced at his watch; it was just past eight. There was no sign of bombers, but perhaps he should go home. He started down the lane and, noticing the drone of an airplane, quickened his pace. He hurried past an empty school with a small patch of sweet potatoes growing in the yard.

The engines sounded louder. He stopped and looked up. He saw one large plane followed by two smaller ones. They were almost overhead. He was panting. His heart and lungs were not what they used to be. He saw a white parachute fall from the large plane; he watched it drift slowly downward. How curious; it must not be a bomb.

For an instant, he saw a blinding flash and heard an earth-shattering explosion. The world went black, and Etsuko Hayato's dust mingled with a mushroom-shaped cloud.

Chapter One

September 7, 1799

It was not the first time she had seen him. The first time was two weeks earlier on a pristine June day in 1799 when she went berry picking with her sister, Carrie. They set out early, each swinging a wooden bucket with a deerskin strap. Having learned to shoot at an early age, Philomena carried a musket slung across her back to protect them from the few remaining bears and wolves.

The sun was just climbing over the ridge. It was still cool. A mantle of fog straddled the ridgeline, and mist rose from the fields. Passing the log cabins of the settlement, they saw smoke from stone chimneys thickening the air. They breathed deeply the tantalizing odor of roasting venison and rabbit. Anxious to be on their way, they hurried through their breakfast of cold corn mush and milk. Their mother laughed and said they could do their chores when they returned.

The first of the settlers had arrived in sparsely settled, Northern Vermont four years ago. Since then, they had experienced good relations with the handful of Abenaki Indians that lived at the northern end of the valley. Thickly forested hills climbed above the Abenaki village, gradually at first, and then angling up sharply to reach a cascade that crashed through a steep gorge into a clear, icy pool.

The settlers located their cluster of cabins in a bend on the east bank of the river that flowed down from the gorge and bisected the valley. Six miles southeast of the Abenaki wigwams, the settlement was in the center of the valley. While most of their homes huddled together like cattle in a storm, several recent settlers built log houses along a muddy, rutted road that extended north and south from the settlement.

The settlers arrived in the valley with several cows and six sheep. They planned to start a flock and use the wool for clothes, blankets, and eventual sale to the towns of northern Massachusetts. Four oxen had laboriously pulled two wagons over the rocky hills and through the lush, green valleys. Crammed into the wood-slated wagons were a variety of tools and farm implements – hammers, saws, axes, hoes, two ploughs – and two pairs of baby pigs, a dozen chickens, and chests of clothes and household goods. The pigs squealed and the chickens cawed as the wagons bumped over the rough terrain. Tied to one wagon, Lucas Scudder's young Holstein bull let out an occasional bellow as if in protest against the loss of Massachusetts' comforts.

Cornfields now spread out on both sides of the river. Young apple trees grew in a communal orchard to the east of the village. Each cabin had a vegetable plot in the back and chickens scratching in front.

Lucas Scudder and Dexter Forshay had guided the first ten families north through the Connecticut River Valley. Skirting the Green Mountains, they passed Brattleboro, Windsor, and Norwich to settle on a land grant issued almost ten years earlier by the then independent Republic of Vermont. The site, south of Craftsbury, was in a hilly area crisscrossed by ridges, valleys, and frothing streams. Through the summers of stinging flies, the winters of razor-like cold, and the monotonous fare of the first years, Lucas had rallied the settlers. Determined to succeed, he dissuaded several families from retreating to Massachusetts. Though stiff-necked and Puritanical, he let no family go hungry, sharing his game with less skilled hunters.

Lucas had grown tired of working for his father and oldest brother in Northfield. To his way of thinking, Massachusetts had grown crowded and could not give him scope for his vision of a thriving settlement carved out of the wilderness. He saw himself as a builder, a creator on a grand scale. He expected that the town would eventually be named after him.

Almost as soon as they had built their homes, the settlers erected a crude log building to serve as a church. Lucas, Dexter, and Owen Harding served as elders and, in the absence of a parson, took turns reading scripture and preaching at meetings. After a year, they constructed a gristmill by the river, and a year later, a primitive sawmill to trim the logs they cut for their homes. New families arrived every year, and now there were over twenty.

The settlers lived much like the Abenaki who, early on, had come to trade. While most Abenaki spoke passable French, a few also knew a little English. Relations were peaceful, and one of the settlers, Israel Smythe, whose wife had died from a rattlesnake bite the second summer, had married an Abenaki woman. They had a baby boy and were expecting another child in a few months. The settler's two older children were delighted with their baby brother, and ran to play with him as soon as they finished their chores.

The first rays of the sun felt good on the backs of Philomena and Carrie. It would warm up shortly, and the mosquitoes and black flies would come out, causing them to brush at their faces constantly, unless a breeze sprang up to carry off the pests. They wore long dresses of drab brown, a bit the worse for wear, and white aprons. They had on stout shoes to navigate the stony meadows and low-lying marshes. Their white caps, with a flounce along the edge, would protect them from the sun and deter the less determined insects.

The sky was a washed-out blue and paler along the ridges. After leaving the settlement, they heard only birdcalls and the sound of their own tramping feet. They crossed the log bridge that led to the western bank of the river. The best berry patches on the eastern side had already been scoured. Looking downstream, they noticed Josiah Royce urinating in the river. Neither girl blushed; it was a common sight. They could have skirted the cornfields and passed through meadows strewn with purple clover and yellow dandelions, but they loved the queer feeling of walking between the rows of thin-stalked plants—their world narrowed to curving leaves and the shimmering sky.

Before entering the cornfield, Philomena glanced north, towards the gorge. She had only been there a couple of times. Last summer, on an exceptionally hot Sunday afternoon, two adults had treated a group of youngsters to an expedition to the pool below the cascade. The boys had stripped to their trousers and jumped in, screaming with delighted shock as they hit the frigid water. The younger girls had swum in their under garments. At seventeen, Philomena had refused to do more than sit on the mossy bank and dangle her bare feet and ankles in the foam-flecked pool.

A dry summer, the adults judged the current flowing through the pool slow enough for the children to swim. Normally, they went to a crook in the river a mile below the settlement. Even at that quiet spot, a boy almost drowned when he ventured near the center of the flow. An older lad cut diagonally downstream, blocked the flailing boy, and pulled him out of the swift current.

Talking intently, Philomena and Carrie hurried along the rows of corn – sidestepping the numerous stumps that dotted the field like flotsam from a shipwreck. They were exhilarated by the bright morning, their solitary excursion, and the rare treat of having chores postponed. Later, Philomena would churn the butter and Carrie would finish her spinning. Philomena loved and confided in her sister. She knew that Seth Lawrence was in love with her. He always contrived to be around her after meeting; and last Sunday, he had been staring at her when she glanced up during a hymn. Her mother had tugged at her sleeve and nodded brusquely at the hymnbook. His attentions thrilled but also bothered her.

"Are you going to marry him?" asked Carrie, trying to be serious but unable to contain a giggle.

"I don't want to get married at eighteen."

"Abby Brewster was eighteen, and Cousin Samantha back in Northfield was seventeen."

"I'm not Abby Brewster – eyeing every boy in the village until she finally hooked beetle-browed Ezra Royce."

Carrie laughed – low and mischievously.

"Pretty soon they'll call you a spinster."

"I don't care what those stringy women with clacking tongues call me. There's lots I want to do before I get married and have a passel of children."

"What's there to do around here except chores and church? Oh, I forgot – corn husking and the harvest dance. Splendid."

"Who said around here, ninny? I want to see someplace other than this valley. Maybe I'll go visit Grandpa. I bet there's lots to do in Northfield."

"Do you like it here?"

Philomena gave no answer as they left the cornfields and crossed into a sloping meadow. She was troubled by Carrie's question. She was expected to marry, raise children, share the farm work with her husband, and take care of her parents when they grew older. That was supposed to constitute a good life, but something was missing. She felt at odds with herself.

"Answer me," said Carrie. "Do you like living here?"

"I do; but then again, I don't. I want something to happen that's different, that's exciting. Seth Lawrence is not exciting."

"You're being ... eighteen."

"Sixteen is the fountain of wisdom? Or maybe God touched you?"

"No, but he will you," shouted Carrie.

She jumped on her sister's back, riding around and pummeling her as if she were an unruly horse. Philomena shrieked and, pulling her sister's skirt, fell to the ground – rolling over on top of her. They wrestled for a few minutes, laughing excitedly, and then stopped, breathing heavily.

"What if Papa saw us?" asked Philomena. "He would consider our behavior quite undignified."

"He would not. We're farm girls, not city women. He'd think it funny."

"I don't know. He's so stern."

"You have to make him laugh," said Carrie.

They continued across the meadow and reached a wooded area replete with raspberry and blackberry bushes. They began filling their buckets. A reddish purple stained their fingertips. Philomena leaned her head back, opened wide, and dropped two blackberries the size of acorns into her full-lipped mouth. They swiped at hovering, whining mosquitoes and picked intently. Dew sparkled from webs in the grass and soaked their shoes. Small birds twittered and hopped about in the thickets bordering the meadow. The sun began to heat their bent backs. When she stood up to stretch and adjust the musket, Philomena felt a bead of sweat trickle down her spine. She liked the sensation.

"What do you think it would be like to be married?" she asked.

Carrie stared at Philomena as if she had just stepped naked from a bath.

"I mean to lie with a man." Philomena waited a second and then turned back to the bush, "You're too young to think about it."

"I think about it a lot. I can hear Mother and Father even though they try to be very quiet. It must be exciting – and pleasurable."

"It must be," said Philomena, "with the right man at the right time." She idly plucked a berry and ate it. "Have you ever ... you know ... touched...?"

Carrie looked at her bucket and then boldly at her sister. "Yes. Have you?"

"Yes."

Absorbed again in stripping the heavy clusters of ripe berries, they fell silent. A few minutes later, Philomena picked an immense raspberry and held it up for Carrie to see.

"Open the door," she laughed and placed it carefully on Carrie's waiting tongue.

"It will never do to eat all the best ones," admonished Carrie, who nevertheless could not suppress a grin.

"We've just eaten a few, and we'll keep it a secret. Surely, that's not much of a sin."

They moved along the edge of the woods. After an hour, their buckets were three-quarters full. Their arms and backs were sore. Philomena suddenly felt uneasy; the back of her neck tingled. She looked into the forest. The maple leaves were a satiny green. Broad sunbeams struck the thick pine trunks. Nothing moved except a grey squirrel dashing from one tree to the next. She shrugged. Then she saw him standing in the shadows, almost invisible and perfectly still. He was watching them, no expression on his lean face. He was tall and looked a few years older. He had glossy, black hair tied behind his head. He wore a buckskin shirt, trousers, and carried a bow. In his other hand, he held a large rabbit.

Philomena exclaimed, "Oh!"

Carrie looked up, "What is it?" Looking in the direction her sister was facing, she saw the Abenaki. Neither girl spoke for a few seconds, and then Carrie smiled and said, "Good morning."

The young man replied awkwardly, "Good morning." He turned and strode into the forest.

"Mama," shouted Carrie as she burst into the cabin carrying a full bucket of berries, "we saw an Abenaki in the woods. He was carrying a rabbit he had shot with his bow." She put the bucket on table. "He was handsome."

"What's that about an Abenaki?" asked Lucas as he ducked into the cabin. He had been clearing a new field to plant with wheat in the spring – the first wheat in the settlement. His hands were blackened from burning and digging out a large stump; his face was streaked with grime. Caleb and Samuel followed him.

Martha glanced quickly at her husband. "Philomena and Carrie saw an Abenaki when they went berry picking."

Lucas looked queerly at his daughters.

"They have been friendly these past four years, but they can be treacherous. They've been known to make off with captives. In future, stay close."

"You girls have had enough fun," said Martha. "The vegetable garden needs weeding – and bring me squash for the stew. Feed the pigs and milk Harriet. Mr. Scudder and the boys will wash and have a dish of samp with honey. Then it's lesson time."

She grinned at the boys and placed a hand on Lucas's arm.

"Your father will help."

"Of course," said Lucas, "seeing as I was so good with my own lessons."

"You were better than some," laughed Martha.

Two weeks later, on a nippy morning with fat clouds scudding above the ridges and larks dipping and skimming over the meadows, Philomena churned butter and then headed to the orchard to check on the young trees. She carried a bucket of potash to spread around the smallest trees. Her father, who had heard of the leaching process patented in Burlington nine years ago, had asked Jedediah Tanner (who was not much good at farming) to convert ashes from fireplaces and stump burnings into potash. Bartering the fertilizer for butter, cheese, and vegetables kept Jedediah's family of five from having to subsist on his poorly tended corn.

Doing chores these past two weeks, Philomena had often thought of the young Abenaki and looked across the valley towards the north. Ignoring her father's warning, she gathered berries below the western ridge one afternoon, but didn't see him. Now her mind was on the upcoming social as she spread the flaky potash with a wooden trowel. The older trees would start bearing fruit in three to four years, and they would have cider again. Glowing memories came to her: the sharp fall days on her grandfather's farm, the tangy smell of apple juice pressed through a cloth, and the sweetness of cold cider. Most of the apple crop was made into hard cider for the taverns, but part had been saved for the children.

He was there; she knew it before she saw him. She was kneeling by a tree and stood up quickly. He was standing at the far end of the orchard, the sun glinting on his copper cheeks. He carried his bow and some pelts. They looked at each other for a moment, and then he stepped forward.

"Good morning," she said.

"Good morning, Miss Scudder."

"Your English sounds very good," she said, looking directly at him. "How do you know my name?"

"We know that your father is the big chief of the settlement. I learned a little English in the country to the north. I went to school with the white medicine men in the black robes. They taught French, but many people also spoke English."

"You mean Canada?"

"Yes, Canada. That is what the English call it."

"What is it like?"

"The same as here - only colder."

"I would like to go to Canada," she said wistfully.

As he approached her, she could see his dark eyes. He looked at her intently and then reached into a pouch slung over his shoulder.

He handed her two wampum strings attached to an eagle feather.

"Thank you," she said. "It's beautiful. What is your name?"

"Susuph."

It began that simply. Through the rest of June and all of July, she saw him more and more frequently. They seemed casual meetings, but she knew that if she went berry picking – musket always slung across her back - or walked along the river to gather wild flowers for the table, he would appear at some spot where they could not be easily seen. She never understood how he knew where she would be. As they talked, his English improved and his vocabulary expanded. He was inquisitive and wanted to know the words for many things. He asked her about her Great Spirit and about books, which he had seen and touched in the school. He thought they were magical. Although he had not stayed long enough to learn to read, he knew that they expressed what was in the minds of men.

"And women," she added, a bit tartly.

"Of course," he replied. "The Abenaki respect women, not like some tribes. They have important work. But they rarely speak in council. Our village is small and poor. It is not like earlier times. The Abenaki have lost much. Many have died – from the wars and the white man's diseases. At least, that is what the old men say."

He told her about the travels of his people, and how they had first come to the valley for spring fishing and fall hunting. Many years previously, they had abandoned a village by the river. Eight years ago, when he was fifteen, the elders decided to reestablish a permanent village, this time in the forest. They hoped for security in the isolated valley so that the village could grow. They wanted many children. They planned to avoid being absorbed into white settlements as had happened to Abenaki bands throughout Vermont. Like her people, they cultivated corn, beans, and vegetables. The hunting and fishing in the valley was excellent – as long as they took care not to decimate the game, but they still traveled to seasonal camps in the hills for a few weeks in the spring and fall.

When the settlers came, his people had been worried. But the settlers seemed friendly, and traded, so the elders had decided to be patient, to establish good relations and not to fight.

"We would wait and see," said Susuph. "We were anyway not sufficiently armed to fight."

"There must always be peace between our peoples," she said, touching his hand lightly.

She told him about the big towns to the south that she had seen as they were coming north from Massachusetts. She told him about her grandfather's farm with the fine cattle and horses, the pigs, the corn and wheat fields and the beautiful apple orchards. She described how the farm was laid out with big stone walls separating the different fields. She told him how she and her cousins loved to play in the hayloft - rolling around and getting bits of hay stuck in their hair and clothes - and how she loved the dry, musty smell and the feeling of being hidden away from the world of adults. When they played hide and seek in the barn, she would burrow under a pile of hay and stay very still. He told her about the games that Abenaki children played. He told her about the time he had killed a bear with his friend Apom.

"Why do you hunt with a bow instead of a musket?" she asked him.

"Muskets and the lead to make the musket balls are scarce. We must use the few we have wisely."

She asked him once if he were married. They were sitting in a clearing. Her bucket was a quarter filled with blueberries and whortleberries; her musket lay beside the bucket. His bow and quiver lay nearby. He got up and walked to the edge of the clearing. He looked out over the tall grass of a meadow, lost in thought, and then came back to sit beside her.

"Yes, once, but she died in childbirth."

"Oh," was all she said, putting her hand on his.

"And the baby?"

"She died too."

"She's walking out with Seth Lawrence," said Martha as she stirred the venison stew and set a loaf of hot corn bread on the hob.

Lucas walked back and forth in front of the fireplace smoking his long white pipe. His father sent him tobacco with the rider that brought mail to the settlement once a month. The sweet odor mingled with the aroma of the stew and filled the kitchen with a smell that calmed his mind. The boys were playing tag in front of the cabin. Carrie had gone to the Forshay's farm about a quarter of a mile away. It was a sweltering evening in early July—not a breath of air stirred in the cabin.

"Seth Lawrence is a hard worker," Lucas commented. "It would be a good match. His family has substance – a promising farm." He paused. "You don't think they ... do you?" He and Martha had been married for twenty years, but there were topics they did not discuss directly.

Martha smiled inwardly. Her husband was, in many ways, a good if naive man, devout, hardworking, and generous to those in need.

Several families had been able to join the settlers because he had loaned them funds. He never asked to be repaid. No settler was turned away who came to his door asking for advice or help. At such times, Lucas was a patient listener, and his advice was generally sound. Above all else, however, Lucas was determined to make a name for himself. He had despised being the youngest of four children. In spite of the farm's ample size, his father had not thought it large enough to divide and remain profitable so he had left it to Mathew, the oldest, with the understanding that the other children would live and work there. His brother had given him important responsibilities on the Northfield farm, but not being "master" gnawed at Lucas. He picked at it like a scab. Lucas was also narrow-minded, like a Puritan, and he had a violent streak that Martha feared. She once saw him knock a man to the ground simply because the man failed to tip his hat and then made an insulting remark when Lucas called him on his manners.

Martha had an open, sunny nature, at peace with the world and her place in it. She had not wanted to come to the frontier - to give up the civilized, comfortable life in Northfield with the friends of her childhood. But Lucas was set on going, and now that she was there, she accepted the life – with grace if not sheer joy. She liked the other settlers – simple, pious, earthy people. If they were not quite her social equals, at least they were honest, hardworking, and straightforward. Sometimes she had found Northfield society a little too sure of itself. Life in the settlement was hard, but the valley held great promise.

"No," Martha replied. "They are both God-fearing and proper young folk. They will wait for the blessing of the church – just as we did – unlike many of our friends who found a simple ring blessing enough."

"Indeed we did." Lucas stared incredulously at his wife, "Would you have wanted to do otherwise?"

"You were so handsome and dashing that it wasn't easy to resist temptation." She laughed softly, as if at some private joke, "I didn't want to shock you. You might not have married me."

Lucas puffed on his pipe and turned to the fireplace where a small fire was burning despite the July heat. Given how difficult it could be to start a fire, the settlers kept one continuously burning.

"Why, the very thought of such a sin! Indeed, I would not have..." He looked at his wife, who smiled coyly, and huffed, "It is not a matter for joking – or teasing me about." Seeing that Martha was still smiling, he crammed on his broad-brimmed hat and started for the door. He stopped and turned around. "Have it your way. Tease me if it pleases you." He thought for a second, "Yes, I would still have married you, although I would have seen to it that we resisted temptation." He laughed, "Both of our temptations."

He walked out of the cabin and told the boys to do something useful. Martha watched him go and continued to smile.

That night, Philomena dreamed that she was lying on a warm, furry skin in a dark space near a small fire. All she could see were the glowing embers. Faces floated in and out of her vision. She thought she recognized Susuph, but she couldn't be sure. She heard soft, melodious chanting, and a disembodied hand gave her a bitter liquid to drink. She choked and tried to spit it out. She shivered even though it was stifling – sweat ran down her sides, and she realized she was naked. Her breasts were swollen, and her stomach was huge – monstrous she thought. A leathery hand gripped hers, and she looked into the wrinkled face of a woman with stringy gray hair in long braids. Now her head felt boiling hot and achy. She felt an immense pain in her stomach that radiated into her legs. She moaned and tried to scream, but a hand clapped over her mouth. She heard a baby crying. She twisted and turned, fighting against the hand that was trying to smother her. She tried to bite the hand. Her mouth formed the words, "My baby ... My baby." A stinking fluid poured from her body. Everything turned crimson. She was drowning in blood. With an intense effort, she tore away the hand.

"Philomena," Carrie whispered hoarsely. She was sitting on the edge of Philomena's bed and gently shaking her sister. She tentatively removed the hand that had stifled Philomena's loud moans.

"Wake up ... Wake up."

Philomena bolted upright, her terror-stricken eyes staring into space. Carrie clapped a hand over Philomena's mouth again. Philomena relaxed.

"I'm sorry," said Carrie, "I thought you would wake everyone. Did you have a nightmare?"

Philomena nodded.

"There was something profound about it. God created life, but to do that, He needed women." She paused. "We come naked into the world but don't spend much time that way thereafter – too bad."

"What is happening?" Martha called up from downstairs. The boys were sitting up in their bed. "Are you girls all right?"

"Yes, Mother," Philomena called back, "I had a ... bad dream."

On a stifling, humid afternoon towards the end of July, Philomena hurried through weeding the vegetable garden and picked a few squash and turnips for her mother. She fed the scratching chickens and carried slops to the pigs. She swept the cabin and the yard. As she worked, she kept looking to the west. She told her mother she was going to gather wild herbs and that she would milk Harriet when she returned.

The Scudder farm was south of the village. She walked north along the rutted track that was called Forshay Road, and passed through the cluster of log cabins. Thanks to the sawmill, several settlers had built solid barns and were planning to replace their cabins with frame houses. Lucas had organized a barn raising in the spring, moving the cows and his horse from their rude shed. He stored hay and corn in the barn and attached a chicken coop to its side. He talked of building a frame house next year.

Four farms were scattered along the track to the north of the settlement. Philomena crossed the bridge just north of the settlement and hurried through the cornfields and pastures on the western side of the river. She climbed a low hill and looked towards the northwest, shading her eyes from the sun. She could just see the Abenaki fields through the haze. Rivulets of sweat ran down her back. She glanced back at the settlement and trotted down the hill. He was waiting in the clearing. His black hair glistened, and his high cheeks caught the broken rays of sun that penetrated the thick woods.

"He's so handsome," she thought.

The clearing was hot and deathly quiet. Dappled sunlight created a pattern of intricate shapes on the ground. They talked with their backs resting against a fallen tree.

"I would like to meet your friend, Apom."

"That can be done. Can I meet your people?"

"My sister Carrie first – the one who was with me that first day."

She reached out and touched his hand as she had done so often. Then, almost without thinking, she pulled him to her and kissed him full on the lips. They lay on the ground kissing and stroking each other's hair. He took off her white apron and began to unbutton her dress. She was frightened, but she helped him. He pulled his doeskin shirt over his head. She noticed two parallel scars on his chest.

Birds chirped in the canopy of trees overhead. In the distance, an eagle screamed. Naked, she spread her legs and touched his penis. He entered her eagerly. She cried out and pulled his head onto her shoulder. Sweat covered their bodies. Afterwards, they lay still, breathing deeply. She wiped the sweat from his brow. They slept. She woke up trembling.

After that afternoon, they met as often as she deemed safe. Her fertile imagination invented one story after another, berry picking, tending the apple trees, mysterious walks (which her parents assumed meant Seth). They flew into each other's arms as soon as they caught sight of each other. He wanted to marry her. She said yes, but she would have to get her father's permission. That would not be easy. He distrusted Indians, but she said he could be brought around – especially when he realized what a fine man Susuph was. She would need her mother's help.

She was nervous when he brought her to the village in late August. They knew she was coming, and several women welcomed her. Dogs growled and then sniffed her. One or two of the young men eyed her suspiciously while the children stared at her from behind wigwams. One little boy approached boldly and held out a gourd. She knelt and drank the clear, cold water. Her taut muscles loosened.

His mother served them in his wigwam, a stew of eel, beans, and squash flavored with wild grasses. Specks of grease floated on top, but she ate two helpings with gusto. Susuph's father had been killed by a mother bear – strange that such a skilled hunter had not seen the cub. His sister had married an Abenaki from a different band and lived with her husband's family. He had not seen her for several years but knew that she was over by the great lake. His mother spoke no English but made herself understood with signs and through Susuph.

"It is past time that my son married again. May you be blessed with many children, and may they come as swiftly as the north wind."

Philomena stiffened but smiled politely. She had planned first on taking Susuph to Northfield. As she stepped out of the wigwam, an old man came up to her, gazing coldly into her face. He sputtered angrily, "C'est maudit! Elle est maudite!" He spat on the ground, walked over to a fire and sat on a large round stone. Philomena stood frozen, an expression of shock and fear flooding her face.

"What did he say?" she stammered.

"Nothing serious," said Susuph. "He is an old man and has seen too much. His wife and two of his children were killed in a raid by your people during the war against your great sachem across the big water. It means nothing; he will come to like you."

She left the village and walked home, Susuph accompanying her part of the way. She had an uneasy feeling in the pit of her stomach but shook it off.

September arrived in a burst of glory. The humidity of August vanished. The days were warm, hot even, but dry and exhilarating. Seth was paying increasing attention to her. She was polite but distant. She went for walks with him, but her mind was elsewhere. They sat on the bank by the bridge and talked idly. He was a kind, frank boy. He said that he wanted to court her and, before the winter, ask for her hand. She replied that she was too young to think of marriage. He looked disappointed, and pointed out that Abby Brewster had married at Philomena's age.

"Well, I'm not Abby Brewster," she snapped suddenly, "you sound like my sister!"

Her tone was cold, and he looked hurt. "I'm sorry," she said, "but I'm just not ready." She touched his hand and then quickly drew back. She hated lying, but what choice did she have? What would Seth think of her when he found out the truth? What would any of them think?

She didn't care. She looked west over the valley. She knew that she loved him.

The seventh of September was bright and warm. It had rained hard the day before, but the sky cleared during the night. When she got up to feed the pigs, the first glimmer of dawn was breaking over the eastern ridge. The pale blue sky was streaked with pink and lavender. Wisps of clouds floated overhead. She could still see the last stars. She wore a shawl but sensed that it would turn hot. She had told Susuph that she would meet him that afternoon in the woods, at a spot where the river emerged from the forest. She wanted to go to the gorge. She carried her musket and a bucket.

They skirted the pool and climbed through thickets and dense stands of mountain pine and tamaracks. The sugar maples showed a hint of color. It was hard work, and she slipped on loose rocks. There was only a faint path worn by generations of Abenaki hunters. The settlers rarely climbed above the pool, which shone dark and mysterious below them. The cascade roared as the stream hurtled over the rocks and plummeted into the waters below. They found a ledge partly hidden by thickets. He pointed to the cascade and told her how, in his despair, he had almost jumped. How in death he expected the water to wash away his pain. She shuddered and hugged him as tightly as she could.

"I had never known such anguish," he said.

She locked her eyes on his as if her will power could direct the future.

"You must promise never to think such thoughts again."

They lay down on a thick bed of moss. It never failed to delight her to take off his shirt and see his burnished, almost hairless chest. She ran a finger over the parallel scars.

"How did you get these?"

"I did them to myself - the day I thought of dying."

A tremor of fear ran through her. She pictured the old man in the village spitting on the ground in front of her.

"I'm frightened," she said. "I don't know why, but I suddenly feel like a shadow has passed over us."

"Don't be scared. It's only an eagle beckoning us."

She touched his cheek, and he undid the row of buttons on the back of her dress. He slipped it over her head, and nuzzled her breasts before entering her. She uttered the little gasp she always did. She put her arms around his back and pulled him to her. She dropped her head back on the moss and felt her heart start to beat faster as her breath changed to short bursts. Her face turned red, and her breasts tautened. She called his name – it was always the same – it was never the same.

He slept briefly, and she listened to the sounds around her, the water, birds, squirrels scampering. She looked up at a bush and saw a vast spider's web, the spider, mottled in color, waiting in the center. Susuph's body lay enfolded in her arms. She felt like she was floating. She felt alone and yet part of something. What happened to her was mysterious and frightening, but this was the universe - or a piece of it that she required.

They scrambled back down the rough hillside. It was long past mid-afternoon. She had to milk the two cows and carry potash to the apple trees. She was hot – her body felt damp. She climbed over a log and slipped on a smooth stone on the other side. She lost her balance and tumbled down the steep slope, rolling over and over – the bucket falling behind her. She heard Susuph cry out, and then she hit her head against a tree trunk.

Chapter Two

September 7, 1799

The first time he saw her, he thought she was the ugliest woman he had ever seen. She was big-boned, not delicate like his Algoma or most of the other Abenaki girls, and had pale skin with spots. Susuph did not know what freckles were. Worst of all was her red hair. He had seen many white men and women but none with such nauseating hair. That had been two years ago, in the spring of 1797, when he had come to the settlement with Apom and Chogan to trade rabbit pelts, baskets and snowshoes for blankets, needles, muskets and musket balls.

They had crossed the log bridge and were walking along the track that wound among the cabins. The bridge had been built as the settlers expanded their cornfields to the west side of the river. Old Eluwilussit had pointed to the bridge as an argument for destroying the settlement before it grew any larger. He said the white invaders would eventually overrun the entire valley just as they had done further south in Massachusetts and Connecticut. The village would have to move again. He had enough of moving and was prepared to fight as their ancestors had done. Suppose they were willing to move: where would they find another unoccupied valley of such beauty, so filled with game?

But Nootau and Keme had prevailed, contending that, while the settlement indeed presented a threat, the settlers had been friendly so far, and the trading profitable. They were certainly not well-enough armed to take on the settlers, some of whom had long rifles. Their best strategy was to bide their time while accumulating supplies of muskets and ammunition. In a few years, the younger boys would be ready to fight. In the meantime, hunting was to be done with bow and arrow.

If the settlement expanded too far west, they concluded, or added too many new families, the warriors would have to choose a propitious moment to attack and burn the cabins. No settler would be allowed to escape, lest word of the raid bring down vengeance as had happened in the past. The grown men would be killed. Since the village already had enough young women, the less ugly settler women would be traded to other Abenaki villages as brides while the others were put to work. The children would be raised as Abenaki. The village could use more young hunters and warriors.

Susuph was shocked at dirty condition some of the white's cabins were in, and how sickly their raggedly-dressed children appeared to be. A proud Abenaki would be ashamed to see his children so shabbily clothed and in such poor health. Other children, however, were ruddy and well dressed in clean wool shirts and trousers. Their yards were tidy with well-attended vegetable gardens. Apparently, the white men did not share among themselves. In a small Abenaki community, the families viewed the fields and gardens as common property. Game was also shared – with the successful hunters, like himself, bringing in most of the meat and skins.

Chogan, who was not a good hunter, had wanted him to come because of his English. He preferred to hunt and let Chogan trade. Chogan had an agile tongue even if he spoke no English, and a quick head for values. Susuph came because he wanted a warm and elegant blanket to give Algoma who was pregnant. He would surprise her with it tonight, and they would have fun. He hoped for a boy, although unlike some Abenaki, he would be happy with a beautiful baby girl. His mother said the baby would come in about five moons.

They were seated on the ground in front of the settlement meetinghouse. They had spread out the trade goods, and Owen Harding and two other men were examining them. The Abenaki were inspecting blankets, wool shirts, and needles. Chogan was talking and Susuph was translating as best he could.

"Where are the musket balls? And muskets?" asked Chogan

"I'm sorry, Chogan," said Owen, "but we simply don't have enough for our own hunting—next time, perhaps."

"Do you think they're lying?" Chogan asked Apom.

"It is possible, but what can we do? If we object, they may get suspicious and never give them to us. Tell them, Susuph that we need muskets and musket balls so that we can bring them fine bearskins."

"Ah, bearskins," said Lemuel Ames greedily. "Perhaps we can spare a few rounds."

He got up and went toward a nearby cabin.

Susuph heard laughing and turned his head. He caught a brief glimpse of four girls walking along the track, talking and laughing. They were about thirty yards away and paid no attention to the trading. They were absorbed in their conversation and had seen Indians trading often enough in the past two years. Two of the girls had bright red hair. They were obviously sisters, and one looked a couple of years older. He pitied the older one; ugly as she was, she would have difficulty getting a husband. He turned back to the trading, filled with anticipation about tonight. He saw the blanket that he wanted.

Five months later, on a brilliant fall day, Algoma died and so did his baby daughter. He had been waiting with Apom outside the wigwam. His mother and two other women were helping with the birth. He heard a scream and then silence. He tried to enter the wigwam, but Apom held him back. After a minute or two, his mother pushed back the flap of the wigwam and came to him with tears in her eyes. She touched his cheek. His grief was beyond bearing. He forced his way into the bark dwelling and saw his wife lying in a pool of blood. He remembered nothing more.

He took to the woods, hunting incessantly, and to the river to fish although the pain was less when he was moving – running through the woods in pursuit of a wounded buck. He doubted if his own wound would ever heal.

One raw March day in 1798, six months after Algoma's death, he woke with his heart on fire—his loneliness and pain more intense than he could bear. He left the wigwam without speaking to his mother, and climbed up the gorge to the top of the ridge. The rushing waters of the cascade bellowed close by, like the constant roaring inside his head. Reaching the summit, he took off his shirt and knelt on a rough rock. A biting wind burned his cheeks and whipped across his bare chest. He prayed and prayed, begging that the pain be taken away. Then he begged for the pain to stay because it was all he had left of his wife. He took a hunting knife from a sheath. He held it high and then carefully cut two parallel lines across his chest. Small round beads of blood dotted the shallow cuts and trickled down his chest.

He started back down the ridge. Leaves swirled around the forest floor. The bare branches of the maples clacked against each other. He stopped on a ledge overhanging the cascade. Far below, he could see the pool in whose icy waters he had swum with his friends on sweltering summer days. The stream fell steeply, spraying off huge rocks into the pool, flowing over a stone lip and coursing swiftly down the slope toward the valley. He gazed intently at the torrent of water and thought how easy it would be. A quick leap and his body would be smashed like a wooden bowl on the rocks, dragged away under the racing current.

He stepped to the edge. The spray soaked his deerskin trousers. What was there to hold him back? But he heard Algoma whispering, this was not the way—he had an obligation to his village, to his mother, to the other children. His suffering, even suffering that had no end, had to be endured. A high spray caught him full in the face. He shivered. He stepped back from the edge and continued down the gorge.

In the fall of 1798, when a full year had passed, his mother told him he should take another wife – even if it meant going across the ridge to another band. She knew that the few eligible girls in the village made him think of Algoma. He refused his mother, something he rarely did.

He saw her again in the early spring of 1799. He had been preparing to throw his spear at a speckled trout when he noticed a woman's figure, still at some distance, out of the corner of his eye. She was walking along the rutted track north of the settlement, carrying a basket with a cloth over it, and watching out for the muddiest places. He ducked among the reeds and stayed completely still. The girl passed by without seeing him, and he recognized her as the tall girl with red hair.

She was carrying a musket slung across her back. What Abenaki woman would be allowed to carry a musket? Algoma had been daring and had always spoken her mind but would never have thought of asking for a musket. The girl was ugly but walked gracefully, her shoulders back and her head erect. She looked around from time to time but seemed at ease. He watched her enter one of the farmhouses about a mile from the settlers' village. He waited in the reeds. About a half hour later, she returned. The basket appeared to be empty; he could not see the cloth. Again, he noticed her gracefulness, the way she walked briskly, but not in a hurry. He liked that.

He took to watching her. It was easy to stay in the vicinity of the settlement, unseen, and follow her when she went berry picking or to the apple orchard. He always carried a few trade goods. If he were to run across any settlers, they would assume he was on a trading excursion. It only happened once, and in a deliberate mixture of broken French and English, he offered to trade two fine pairs of snowshoes for musket balls or a blanket. The man had a thick beard and wore a heavy jacket with a rip under one arm. He was coming from the cornfields. He guided Susuph back to his cabin and offered him a worn blanket. The snowshoes were worth more than the blanket, but Susuph agreed to the trade. As he walked away, he noticed the man smiling in a smug fashion.

He wanted to talk to her, but he was hesitant. He felt intimidated. She was so much more independent than the Abenaki girls. And that musket. It did not scare so much as amaze him. One day in June, she crossed the bridge with her sister, the other one with red hair. He was getting used to, if not actually liking, the red hair. It was so different. They both carried buckets. Going berry picking, he presumed. He knew where they would go so he hurried ahead and waited in the woods. Perhaps it would be easier to talk to both of them.

He stood in the shadows, watching for a long time. They would notice him eventually. The pain of Algoma would never leave him, but it had lessened. He thought of her less often – not like the first six months when the thought of her followed him day and night. He would lie for hours on his bearskin, trying to feel her skin next to his, hear her voice whispering in his ear, and taste her moist lips; but he could not quite capture the sensations. They were always just out of reach no matter how much he strained. When he did drift off to sleep, he dreamed of her. He would stretch out a hand or a finger to touch her, but she floated backwards. He would see her form but could not make out her features. They were shrouded in darkness. He always woke up exhausted.

Slowly, the dreams faded; and his thoughts turned back to his friends. He invited Apom hunting. Then he saw the red-haired one, and he started going out alone again. Apom thought that his bitterness had returned and was worried.

Susuph sensed when she felt his presence. She stood up. He heard her say, "Oh!" What should he do? Had he frightened her? The sister stood up, smiled, and said, "Good morning." His heart beat wildly. Hunting a bear was easier than this. He stammered out something; he thought it was "Good morning" but he wasn't sure. He turned and fled.

How could he be such a fool? What did he think he was doing standing in the shadows? Of course, she would be afraid—an Abenaki suddenly appearing in the dark of the forest. Yet they didn't seem afraid, and the sister smiled and greeted him. The musket stayed put. She might have been too startled to move – like a buck that, finally detecting him, hesitates a fatal instant.

Whether she was afraid or not, next time it would have to be in full daylight, in a place where she would feel safe. Near the village but where he would not be seen. The apple orchard – that was it. She went there often to care for the trees. She put some kind of ash around the small ones and weeded. He would also have to find out her name. He had seen her several times with the man who appeared to be the sachem. He would ask Chogan, casually, about the sachem.

He learned that the big chief's name was Scudder—his daughter must be Miss Scudder. He must bring her something to show that he came in peace. He knew where there was an eagle's nest – high up on the ridge. For two weeks, she did not go to the orchard. She went once to the woods and gathered berries, but he did not want to approach her so far from the settlement. Finally, late one morning, she took a bucket with the ashes and walked in the direction of the orchard. He approached the orchard and waited. She sensed his presence again—she did not appear to be frightened. He caught his breath and stepped forward. She spoke:

"Good morning."

"Good morning, Miss Scudder."

She was the most amazing person he had ever met. She talked to him in a way no one ever had before. He could not describe it, even to himself. He followed her constantly. They met more and more frequently. She always seemed glad and excited to see him. When he talked to her, the pain of Algoma almost disappeared. It took a while before he found out her first name. They were sitting in the clearing one afternoon in July. The clearing was their favorite spot, secluded, quiet, a little stream flowing nearby. He screwed up his courage:

"You have a second name, don't you?"

"Yes," she laughed a laugh that brought a warm glow to his copper cheeks, "and you don't know what it is."

"How do you know that?"

"Because you keep calling me 'Miss Scudder'. It's Philomena."

"Phi-lo-mena. Philomena. I like that."

"Why, thank you." And she laughed again.

She seemed to like to touch his hand; he was not used to that. Algoma had not been so forward at first. He did not know what to make of it, so he did nothing. She also liked to talk and was very inquisitive. She asked him about the village, what Canada was like, how the missionary school, where he had gone from time to time, had been.

"The same as here – only colder," he said, referring to Canada.

Then, one hot afternoon in August, everything changed. They were talking about his meeting her sister. She touched his hand, as she had done so often; then suddenly she was pulling him toward her and kissing him. He was stunned. For an instant, he thought of Algoma. Then, without quite knowing what he was doing, he lay with her on the ground and began to unbutton her dress. His thoughts careened around inside his head. His fingers were awkward; she had to help him. Then he was lifting off his shirt and lying on top of her.

Everything seemed far away. Somewhere he thought he heard an eagle scream. She touched his manhood, sending shivers through him. He heard the eagle again and wondered if he were imagining it like the nightmares that had haunted him for so long. Unused to making love face to face, he entered her eagerly and heard Philomena's sharp cry, first of pain and then replete with desire and longing—her eyes bright and hot as he began moving inside her. His breath quickened and his heart pounded rhythmically with the beat of war drums he heard at some great distance. Was this also a dream? She moaned and he quickly forgot about the drumming as he pressed himself tightly against her pelvis. Philomena's heart beat in time with his, and she was reminded of the clanging of a blacksmith striking blazing iron on a forge. Drenched in each other's sweat, their climax started slowly and then came with a rush as their voices rang through the forest. Their passion fading, they lay clinging to each other and fell into a dreamless sleep. A few minutes later, a sixth sense woke Philomena and she saw a timber wolf eyeing them from the edge of the forest. She moved slightly, grasping her musket, and Susuph woke. As he started to get up, the wolf growled sharply and disappeared into the woods.

Susuph wanted to marry her. The pain was gone. He could look forward to life again. They would have children. He brought her to the village so that she could see what their life would be like. She seemed to find it agreeable, except for that damn old fool, Kitchi, frightening her with his curses. If they destroyed the settlement – and he hoped it could be avoided, she and her family (except the sachem) would come to live in the village. Neither her mother nor her sister would be traded. That would be her privilege as his wife.

They climbed the gorge on a warm September afternoon. She said that she had not been to the gorge since the previous summer. They found a mossy ledge and made love. Although it was late in the afternoon, he thought of stopping briefly by the pool to swim. He was not paying close attention to the path as they made their way back down. She began to climb over a log, and suddenly he saw her tumble down the steep slope. He cried out and went running and sliding after her. She hit her head against a tree and lay there, still as death.

"No!" he screamed in terror. "No!"

He knelt beside her and felt her chest. She was still alive. He kissed her cheeks and then her lips. He felt hot tears rolling down his cheeks, falling to the moist earth.

"Philomena," he said softly and then urgently. "Philomena!"

She made no sound.

"Philomena, listen to me. Philomena, please don't go away. Please don't die. Please."

He looked around in desperation. There was only one thing to do. In this situation, the white man's medicine would be stronger than Pajackok's. He took her into his arms and started down the hill. She had dropped her bucket when she fell, and he left it. She was breathing slightly, and made no other sound. She was big and heavy, even for him, and the going was rough. He slipped in places where the seldom-used path disappeared. The musket slung across her back made it even more difficult so he gently took it off and leaned it against a tree. He would return for it later and give it back to her. The roar of the cascade pummeled his ears. He pleaded with her as he walked. He loved her, and didn't know if he could live without her. She had brought him back from the land of death.

The sun was setting as he reached the bottom of the gorge and the terrain became flatter and smoother. He stopped briefly for a drink at the stream. His arms ached. He laid Philomena gently on the bank and scooped a handful of water into his mouth. He moved more quickly now, but it was dark when he reached the settlement. He had been carrying her for over two hours, and he could barely tolerate the grinding pain in his biceps. He stopped from time to time to check her breathing; it was slow but rhythmical. He skirted the cabins in the bend of the river and walked rapidly down the Forshay Road. He wanted to move quickly but was careful not to bounce her.

He could see light in the window of her father's cabin and under the door. Two cows moved restlessly in their stalls; a pig grunted. He approached warily and laid her on the ground in front of the door. Voices murmured inside the cabin. Tortured with guilt for abandoning her, what choice was there echoed through his confused, fearful mind. He kissed her on the lips, knocked loudly on the door and disappeared into the darkness.

Chapter Three

Sean Reynolds
(1783 – 1826)

September 7, 1799

It was not the first time he had followed her, nor the first time he had spied on her with Susuph when they lay together. He thought of it as dirty because he had watched farm animals doing it and they were dirty.

"Just look at the pigs," he thought. "They're always wallowing in the mud."

When he was younger, he had tried wallowing in the mud. He had wanted to see what it was like, what the pigs felt. His father had caught him and whipped him within an inch of his life. Now he followed the chickens around the yard and examined their droppings. He found them fascinating. He picked them up and smelled them. He wondered why they smelled different from his own.

"Daddy told me not to do that," Sean said to himself. "Told me he'd whup me good if he caught me again. Like with the pigs. I'll just make sure he don't catch me. Pretty smart, huh?"

He had seen Philomena touch Susuph's thing. He knew that was especially dirty, but he liked touching his own thing and watching it grow big. He didn't understand why it happened. His mother found him in bed once touching it. She smacked him hard.

"That's dirty," she said. "Get out of that bed and don't ever do it again." She shook him. "Do you want to go to Hell?"

He had cried. He liked pretending to be sad. She had held him to her breast. He had also liked that – so warm and comforting, like lying naked in a stream on a hot day, which he did in one of his secret places.

"Sean, do you understand?"

He nodded, but he did it anyway, only in the woods now. He shed his trousers but kept them close by just in case. Few people wandered in the woods, but he could never be certain. Last thing he wanted was another whipping.

"Pa is very strong," he thought.

Susuph took off Philomena's clothes every time they were together. Sometimes Susuph looked around as if he suspected Sean was there, but he never left her to find out.

"Why does she let that Indian take off her dress but not me? It was funny that time I snuck up on her at the river. She jumped like a rabbit when I pulled at her dress. I'm good at sneaking around. I can make myself so nobody can see me. She sure shrieked."

"Sean," Philomena had snapped. "Don't do that."

"Sean, I'm sorry," Philomena said, her voice softening, "but you mustn't touch my dress. Do you understand?"

He knew how to walk without making any noise, and how to hide. It wasn't any trouble to follow her without being seen. He had to be more careful when Susuph was around. Susuph used to follow her, but now they took to meeting, which made it easier. It seemed to Sean that they had a ritual, and it didn't vary. He knew that toward the end of the ritual they would get naked. He would take his clothes off at the same time. He had to be careful not to make any noise, like he did when he was alone in the woods. He wondered why they often bathed in a stream after the ritual. He also wondered what would happen if he told anyone what Elder Scudder's daughter did with an Indian. Maybe the boys wouldn't tease him.

"Or call me 'Fuddle Brain' and 'Dim Wit'. If they kill the Indian, Philomena will take off her clothes with me. It's not fair. I'm as smart as any of them. Let them follow an Indian without being seen."

When he killed a cat and nailed it to a tree in Josiah Royce's farmyard one night, no one saw or suspected him. "You can't be a dimwit and do a thing like that." Jethro and Tilly Royce had set up a howl about their poor dead cat. "You'd think I had skinned it. Now there's an idea. Next time." He figured that would settle the score for the teasing and for excluding him from their games. Not even the youngest would play with him, except for blind man's bluff and then only if he played the blind man. Then they would trip him and laugh, or poke him with a stick. He was, however, good at catching the other children, even if they stood still as scarecrows. He sensed them. He didn't know how. Perhaps their smell or breathing. He had to concentrate, but he always caught them. He liked blind man's bluff.

Some of the older girls were nice to him. They often told him to go away or simply ignored him, but they didn't taunt him. Occasionally, they let him listen to their gossiping. He missed a lot of what they said, but he liked listening to their voices – like birds chirping. He liked birds. He found a robin's nest high up in a maple tree. He brought the sky blue eggs back for the chickens to sit on and hatch, but they wouldn't do it.

"Stupid chickens," he thought.

It had always been the same with the children, even in Northfield, although he didn't know that was the name of the place. He remembered the trip, the long days of walking. He thought it would never end. He liked the mountains, having never seen anything remotely like them. He wondered if mountains existed anyplace else in the world. He wanted to go to school, but his father wouldn't allow it. He wondered what they did in school. He peeked through a window, but it made no sense. The students just sat at their desks. No games except in the yard when all hell broke loose. The kids didn't go every day, and they didn't have a separate building, like in Northfield. They used the meetinghouse where one of the Elders read from the Bible and everyone sang. Meetings were fun. He sat between his mother and father and felt like he belonged. He was quiet except the time he laughed loudly at something Elder Scudder read about begetting. His mother pinched him. He didn't laugh again, at least not out loud.

He did go to school once – a long time ago – in Northfield. He couldn't understand what the teacher wanted him to do so he pounded on his desk. The teacher shouted at him. That was fun so he pounded some more. The teacher sent one of the kids for his father.

He didn't talk much. He didn't like to talk, but occasionally he had something to say. He planned to talk about what Philomena did with Susuph. That would be a red-letter day. He would talk exactly as he thought. Mostly the words came out jumbled, but this would be different.

It was a warm afternoon in September. Sean didn't know it was September, but he could tell that summer was slowly coming to an end. Some of the ducks and geese were already starting to fly in huge V-shaped formations across the sky. He sat by the river and watched them. He was sitting in the reeds when he saw Philomena walk by, headed toward the forest. He followed her. When she reached the last farmhouse, she looked around as if checking on something. He didn't know what. Then she went quickly into the woods. She went a short distance along the stream. Susuph stepped from behind a tree. She ran into his arms and hugged him. They started up the slope.

Sean stayed well behind. It was easy to follow unnoticed. They were engrossed in a conversation that he couldn't hear. They climbed up the gorge until they reached a ledge near the cascade. The Indian said something to Philomena, and she looked over the pounding water. She turned back to hug Susuph tightly, pressing her cheek into his chest and gripping him around the back. Sean quietly climbed higher and found a thicket from which he could see the ledge. He watched them take off each other's clothes. Soon after, he heard her cry, "Susuph, oh Susuph. I love you." His brain was in a whirr as he huddled in the thicket hugging himself with his arms. He made little gurgling sounds. He watched them sleep and then dress.

They started back. He saw her fall and tumble down the hill. He followed Susuph while he carried her back to the settlement. He saw him lean her musket against a tree. He watched him leave Philomena at her father's cabin and pound on the door. He didn't see him again after that. The cabin door opened, and Sean saw Philomena's mother framed in the light from the fireplace. She screamed. Elder Scudder came to the door, looked wildly around, and carried his daughter inside. Sean waited.

The door opened again, and Caleb flew out and ran for the barn, carrying a lantern. In a few minutes, he rode a horse out of the barn and raced toward the settlement. Sean waited. Minutes passed. He waited. Then something told him the time had come. He went to the door and knocked. The door opened. Elder Scudder glared at Sean.

"Saw them. Saw them." babbled Sean. "Came from woods. Wrestled. Like this." Sean jumped up and down and whirled around, flailing his arms.

Lucas stared at Sean, uncomprehending.

"Wrestled … wrestled. She hit. She hit. Yelled him stop." Lucas understood. He pulled Sean into the cabin and slammed the door.

"Who did this?" he demanded. Then he forced himself to be calm so as not to frighten the half-witted boy. "Sean, take your time. Who did this and what exactly did he do?"

Sean grinned.

"Indian," Sean continued. "Indian. Wrestled. Roll on ground. No clothes. No clothes," Sean babbled with growing excitement. This was his moment. Why couldn't he talk the way he thought? He must try harder. He forced himself to mouth his thoughts. "No clothes. Dirty thing. Pigs. Na … na … naked. Roll. Ground. Sleep. On her. Hit head."

"Oh my God," howled Lucas. "The depraved savages!" He grabbed the boy by the lapels of his coat and pushed his face close to Sean's. Martha stood behind him, frozen in fear. Carrie, her hands trembling, was wiping her sister's forehead with a cloth. Philomena, still unconscious but breathing steadily, lay on a blanket by the fire. Another blanket covered her up to the chin. Samuel huddled near the fireplace.

"Who was the Indian?" Lucas breathed his hot anger into Sean's face. "Think Sean. Who was the Indian?"

Sean whimpered and then stammered: "Su – Su – Susuph. Name. Clothes put on. Down mountain. Down mountain. Roll … roll … roll. Carry … carry … carry. Head … head."

"The savage must've knocked her unconscious. Did the Indian hit her on the head, Sean?"

"Tree. Roll … roll. Arms … arms. Sleep … sleep."

"Think hard, Sean. Did he hit her?"

"Think. Sean think. No … no. Dirty thing. Pigs."

Martha put a hand on Lucas's arm. He brushed it off.

"Did you carry her home, Sean?"

Sean laughed.

"Carry … carry."

"We've got as much from him as possible," said Lucas. He put an arm around Sean's shoulder. "You did well, lad." Sean beamed.

Lucas pounded one fist into the other. He walked to the fireplace and looked down at Philomena.

"My daughter," he said between clenched teeth, "you will be avenged. Have no fear on that score. Your precious honor will be avenged."

The door opened and Oliver Lawrence entered, followed closely by Caleb. Oliver knew a little doctoring. He had studied with a doctor in Northfield and had read a couple of medical texts. He was called on in the settlement to care for sick people and animals. He knelt by Philomena, felt her forehead, and took her pulse. He put his ear to her mouth. He saw the bruise on the side of her head. He stood up.

"She has a fever and a nasty bruise from hitting her head, but her heart is beating normally and her breathing is steady. I think she will live, but I cannot tell how long she may be unconscious. Keep her warm and comfortable. Make a tea from comfrey and sage. Try to get a little down her throat. Hold her mouth open and put in a little at a time with a spoon. It will help with the fever and let her rest easier. Rebecca knows more about herbs than I do. She might add some tansy or thyme. A spoonful of whiskey or brandy, if you have any, will help revive her. Do you know how it happened?"

"She was attacked and … and … taken advantage … damn it, raped by a skulking Abenaki."

"Dear God," gasped Oliver.

"She fought the whole time. Sean apparently witnessed it and has been frightened out of the few wits he has. It's impossible to get more out of him. The savage either struck her or she may have fallen trying to escape and hit her head. We may find out more when she wakes up, but I'm not waiting for that."

"How did she get home?"

"Sean must've carried her," said Lucas, "although I can't get him to say for sure."

"Hard to imagine the savage bringing her home," said Oliver. "Philomena must've been unconscious at that point so the truth may never be known." Oliver paused thoughtfully. "What are you going to do now?"

"Do?" Lucas's voice rose in a fury. "Do? The bastard will hang." His voice rose higher. "The whole heathen tribe will pay for this. We'll do what we should have done a long time ago." Lucas glared at his wife and spoke sharply to Caleb, "Boy, take the horse and spread the word among the farms between here and the village. Then ride to the village. Ask all the men to come here as quickly as they can. Ask someone to ride to the farms to the north and then come back. Hurry, damn it!"

"Philomena should be in a bed," said Oliver. "If it's warm in the loft, that would be best since it's quieter."

"We put her by the fire to keep her warm," said Martha. "She did not seem to have too much of a fever."

"The fever is moderate," said Oliver. "You did right, but I think she should be moved now—carefully."

Lucas gently lifted his daughter and carried her up to the loft. He lay her in her bed and pulled the coverlet to her chin. He went down again.

Carrie, weeping softly, climbed up and sat by her sister. Martha joined her. Singly and in small groups, the settlers arrived at the Scudder farmhouse. Hearing the news, several decided to patrol the settlement and outlying farms rather than attend the meeting. They asked neighbors to speak for them. One farmer had a desperately sick cow that he dared not leave. The settlers arrived in an ugly mood. The sixteen men barely fit in the room that served as kitchen, dining room, living room, and makeshift bedroom for Caleb and Samuel. Lucas and Martha slept in a small room behind the kitchen while Philomena and Carrie used the loft. The men listened in shock and growing anger as they heard what Lucas had to say. Owen Harding asked to hear from Sean.

"He's barely comprehensible," said Lucas.

"Let me try," Owen said.

Owen had taken Sean along on hunting trips and was often able to calm him when no one else, including his parents, could. Owen spoke to Sean in a slow, gentle voice.

"Tell us what you saw."

Sean smiled and repeated what he had told Lucas.

"What were you doing in the woods?" asked Owen Harding.

"Picking berries."

"Not the season for berries," said Dexter Forshay.

"Why didn't you run for help?" asked Owen.

"The lad was too frightened and confused to think of running for help," snapped Lucas.

"Did you carry Philomena home?" asked Owen.

Sean hung his head.

"I'm not sure we can rely on Sean's account," said Dexter.

"He may be slow," said Barnabas Young, "but he isn't blind. He probably has some of the details mixed up, but in general, I believe the boy's story—enough to go and bring that savage in."

"I agree," said Lemuel Ames.

"So do I."

"Count me in."

"There are things here that don't make sense," said Owen. "Is there any sign that her dress was torn? Why would a…" Owen hesitated. "…an attacker bother with removing a dress? It's not clear that Sean brought her back. Why would Susuph? What was Philomena doing near the gorge by herself?"

"Am I supposed to understand what goes on in the mind of a degraded savage?" snarled Lucas. He glared at Owen. "Are you suggesting that she was with this savage of her own free will? That she …?"

Several men hissed at Owen.

"How dare you?"

"Lucas Scudder's daughter!"

"A fine, modest girl."

"Have you taken leave of your senses?"

"I'm not suggesting anything," countered Owen, "except that we ask Philomena about this when she recovers."

Several men nodded their heads. Eyes burning, Lucas confronted Owen.

"We cannot wait. By the time she wakes up, the stinking savage may have disappeared."

"That's unlikely," said Owen, "since he has no idea that Sean saw him."

Dexter pulled Lucas away from Owen.

"Calm yourself, Lucas," said Dexter. "Owen is not casting any doubt on Philomena's honor. He's simply trying to clear up some uncertain aspects of the matter. But you're right. We cannot wait for Philomena's recovery to bring in Susuph for questioning and a trial. We'll get the truth out of him and clear up the problems with Sean's account."

Dexter turned to Owen.

"Would you agree?"

"Yes." He hesitated. "It may be that Sean carried Philomena home and is unable to tell us clearly. We should indeed question Susuph in great detail."

"What about the rest of the village?" someone in the back of the room called out.

There was silence for a moment.

"The damnable savages all need a lesson," raged Lucas. "Not one of 'em is worth six pence. Turn your back 'n they'll cut your throat. Burn the village! Drive them out of the valley. Kill a few while we're at it."

"You go too far, Lucas," said Dexter.

"Too far?" Lucas slammed a fist on the table. "Was it your daughter, Dexter, the savages raped? Is it your daughter lying upstairs, clinging to life by a thread? Who knows if she'll recover?"

"Philomena was raped not by savages but by one renegade. He must be tried according to the law. It would be neither fair nor reasonable to hold the village responsible. I understand your fury. I would feel the same, but please try to think rationally."

"To hell with you, Dexter. You've always favored the savages. Look at the outcome. My precious Philomena raped and battered. You may be too damn weak-kneed to exact justice, but I, for one, am not!"

Lucas glared at Dexter and then scanned the other men, trying to ascertain support in their expressions. Several men nodded, and an angry buzz went around the room.

"Savages!" murmured one man. "Lick your boots one minute; steal all you've got the next."

"Out with the lot of them. This is our land now."

"Frenchies and papists if not out-and-out heathens. We'll show them a 'Parlez-vous?' or two."

"Hang on," said a stout, balding man. "One of them brought my family a haunch of venison when I had the fevers."

"Be quiet, Baxter! A year in the valley and you claim to know something. How did they know you were with the fevers? Lurking around, that's how. Gives me the jitters."

"I do know something," broke in Owen Harding. "We've all benefited from trading with the Abenaki. I don't intend to sacrifice these profits because of one man's crime. If Susuph is guilty, he'll pay with his life. If the others are left in peace, they will accept our justice. Life will go on as before. I pray for Philomena's recovery, but listen to what I say, Lucas, if you want me along."

"Here, here," murmured a couple of men.

"Owen makes sense," said Lemuel Ames.

"No use killing the golden goose," added Peter Rawlings.

Lucas sensed the tide turning against him. The opinions of Owen Harding and Dexter Forshay carried great weight. Like Lucas, they were elders in the church. Their fathers had each contributed the same capital to the enterprise as Lucas's father. It had been Owen who, as they crossed the eastern ridge and saw the valley spread below them, had gotten down on his knees and thanked God for his providence.

Lucas fought his rage and grumbled: "As you wish. But there had better be no trouble from the bastards. We'll take twelve men. The rest will stay on guard here. We'll leave mid-afternoon tomorrow and move into the village just before dark. We'll capture Susuph and get out. We'll allow a few of them to attend the trial and the hanging. They'll learn to respect our justice … and what happens to transgressors. Lemuel, tell the men who are not here."

"What you're planning hardly sounds like the arrest of a suspect," said Owen.

"Do you think, for one minute, asked Lucas, "that they'll let us walk in there and demand they hand over Susuph? As if we were on a trading mission? We'd have to fight our way out with dead on both sides. Is that what you want?"

"Of course, not."

"Then let's rush the village and be gone with Susuph before a fight can start. Naturally, we'll be ready if one does."

"What makes you think they won't come after him?" asked Owen.

Lucas maintained a blank expression.

"We can defend the settlement. Once the trial is over and Susuph has been hanged, it will blow over—business as normal. After all, it's their golden goose as well."

"Lucas is right," said Josiah Royce.

"We should do it his way," said Peter Rawlings.

The twelve settlers moved through the woods like ghosts. They were farmers, but hunting had taught them stealth. They took care not to step on dry branches, and they edged their way through thickets. Tense and alert, the men looked around constantly. They walked in single file without uttering a word. They were dressed in dull colors: high black boots, muddy trousers, sweat-stained shirts, and broad-brimmed felt hats pulled low over their foreheads.

They had crossed the river on the log bridge just north of the settlement and headed west. Keeping their heads and shoulders low, they darted through the high grass and sheltered in small clumps of silver maples and red oaks. They kept an eye out for Indians hunting in the meadows or crossing the valley to fish in the river. Reaching the forest cover in about thirty minutes, they turned north toward the Abenaki village. Through the trees, they could make out the Indians' cornfields and gardens of beans and squash. Alongside a stream, six bark wigwams clustered in a clearing a short distance from the fields. Pale streaks of rose smeared the western sky as the sun settled behind the ridge. Lucas whispered that they should wait until the light was dim.

"They'll be preparing to eat and won't suspect anything. We'll move quickly and confuse them. Let them see our weapons. They'll think twice before starting anything."

Five of the men carried Kentucky long rifles – accompanied by pistols and knives shoved into their trousers. The rifled bores gave these guns greater range and accuracy than the ageing muskets of the other seven men, who also carried tomahawks and knives. Lucas's rifle had an ornately engraved barrel and stock. His father had given him the gun when Lucas left Northfield. Lucas and Dexter led the party. The men's faces were hard and angry.

As the glimmering light began to fade above the western ridge, the men cautiously made their way toward the low fires of the village. Through the spruce, birch, and sugar maples, they saw women bending over the fires and children playing among the wigwams. Several elderly men were talking by a fire. From the direction of the gorge, two young men entered the open space in the center of the village, a two-pronged buck slung between them. The children crowded around, shouting and laughing, and then continued their game. The settlers, led by Lucas, approached to less than fifty yards.

One of the women looked up from stirring a pot and stared at the forest. She said something to a woman standing next to her. The second woman glanced at the forest. The settlers froze. The women laughed and returned to their work. The settlers moved forward again. A mongrel dog rushed, barking, from a wigwam. The women ran to their children. Several men came to the edge of the village with muskets. Framed against the firelight, they peered into the darkening trees.

"Forward, in God's name," shouted Lucas, who broke into a run.

The others followed. They raced through the woods, one or two stumbling over roots. They crashed through a thicket of brambles. Another dog barked. The Abenaki men shouted at their women to get the children into the woods. The settlers burst from the forest about ten yards from the first wigwam. One of the Abenaki raised his musket and fired. A musket ball hit Lemuel Ames in the shoulder, and he fell backwards. A second Abenaki aimed at an oncoming settler and pulled the trigger, but his ancient musket misfired.

"Bastards," screamed Lucas. He stopped, raised his rifle, and shot a young man through the chest. He raced forward, pulled out his pistol, and shot a woman through the back as she was shepherding some children away from the fires. He quickly reloaded his pistol and seeing a child running past a fire, shot her through the head. Crouching behind a log, an elderly Indian fired his musket at Lucas, hitting him in the thigh. As the Indian reloaded, Oliver Lawrence shot him from the edge of the clearing. The old Abenaki looked up, surprised, and sank behind the log. Bleeding from the stomach, he crawled toward a woodpile and hid behind it. He lost consciousness and bled to death.

The two young Abenaki carrying the buck were shot as they dropped the deer and raised their muskets. Growling and barking, the dogs snapped at the intruders. A settler, screaming oaths, clubbed a dog with the butt of his musket. The dog sank to its knees and rolled over dead. Another young man was clubbed as he emerged from his wigwam. His jaw cracked in two, and a tomahawk finished him. His wife and three children cowered inside. A settler poked his head in the wigwam and shot her.

The Indian, whose musket had misfired, gripped the barrel and charged at Lucas. As he was swinging the gun, Dexter aimed his long rifle and shot the Indian through the face. He fell sideways, his musket flying into the smoky air. Dexter heard a scream of agony behind Lucas and ran toward the trees. An elderly woman had plunged a knife into Lemuel Ames's chest and then slashed at his throat. Dexter shot her in the back with his pistol. She fell on top of Lemuel's body. Dexter reloaded his rifle and killed a young man who had just shot Peter Rawlings in the chest with an arrow. Peter staggered backwards, screaming and tearing at the arrow as he died.

An old man carrying a child scurried past Lucas who was limping from his wound. Lucas pulled a hunting knife from his trousers, threw it, and caught the man between the shoulder blades. As the old man fell forwards, Lucas raised his rifle to club the child.

"Stop, for God's sake," screamed Owen Harding. Lucas turned toward Owen. A woman picked up the child and ran into the woods.

"Look out," Lucas hollered. Owen turned to see a teenage girl aiming a musket at him. She fired, but the bullet only grazed his arm. He raised his pistol but, staring at her in horror, fired into the air. The girl fled into the woods.

Israel Smythe stood frozen at the edge of the clearing. His wife's sister ran past him clutching a child. She didn't seem to notice him. Rowtag, his brother-in-law, stepped around a wigwam and glared at him. Israel opened his mouth. Rowtag raised a bow and shot Israel through the chest. A second later, Josiah Royce clubbed Rowtag from behind.

Screams rent the air as the settlers rampaged through the village clubbing and tomahawking women and children. Then it was over, and silence fell like a thick snowfall. The settlers gathered in the center of the clearing. They did not look at each other. Twenty-one, including all the young men, of the thirty-two villagers lay motionless on the ground. The rest had scattered into the forest. Owen Harding counted the bodies of five women and seven children as he walked through the clearing weeping visibly.

Lucas saw Susuph lying on his back, his eyes staring in frozen disbelief. Lucas raised his rifle and clubbed the dead man. Then he took out his knife and knelt beside the body.

"Have you gone mad?" snapped Dexter.

Lucas paid no attention. He grabbed a hank of the young man's hair, stretched it, and cut off part of the scalp. He stood up and ordered, "Burn the wigwams."

The next morning, the remaining Abenaki returned to the smoking clearing to chase away the scavengers and bury their dead. A bent old man picked up a musket with a charred stock. He looked at it bitterly. It had not belonged to any of the villagers.

The survivors fled north. A heavy fall rain formed rivulets of ash-laden water that flowed into the stream. Wild grass covered the black circles. The village was never rebuilt, and for years, the small bands of Abenaki who lived in northern Vermont avoided the valley.

After the raid, settlers began referring to both the gorge and the settlement as Scudder's Gorge.

Philomena was unconscious for two days. Martha and Carrie sat by her side day and night and forced spoonfuls of tea into her mouth. When she awoke, she was thirsty and didn't know where she was.

"Susuph?" she asked. "Susuph?"

Carrie was sitting by her side. She took her hand and stroked her brow.

"You don't have to worry about that savage anymore," said Carrie in as reassuring a voice as she could muster. "He's dead."

She told Philomena what Sean had said and described the meeting. She told her what she knew about the raid. She didn't mention the scalp that Martha had forced Lucas to bury. Philomena listened with growing horror. Tears sprang to her eyes.

Carrie held her hand tightly and kept saying, "It's over now. You're going to be all right. He's dead."

"Susuph," was all that Philomena could say.

Lucas entered the cabin and, hearing voices in the loft, climbed the ladder and looked at his daughter. His expression softened.

"You're awake."

He smiled and sat by the bed.

Philomena looked at him with horror and disgust. She said nothing for a second, and then she sat up in bed and pounded his chest with her fists.

"Murderer! Murderer! Murderer!" she screamed. She broke into violent sobbing and continued to hit him. Tears streamed down her face. Lucas didn't move.

"I loved him," she sobbed uncontrollably. "I was going to marry him. You killed him. I loved him. I loved him. I will always love him."

Lucas stood up and glared at his daughter with anger and hatred.

"We will speak no more of this," he commanded before climbing down the ladder.

Philomena died in the early May of 1800, four hours after giving birth to a healthy boy with copper cheeks. A few days earlier, she had given Carrie a letter that she had written back in December. She named the baby "Remember".

Lucas died in 1821, having never mentioned Philomena's name again. At seventeen, Carrie married and raised Remember as one of her own family. She passed the letter on to Remember at her death.

Chapter Four

Everett Scudder
(1879 — 1945)

1891

"Augustus, look – a colt."

The two twelve-year-old boys peered through the trees at a chestnut colt that galloped around its mother and up to a frayed split-rail fence. The colt hung his head over the fence and looked in the direction of the boys. Then, flicking his tail, he galloped up and down the small pasture until he tired of the game and went to suck at his mother's teat.

"What a beautiful colt," said Augustus. "I wonder who's moved into the Macleod place. It's been empty for over six months - since old Randall died, and Mrs. Macleod went down to Montpelier to live with Jessie."

"Maybe Jessie rented it to someone," said Everett. "I can't imagine he moved back. Pa would have said something. 'Sides, he hated farming."

The boys crept close to the edge of the woods and stared across the open meadow toward the fence. They knelt down in the long grass at the edge of the meadow. Augustus laid down the .22 rifle his father, Robertson Baxter, had given him for Christmas, and parted the tall, swaying fronds. There was nothing in sight except the colt, the tired-looking mare, and, in another small field bordering the road, three black and white cows with a small calf wandering between them. It was late May, and dandelions bloomed throughout the meadow.

The small pasture, where the colt vigorously sucked its mother's milk, was hilly, the grass faded and worn. Until he died last October, Randall Macleod had kept a dozen milk cows, which Jessie sold on his father's death. The meadow and woods (where the boys were hiding) formed the eastern boundary of the Baxter farm, which stood on the north side of the Forshay Road. Dean Scudder's farm was across the road and about three quarters of a mile closer to town.

The Macleod place was squeezed between the Baxter's and a swath of marsh, hillocks, and woods that gradually gave way to the steep, forested hills that rose to the eastern ridge.

Robertson Baxter generally left this meadow fallow, except when his herd was larger than usual or the Almanac predicted a severe winter— then he planted hay there. The copse separated the meadow from the other Baxter pastures. Augustus and Everett frequently crossed the copse and meadow, skirting the Macleod farm, to climb toward the ridge. Ignoring their fathers' admonitions, they had gone too far last October and were still in the woods after dark. Badly frightened, they had finally crossed the marsh to meet their fathers and Augustus's older brother, all carrying kerosene lanterns.

They ran into their fathers' arms. Relief giving way to fury, Robertson and Dean were tempted to whip the boys then and there. Spared that humiliation, the boys, on arriving home, were marched grimly to the woodshed. Grace Baxter and Kate Scudder each thought to intercede, but one look at their husbands' angry faces deterred them.

Scratching a living from over-grazed acres had made Randall Macleod a querulous old man. Whenever he saw the boys anywhere near his property, he threatened them with the ravages of hellfire should they dare to set one foot on his land.

"His brain is as loose as his tongue," Augustus would snicker and then shout back gibberish at Randall as Everett pulled him into the woods.

"You'll get us shot someday," Everett would say. "Can't you hold your tongue."

"That old coot couldn't hit us if we were standing on his porch."

The day their fathers had to look for them, Randall stepped onto his porch and hooted as the boys, heads bowed, followed their fathers across the meadow.

"You brats are going to get it now. Whip 'em good, Robertson. Spare the rod, you know." He laughed uproariously and stomped up and down.

"We'll get the old fool," Augustus whispered to Everett, but within a month, death had cheated them of the opportunity.

Everett nudged Augustus and whispered, "Someone's coming."

An unpainted barn stood along one side of the pasture where the colt was frolicking. The house was at right angles to the barn, and the back porch looked across the pasture to Robertson's meadow. The porch also had a view west, toward the Scudder farm. A tall man with long black hair, swarthy skin, and a hooked nose rounded the barn and walked briskly toward the pasture gate, carrying a bucket. He wore faded jeans and a wool shirt.

"Time to skedaddle," Augustus whispered back. The boys backed up on their knees a few feet and then crept through the woods. The tall man stopped at the pasture gate and looked toward the woods. He shrugged and opened the gate.

The boys left the woods about a half mile from Macleod's, crossed the meadow and headed toward the forest. The marsh had started to dry, but mud holes still sucked at their boots. They climbed a small hill and looked back. They could see the colt prancing around his mother, but the tall man was gone. A mangy dog was standing on the porch.

"Race you down the hill," shouted Augustus as he took off, swinging his rifle as he ran. They tore down the hill, their strides lengthening with each step. Augustus, in the lead, continued across a field dotted with wildflowers, stopping finally at a brook that cut a narrow channel through the field.

Everett gasped! "No fair. You didn't start even."

Augustus caught his breath. "So?" He poked Everett in the ribs. "You just learned something." He knelt down and drank from the brook.

Everett cupped some water in his hands; it was cold and clear. Pretending to drink, he splashed Augustus in the face.

"So did you."

Laughing, they entered the forest. The gradual slope soon rose steeply. They wove around thick pines and delicate hemlocks, the dark woods brightened by the white flourishes of slender birches. They breathed hard as they climbed. Mindful now of their fathers' warnings, they stopped after about a half hour and rested on a boulder before starting back down.

"When we're older, we'll climb to the top," said Augustus.

"By then, we'll probably be working too hard to have the time."

Scrambling down a rocky slope, Augustus grabbed Everett's sleeve and pointed. A large, tawny hare sat on the other side of a thicket about thirty yards away. Augustus raised his rifle. The hare crouched and sprang. As it lifted off its hind legs, Augustus fired. The hare froze in the air and fell, crumpled and lifeless.

"Got it," crowed Augustus.

He ran through the thicket, pushing brambles out of his way, and picked up the hare. Drops of blood fell on Augustus's shirt as he held it aloft.

"My father loves rabbit stew."

Everett clapped him on the back. "Let's go," he said quietly.

The boys attended a one-room schoolhouse. The next morning, Monday, Robertson Baxter hitched his two workhorses to the wagon. Augustus and his two younger sisters piled onto the seats that lined both sides, and Robertson drove down the Forshay Road toward town. Ogden, his oldest, had finished eighth grade and worked full-time on the farm. At the Scudder house, Everett and Frieda climbed aboard while the three Forshay children got in a mile further on. Two years older than Augustus and Everett, Richard Forshay occasionally deigned to play ball with them.

"Full of himself," commented Augustus, "like all the Forshays, except little Belle, who's still young."

Robertson slapped the reins, and the horses broke into a trot. They passed small farms with narrow fields dotted with a few Holsteins. The road curved north to parallel the river through a mile of farmland and open country before reaching the first houses in town. Several paths wound down to the river through fields of tall, waving grass. The youngsters bounced on the hard benches, chattering noisily. School would soon be out for the summer.

Entering town, they turned onto Mill Street, which led down to the sawmill on the river. Wooden scaffolding surrounded the new Catholic Church that would serve the growing community of Irish and Italian immigrants who were building modest frame houses along Mill and neighboring streets. The men worked mostly in the sawmill or the granite quarry that had been carved out of the western ridge.

"Gloomy looking place," said Everett, looking at the dark brick structure that still lacked a roof.

"We should sneak over at lunch and look around. Might find something good."

The passengers jumped out at a one-story building, and Robertson continued down Cedar through an area of new clapboard houses. He had to pick up some tools at Sellick's Hardware. Children of all ages romped in the dirt yard in front of the school. The younger ones played tag while the older boys threw a baseball. Wagons from several directions stopped in the rutted road to drop off excited students. Children also arrived on foot, carrying book bags slung over their shoulders.

At precisely eight o'clock, a tall, gaunt man wearing a shawl over his stooped shoulders stepped out of the schoolhouse and vigorously rang a large iron bell. Mr. Osborne had taught elementary school for many years in Burlington. He and his wife had come to Scudder's Gorge six years ago to "partially retire and find a quieter life." When Vera Howell died four years ago, Mrs. Osborne had taken over the library and fiercely pursued overdue books. They had no children of their own, and Mr. Osborne was known to observe that "they didn't much care for them". He may have heard of the new concepts of education, such as inspired the recently founded Horace Mann School in New York City; but Mr. Osborne would never be caught practicing them.

"In your places – and be quiet," he barked as the exuberant children filed into the classroom.

The students were separated by age, and Mr. Osborne assigned tasks to each group. Having outgrown their desks, several older pupils sat uncomfortably with their legs sticking into the aisles. He instructed the third and fourth graders to study passages from their McGuffey Readers while he used the blackboard to work with first and second graders on their spelling. He told the seventh grade to read a chapter in their American history book and then write a summary of what they had read. Augustus and Everett bent their heads to the task. After a few minutes, Augustus whispered out of the side of his mouth:

"Geez, the 1824 tariff. Does it get any duller?"

"Even grammar is better than this," said Everett. "I don't understand why Henry Clay cared about northern companies. He was from Kentucky."

"My father says that Daniel Webster was better than any other politician back then."

"Mr. Baxter. You are talking, sir. Come to the front of the room."

The boys looked up to see Mr. Osborne standing squarely, hands behind his back, glaring at them from the front of the classroom.

Augustus walked slowly up the aisle.

"Hold out your hand."

The schoolmaster gave him five loud strokes on the palm with his ruler. Augustus winced but kept silent.

"You may return to your seat, Mr. Baxter, and you will, I am confident, pay greater attention to your reading in the future."

Augustus winked at Everett.

"Why me?"

"Just lucky, I guess," smirked Everett, keeping his head bent over his book. "Maybe he doesn't like Daniel Webster."

"Mr. Scudder."

Augustus and Everett were grousing about Mr. Osborne at recess when Cornelius McCabe, two years younger and generally scorned by them, approached their corner of the yard, bubbling with excitement. His family owned a small dairy farm about a mile east of town.

"Not now, Cornelius," said Everett.

"Can't you see we've got important business to discuss," snapped Augustus. "Beat it."

"I guess you fellows haven't heard the news," taunted Cornelius, sidling up to them, ready to run if one of them took a swipe.

"What news?" asked Augustus in a bored voice.

"About the Indians."

"What Indians?" they both said at once.

"My Pa said some Indians have moved onto a farm out your way. He said it was a goddamn shame, but he guessed no one else would take the miserable place."

"Watch your language," said Everett.

"Yeah, and we already knew all about that," added Augustus.

Downcast, Cornelius left, but his spirits picked up as he joined a game of blind man's bluff.

"Do you think he meant the family that's taken the Macleod farm?" asked Everett.

"I don't know, but we sure as hell had better get out there and take a look."

What with farm work and school, it was Saturday afternoon before the two boys returned to the copse. They walked quietly to the edge of the meadow and, once again, knelt down to peer through the tall grass. A brisk wind blew high clouds over the ridge and set the meadow grass billowing.

"Better lie down, or someone might see us," said Everett, stretching out in the grass and looking cautiously over the waving stems.

Augustus lay down, his .22 by his side. The colt and mare were in the pasture, and today, four cows instead of three grazed in the far field. The sun started to warm their backs. They had worked hard that morning, weeding vegetables, cleaning barns, and helping spread manure—the warmth adding to their drowsiness. A few bees droned around the wild flowers, and robins skimmed over the meadow. A red-tailed hawk rode the drafts, its whitish underbelly just visible. A field mouse ran in front of them, a few yards away.

"What are you fellows doing there? Sleeping?"

They turned over fast to see a boy their own age standing behind them – grinning as though pleased with himself. He was thin, with narrow shoulders and tawny skin. He had jet-black hair and a hooked nose. His hands were calloused.

Augustus and Everett sat up. "Who are you?" they both asked.

"Who are you?"

"We live around here," Augustus said.

"I live over there," said the boy, pointing to the Macleod farm.

"You must be ..." said Augustus.

"What's your name?" interrupted Everett quickly.

"Thomas. Thomas Zaltana."

"You have ..." said Augustus.

"An English name. That's right. What's yours?"

"Augustus Baxter."

"Everett Scudder."

"Can you shoot that thing?" asked Thomas.

"Like Annie Oakley. Wanna' see?"

The three boys walked along the edge of the meadow for a hundred yards and then headed toward the forest.

"My Pa won't let me shoot anywhere near houses," explained Augustus.

They crossed the marsh and climbed a hillock. Looking back, Everett asked, "Is that your colt?"

"The family's. My father bred the mare to a farmer's stallion over in Frenchman's Hollow where we used to live."

"Nice colt. What are you going to do with it?"

"My father wants to sell it in a couple of years. He thinks it could race."

They skirted the perimeter of the forest until they found a wide, level stretch of open land. They piled up a dozen pinecones and fixed three in the crooks of maple trees. Taking long strides, they measured off twenty yards. Augustus aimed and fired, hitting a cone dead center. Thomas and Everett each hit a cone. They set up three more cones and paced off an additional ten yards. They each hit their target. At forty yards, Everett missed; and at fifty, Augustus grazed the branch but missed the cone. When Thomas hit a cone at sixty yards, Augustus jumped in the air and whooped, "Let's save our ammunition for squirrels and rabbits."

He pumped Thomas's hand and pounded him on the back.

Fast friends from that moment on, the three boys spent every free hour together during the bright, buggy days of June. Augustus and Everett would walk through the copse, and, upon reaching the meadow, Augustus would put two fingers in his mouth and make an ear-piercing whistle.

"How do you do that?" asked Everett.

"Talent."

Thomas would come running around the barn, and they tramped through the meadow toward the forest. Augustus often brought his .22, and Thomas was sometimes allowed to borrow his father's old Springfield. They hunted rabbits and squirrels and once shot a small buck. They carried the game back to the Zaltana farm where Thomas's father and brother helped them skin the animals and dress the meat. They divided the catch, but Everett somehow always managed to see to it that Thomas's family got the largest share. Stuffing the meat into leather pouches, Augustus and Everett strode proudly home.

Thomas's father, Hugh, and his older brother, Carl, struggled to wrest a living from the tired Macleod farm. Having invested most of their savings in the three cows, all of which were producing milk, they had sold the calf to help pay for the fourth cow. Although starting late in the season, they had put in a small crop of hay and a vegetable garden. They wanted to buy some chickens to have eggs for the family and to sell. They hoped to keep the colt until it was old enough to bring a handsome price. When he signed the lease, Hugh had negotiated an option with Jessie Macleod to buy the farm for a modest price. He wanted to own his own land no matter how poor. His forefathers, his grandfather had told him, had farmed in this valley but had been driven out by white settlers.

The Zaltana family had tenanted a farm in Frenchman's Hollow for almost ten years but had lost their lease when the farm was sold. It had been a smaller, but richer place than the Macleod farm. But here they might be able to save enough to buy the property. It was an article of faith for Hugh Zaltana that to survive in the white man's world, you had to own land.

Like every other farm family, all the Zaltanas had their share of farm chores. Hugh and Carl did the heaviest work, but Thomas and his little sister, eleven-year-old Tehya, bore the chief responsibility for the vegetable garden. Hugh and Carl spent long hours repairing the barn and house. They also roamed the valley looking for seasonal work to supplement the cash income from the farm. If he were going far enough, Hugh took the mare although she didn't like leaving the colt. Hugh rode bareback. The mare balked and bucked, but once he nudged her out of the yard, she trotted down the road.

"Why does Tehya have an Indian name and you and Carl don't?" Augustus asked one hot afternoon. It was early July, and instead of hunting, they were walking down the dusty road toward the swimming hole in the river.

"We all have Indian names only Carl and I don't like to use them. Tehya is too silly to know the difference."

"What's your Indian name?" asked Everett.

"Ahmik, which means beaver. Carl is Minigan – grey wolf."

"What does Tehya mean?"

"Like what gold is – or a jewel. Sort of ..."

"Precious," said Everett.

"Yes," said Thomas. "That's it, precious. How did you figure it out so easily?"

"Well, she is, isn't she?" asked Everett.

It was a two and a half-mile walk to the swimming hole. A few wagons loaded with supplies passed them coming from town, but none going toward the river. Augustus and Everett greeted the farmers politely by name. Thomas nodded but said nothing. On one rickety wagon, Augustus and Everett recognized neither the farmer sitting up on the high seat nor his two grown sons lounging in the back. A barrel of flour, a bag of sugar, tins of coffee, tools, and a bolt of bright yellow cloth were stacked along the sides. The three men had stopped at Elihu's Tavern on the outskirts of town, and the two in the back were singing in a loud voice:

> The drums will rattle, the bands will play,
> The boys hurrah, and the girls look gay,
> And we'll all rejoice when
> The boys come marching home.

As the wagon approached, the three boys stepped out of the road to avoid the billow of dust rising from the horses' hooves and the metal-rimmed wheels. They waved to the strangers. The driver turned his head, nodded to them, and muttered something inaudible. His sons stuck their heads over the slatted sides and nudged each other in the ribs.

"Will ya' look at that, Aaron? Wonder where he come from?"

"Yeah, I see. Big as life and twice as ugly. And acting like he's white."

"Hey, Pa," said Derek, in a slurred voice. "Do ya' see that buck? Wonder where his tomeyhawk is? Hey Injun ...," he started to call to Thomas.

"Shut up! Yes, I saw. Now both of you shut your damn fool mouths." He slapped the reins, shouted "Git Up!", and hissed at his sons, "Them other two are a Scudder and a Baxter. If they want to pal around with a nigger, you jes keep shut about it."

The boys had heard snatches of what the men had said and stared at the wagon as it rolled down the road, dust swirling behind it.

"Jerks," said Augustus. "Let's go. I want to swim."

He and Everett started, but Thomas continued to stare at the wagon. Everett came back and put a hand on his arm.

"It doesn't mean a thing," he said.

"Yes it does."

Dripping with sweat, the boys reached the swimming hole, stripped down to their shorts, and dove in. The swimming hole was simply a bend in the river where a pool formed away from the current. It was crowded today, mostly with boys, but a few girls were also swimming. Two farm wagons and a carriage stood on the bank. The wagon horses were munching contentedly out of feedbags while the carriage horse had been tied loosely enough to a tree to graze in the shade.

The three boys rose to the surface and started splashing each other. A couple of other boys joined in, and soon there was a general melee that included the girls. Three adults kept a careful lookout. Swimming here was safe as long as no one ventured toward midstream where the current could sweep a child away in an instant. Close calls had occurred, and a couple of kids had drowned - although not in recent memory. Since children were forbidden to swim without an adult present, a rite of passage had emerged, one that involved sneaking to the swimming hole after dark.

After the water fight, the children started jumping off the bank, bursting to the surface, and climbing out at a shallow, sandy beach to run up the bank and jump in again. The three friends swam for about an hour and a half and then lay on the bank to dry off. The blazing sun felt delicious as they stared into a cloudless sky arching overhead like a blue cathedral vault. They dried quickly and stood up to swim again, but the adults were calling in the children.

Chores needed doing.

On the way home, Augustus remarked slyly, "I think the time has come."

"For what?" asked Thomas.

"You'll see," said Everett.

"We meet at the Scudder barn Sunday after supper," instructed Augustus.

Everett swatted at a mosquito as he stepped onto the front porch; he waved to his friends and went inside. His father was in the parlor reading copies of the Burlington Free Press that a friend sent once a week. He put the paper on a cherry side table and heaved himself out of the overstuffed armchair.

"Time for the cows."

As they walked across the yard, Dean said to his son, "What do you say to sneaking off for a little fishing tomorrow after lunch? We can be back in time for milking."

"Oh, yes sir. Thank you."

Everett's eyes glowed with excitement as they approached the barn, a post and beam structure that had replaced the old sheep barn over ten years ago. Since the time of Lucas, the Scudder family had farmed along the Forshay Road. Remember had been Lucas's only male heir to survive into adulthood. His son Nathaniel had sold the farm near town in the 1840s and purchased a much larger property about three miles further out. Nathaniel raised sheep until the early 1870s when he and his son, Dean, began dairy farming. They grew corn and hay as fodder and vegetables for family use. Although he was a full-time dairy farmer, Dean had served two terms as mayor of Scudder's Gorge in the '80s.

The large, white frame house, which Nathaniel had built in the late '60s after his original house was burned by lightning, was set on a slight elevation, and looked south past the chicken coop and pastures. Albert Forshay, Richard's father, had apple orchards a mile to the east. Between these apple orchards and the river clustered a few smaller dairy farms. Typical of Nineteenth Century and earlier farmhouses, the Scudder's had a small front yard close to the road and a large back yard, studded with tall maples, between the house and barn.

Travis, the hired man, had already started. Dean and Everett each took a tin pail and a stool and sat down next to a cow. No one spoke as they concentrated on pulling the teats and watching the milk splash into the pails. It was steaming in the barn, and sweat began to drip from Everett's brow. Flies buzzed around the pail; he stopped from time to time to wipe his forehead with a handkerchief and shoo away the flies. The cows stood quietly in their stalls and idly swished their tails.

The next afternoon, Dean hitched up the buggy right after lunch and loaded high rubber boots, two fly rods, a box of hand-tied trout flies, two nets and two wicker baskets in the back. Everett climbed onto the seat next to his father, who handed him the reins while he lit his pipe. They set off toward town and Everett, feeling proud, sat stiff and straight. He waved at Richard, who was swinging on the front porch, when they passed the Forshay farm.

Everett watched the green fields of corn and hay roll by, and listened to the clopping of Bertha's hooves on the hard-packed dirt road. A breeze off the river relieved the stifling heat. Dean glanced occasionally at his son. He thought there was something on his mind, but he waited. Some things cannot be hurried.

Everett started to speak, stopped, and then started again. "Dad, why do people hate Indians?"

Dean sighed, a pained expression crossing his face. "Some folks do, son. Most don't, at least not anymore. Some never did." He puffed on his pipe. "Did something happen with Thomas?"
"Not exactly happened, but yesterday, when we were walking to the swimming hole, a wagon passed and some men insulted Thomas."

"What did they say?"

"I couldn't hear everything, but they called him "ugly" and "a buck." One of them called out, "Hey Injun." That's when I was sure it was Thomas they were talking about. Oh, and something about him acting white."

"Was that it? Did anything else happen? Did they threaten you?"

"No, sir. They didn't even stop the wagon. The two men who did the talking were sitting in the back. The driver, I think he was their father; anyway, he was much older, told them to shut up. There was more, but I couldn't hear it. Thomas was pretty mad."

"As near as you could tell, were they liquored up?"

"I guess so. Their voices sounded funny, and the men in the back were singing pretty loud as they came down the road."

"I see. Go on."

"Thomas was glaring at the back of the wagon; and I told him that it didn't mean anything, but he said that it did. I wanted him to know that he was my friend."

"Did you tell him that?"

"No, not exactly. I didn't know what else to say because I was ..."

"Embarrassed."

Everett looked at Bertha's ears and then said in a quiet voice, "Yes, sir."

"That's all right son. I know how you felt, and you did the best you could."

Dean shook the reins, and Bertha trotted a little faster. A blackbird swooped in front of the buggy. Winding its way through the meadows, the river gleamed like a silver thread woven into a tapestry. Dean looked toward the horizon and then at his son. From Everett's description, it could have been any of a number of farmers.

"Unlike some other places, son, people are free in our country to say what they think. It's in our constitution. But having that right doesn't necessarily make people intelligent. There are plenty of stupid people in this world who, especially when they get some liquor in them, can say some cruel and hurtful things. There's not much you can do as long as they're just talking. I guess the best thing now is to find some way to let Thomas know that you're his friend. He's a good, hard-working boy.

They're all hard-working people, the Zaltanas. Most people would be better off with their mouths shut."

Everett was silent. They had entered town, and Dean greeted a few people as they drove down Cedar Street. They passed the schoolhouse, deserted for the summer, the small granite and marble town hall, the red brick professional building and Tyrell's General Store. As they left town, Everett said:

"Thanks, Dad."

Dean let out a puff of smoke and looked at the river. It was lower than usual. They needed rain.

"You're a bit young yet, and I would normally have waited, but there's a letter I want to show you when we get home. It was written by your great-great grandmother some ninety years ago. It's a troubling letter, but I think you're mature enough to read it. The Scudder family has a great responsibility which I am confident you will live up to."

They drove north for another mile. Dean stopped the buggy in a clump of trees. He unhitched Bertha and tied him to a tree so that he could graze. He and Everett put the rods together, attached the reels, and tied delicate feather flies to the end of each line. Putting on their boots and slinging baskets over their shoulders, they waded into the stream – not far out since the current could be strong even in this fairly level stretch.

"Let me see you cast," said Dean.

Everett played out some line with his left hand and flicked his fishing rod back and forth until his line curved in broad arcs over his head. He gave a strong toss of his wrist and the fly sailed into the middle of the stream. He let it rest briefly and then started reeling it in. The bright yellow fly skimmed and danced along the surface of the water.

"Very good," said Dean. "Nice cast. Just lift your wrist a little higher on that last snap, and your line will go further. Now, I'll move downstream a piece, and we can both cast at the same time."

Dean waded about twenty yards, selecting a spot where he could block Everett if he fell into the current. He spotted a dark shape in an eddy near the far bank. He let out his line and cast in a long, graceful arc. The line made a zinging sound as the reel spun, and the fly landed within a few inches of the trout. Dean gently jiggled the fly, but the trout ignored it. Dean brought the line in and then cast it out again. This time the trout struck and, feeling the bite of the hook in its mouth, swam desperately upstream. Dean's rod bent in a taut bow. He reeled in line, but let out a little when the tension got too tight. The trout leaped out of the water, fighting the hook, its belly flashing in the sun. Dean pulled back his rod to keep the line taut. Everett watched, transfixed. Dean brought the fish closer and closer, reeling in quickly when the fish swam toward him, and more slowly when the fish fought the line. When he saw the dark, speckled form of the now exhausted fish swimming within a few feet, he reeled the trout close to his boots, caught the writhing fish in his net, took out the hook, and plopped the fish into his basket.

"Gave you a good fight, Dad, but you sure held him."

"Yes, it had a lot of spunk. Catch a couple more, and we've got dinner. Your mother loves trout."

Everett cast, and a trout struck. He fought the fish awkwardly with the line too tight and the rod straining. Dean resisted offering advice. Experience, he felt, was the best teacher. The fish jumped, and Everett jerked the rod sharply backwards. Flailing and tugging viciously, the trout dove back into the stream and snapped the line. Everett was crestfallen. Dean's heart ached, and his throat tightened. He waded over to his son and put an arm around his shoulder.

"I can't tell you how many times that's happened to me. My father used to ask me if I was selling the flies on the sly. Just play him a little more gently and let him have some line when he's running so as to keep the line from getting too tight."

Everett nodded, and the next time a fish struck, he followed his father's advice. The fish fought hard, leaping and plunging. Everett's muscles ached, but he kept the line at just the right tension, playing out when the pull was too hard, and reeling in whenever he could. The trout eventually tired, and Everett pulled it in.

"Nicely done, son. It's a beauty."

They caught several more, and Dean declared, "Supper's as good as on the table." They packed up their gear and turned Bertha toward home.

Sunday dragged on forever. After the morning chores, church and lunch, Everett cleaned the barn until mid-afternoon. It was close, dusty, and reeked of dried hay and manure. He wished the afternoon were over. Augustus and Thomas came over for a while; the three boys threw a baseball and then sat under a tree whittling.

"Don't you boys want to go swimming before you have to get back to chores?" asked Kate.

"No, not today, Mom. It's too far to walk. We just want to sit awhile."

After supper, Everett helped with the dishes, carried the slops to the pigs, and then told his mother that he was going over to the Baxter's. Checking the yard quickly, he hurried around the barn and waited on the side hidden from the house. Augustus and Thomas ducked into some trees before reaching the Scudder farm. They slipped quietly to the barn by following the split rail fence that separated the back yard from the upper pasture. They walked bent over along the fence, looking constantly through the rails to see if anyone was around.

The three boys crossed the pasture and hurried through rows of tall corn stalks. They skirted a hay field and scurried into a copse at the edge of the Forshay place. Peeking out to be sure the coast was clear, they made a wide circle behind the house, climbed a rail fence, crossed a narrow potato field, climbed another fence and entered an apple orchard. The trees were laden with young apples. Bright rays of light shot out from behind the ridge and painted the sky in delicate blues, pinks, and crimsons.

They left the apple orchard and started down even rows of tangled strawberry plants thick with hanging red berries. Augustus bent over and picked three, which he shared with Everett and Thomas. They struck the road a half mile beyond the Forshay farm. It was dark and still blistering hot when they reached the deserted swimming hole. Quickly shedding their clothes, they jumped in and splashed around noisily. They had a contest to see who could swim the furthest underwater. They sat on the bank, drying themselves with their shirts.

"I wonder what's up there," said Augustus, lying on his back and staring at Orion's Belt.

"Spirits," said Thomas.

"What kind?" asked Everett.

"All kinds."

"Last one in's a monkey," shouted Augustus.

They sprayed each other, bringing the heels of their hands down hard on the water. Everett edged backwards. The chirping of crickets floated across the water. The rising moon cast a pale light on the black river so that the boys could see each other's heads and shoulders bobbing in the water. The current suddenly sucked Everett in. He shouted and went under. He came up gasping and flailing. He went under again. A strong arm circled his chest and jerked him back toward the bank. He flung his arms madly.

Thomas cuffed him sharply on the side of his head and propelled them both backwards. Augustus swam up and grabbed Everett's legs. He and Thomas maneuvered him into the quiet pool. Everett coughed up water and spit. His throat burned and his lungs felt like an iron spike had been driven into them. With his friends' help, he crawled onto the beach. He knelt on his hands and knees, gasping and spitting. His body shuddered, and he retched onto the sand. He collapsed. Thomas and Augustus sat facing him.

"Thank you." He sat up and shivered. "Thank you both."

No one spoke for a minute. Then Augustus asked, "What awful stuff did you have for dinner?"

They started laughing, and when they stopped, Everett waded into the water and immersed himself. They kicked sand over the spot where he had thrown up and started home.

"Well," said Thomas. "We did it."

The road shone brightly in the moonlight. When they reached the Scudder barn, they formed a circle and put their fists in the center.

"One for all, and all for one," said Augustus who had been reading Dumas that summer.

Everett took his shoes off and quietly opened the kitchen door. He closed it softly behind him and turned to see his mother sitting in the dark at the kitchen table.

"Did you have a nice swim?" she asked.

"I ... we ... uh..."

"Don't even think of lying to me."
"How did you know?"

"When you didn't come back at dark ... and you're the right age."

"I almost drowned. Thomas and Augustus pulled me out."

He started to cry and fell into his mother's waiting arms. She held him tight and stroked the back of his head.

"Go on up to bed. Your father was tired and went to bed early. If he finds out, he'll skin you alive." She pushed him toward the passageway. "And if you ever do it again, I will."

One afternoon, late in August, Robertson Baxter drove his wagon into town. He had half a dozen bushels of squash, peppers, and tomatoes to deliver to Tyrell's. He wanted to spend a few minutes with Cory Smythe, his lawyer, concerning a piece of property he was negotiating to buy on the west side of the river. He took Augustus and Everett with him. He stopped the team at a narrow brick building on Cedar, handed the reins to Augustus, and got down.

"You boys drive on down to Tyrell's and unload the vegetables." He gave them each a penny. "Then pick yourselves out a candy. I won't be but a minute. We have to pick up some sugar and a few other things for your mother."

Beaming, Augustus picked up the reins and flicked them.

"Be sure to give Bravo and Sonny their feedbags."

Robertson proudly watched his son, sitting high up on the wagon seat with Everett, drive the short distance to Tyrell's. He waited until they got out the feedbags before entering the building. It took both boys to slide each basket to the back of the wagon, lift it, and carry it into the store. Sweat trickled down their backs, and their shirts were soon soaked. Carrying a basket brimming with tomatoes, Everett said, "Maybe your Pa will let us swim on the way home."

The store was dim and cool. Baskets of vegetables stood on tables. Various-sized barrels of flour and sugar lined a wall. Canned fruit, meat, and vegetables crowded the shelves. Three large wheels of cheese were on display while more were kept in the cellar. Tall, narrow-necked jars of hard candies stood on a glass counter that contained, among other items, pocketknives, fishing hooks, packets of writing paper and boxes of loose pencils. Ferris Tyrell stood behind the counter at a black cash register; behind him were tins of coffee and boxes of ammunition. A brass scale rested on an adjacent counter. Except on the hottest days, a fire burned in the cast iron stove set squarely in the middle of the store. A pipe rose from the stove to the ceiling. Several farmers sat talking in front of the unlit stove.

"That's the last one, Mr. Tyrell," Augustus said.

"Good. Set it with the others and help yourselves to a piece of candy."

The boys offered him their pennies, but Mr. Tyrell shook his head.

"On the house."

"Thank you, sir," they said in unison and selected a hard candy each.

They sat on the porch steps and watched a Phaeton pass. Four wagons stood outside the store. An old wagon creaked up Cedar, the driver a sour-faced farmer in a soiled denim shirt. Two men leaned against the sides in the back. The driver spit a long stream of dark liquid that kicked up a puff of dust.

Everett nudged Augustus, "Those are the same fellows that insulted Thomas."

"Holy cow! We better hide someplace where they can't see us."

Scrambling like lightening off the steps, they scrunched down in their wagon, pretending to be asleep. The farmer swung his team into the yard and climbed down. Walking to the back of the wagon, he growled at his sons.

"Out, you lazy half-wits and start unloading these potatoes."

The farmer stomped up the stairs, his sons each hefted a heavy basket and followed him. On their second trip, a slight man in his early thirties stepped through the door and bumped into Derek, who stumbled back a half step. He barked at the young man, who was already mumbling an apology.

"Watch where you're going, you idiot!"

Wiley Fitzgerald was a shy man who had lived his entire life on his father's farm, a scraggly affair across and down the road from the Scudder place. The Fitzgerald farm consisted of scrawny chickens, a couple of cows, and a vegetable garden. Neither father nor son was good at farming, but Wiley was a crack shot and always found game.

"I'm sorry," Wiley mumbled again, and walked around the porch to the side of the store. He sat down and put his head in his hands. The men inside had been talking politics, and Wiley didn't understand politics. Besides, he had stopped at Elihu's for a beer on the way into town, and he didn't do that very often. As a matter of fact, he didn't come to town all that often. His head hurt. Aaron and Derek had unloaded the potatoes and waited on the porch for their father to finish buying supplies. They saw no one else on the porch.

"They's two grown ones on that farm so we need maybe two ... three more men," said Derek.

"You think those scumbag Indians have got guns?" asked Aaron.

"Sure they do. That's why we got to move fast and scare 'em good with enough men. We don't want this party turning into a fight."

"So the idea is we ride up to their place tonight, shoot out a few windows, throw in some torches, and mosey along? That ole house'll go up like a cracker, and the niggers'll hightail it by morning?"

"We have us some fun 'n gets the farm to boot." Derek smirked.

"Mebbe get us a buck to hang on the wall."

"Now wait just a minute. We want to scare 'em and drive 'em off but no killing. That could cause us a heap of trouble."

"Aw, I was jes kidding. I ain't gonna' kill nobody – 'les they accidentally gets in my sights. 'Specially that nigger brat that was sashaying with those highfalutin rich kids. Think they're somebody 'cause their pa's got money and their ancestors settled this dump."

Augustus and Everett exchanged glances, their faces ashen, and pressed hard against the wagon's floor.

Derek continued: "We're gonna deal with these damn Indians jes like they did out at Wounded Knee. 'N I see just the fellow to help us."

A short distance away, a heavyset man with dark hair and a red, bulbous nose ambled down the road carrying an ax over his shoulder. Since timbering had fallen off, and was, in any case, a seasonal occupation, Cody Murphy chopped wood for elderly residents and did occasional stints as a carpenter in the Taylor furniture factory. He was a drifter and brawler, periodically making himself scarce, but he always returned to take up residence in a dilapidated cabin, one of four that festered in the woods where North Valley road ended and the trail to the gorge began.

"What do we want him for? The bastard'll kill you soon as look at you."

"Exactly," Derek grinned. "'N he's got friends jes like him."

Derek stepped off the porch and, still grinning, hailed the lumberjack. "Hey Cody, you murdering son of a bitch. I'll bet even an ignorant mule like you has heard of Wounded Knee."

Cody raised his ax threateningly and laughed. Derek strutted the twenty yards that separated him from Cody and clapped the beefy, sometime-lumberjack on the shoulder. Aaron hurried to join them, and the three strolled up the street before stopping to talk. Derek and Aaron stood with their backs to the store. Derek gesticulated with his hands while Aaron held up one hand and rubbed his thumb and forefinger together. Cody nodded, raised his ax, and pointed toward the gorge.

"Are you boys asleep?" Robertson peeked over the side of the wagon.

"No, sir," answered Augustus. The boys shot up from their crouched position.

"You both look like you've seen a ghost. Is everything all right?"

"Yes sir."

"Well then, come on in the store with me. We've got some purchases to make."

Looking around cautiously, they climbed out of the wagon and followed closely behind Robertson. The sour-faced farmer, carrying some parcels wrapped in brown paper, pushed open the door just as Robertson reached for the handle. Robertson stepped back to let him pass.

"Afternoon, Adam," he said politely. "Hot day."

"Indeed, Robertson, indeed."

Adam Jenkins nodded curtly and carried his packages to the wagon. He looked up the street and scowled. Robertson greeted the men sitting by the stove and went up to the counter. Augustus and Everett drifted off to a corner and pretended an absorbing interest in a display of buggy whips.

"We need to stop them," Everett whispered urgently.

"I'll ask Pa if you can come to dinner, and we'll figure out a plan."

"I already have an idea."

Everett put his mouth close to Augustus's ear.

"Afternoon, Ferris. How's business?"

"Afternoon, Robertson. Me and the missus are scraping by and could do better if the good citizens of this town would try these new brands of canned goods."

"They'll catch on. Now I need two pounds of sugar, three pounds of coffee, a tin of ..."

Adam came back into the store and picked up two more parcels on the counter.

"Sam will help you with those," Ferris said to Adam, nodding at a barrel and several bags waiting near the door.

"Obliged. Good day, Ferris ... Robertson." Adam nodded to the men by the stove. Robertson continued with his list.

Sam Fowler, Ferris's stock boy, carried the small barrel of flour, bags of rice, and a bushel of beans, out to the wagon. Adam muttered his thanks, climbed onto the high seat and looked up the road to where Aaron, Derek, and Cody were still talking.

"Damn, no account sons," he barked and, flicking the reins, turned the wagon in their direction. "Never amount to anything."

Wiley Fitzgerald got up from the edge of the porch, rubbed his temples, and got on his mule to ride home.

"... and throw in a couple of cans of those creamed onions," grinned Robertson.

With the milking and other chores finished, Everett burst out the kitchen door and ran down the road toward the Baxter's. Kate had cautioned him to be home not long after dark. The boys threw a ball back and forth before dinner and talked over their plan, which hinged on Everett's notion that surprise and bravado would carry the day. Everett couldn't stop thinking about the letter his father had shown him, written by Philomena Scudder, his great-great grandmother, shortly before her death. He had a dim memory of his grandfather, Nathaniel, who had died when he was four, so a great-great grandmother seemed impossibly distant. His father had made several comments about the letter—and despite its age, the words simply could not be ignored:

> *Judging any person for who, rather than what, they are, is a great sin. Taking an action before you know all the*

pertinent facts will lead to terrible mistakes more often than not. It is easier to avoid than to undo a wrong. It may seem harsh, but Lucas Scudder's crime does not end with his generation. It places a responsibility on all Scudders to ensure that racial hatreds and the crimes that spring from such hatreds have no place in our community. You have a small amount of Indian blood in your veins. Be proud of it.

"I wish we could get hold of another gun," said Augustus.

"It would help, but no matter what, this is what we have to do."

Everett threw the ball hard at Augustus. He was the best pitcher among the boys in town.

"One for all and all for one," said Augustus.

The boys ate quickly and declined a second helping of chicken stew. They helped clear the table and asked to be excused. Augustus ran for the .22.

"It's too late for hunting," Robertson said.

"We're just going for a little target practice."

"All right, but only while there's good light."

Robertson paced up and down the kitchen. "Something's up with those two," he said to his wife. They've been jittery ever since I met them at the store."

"Why don't you have a talk with Augustus when he comes back?"

A few stars were glimmering and the sky was turning a deep purple as they picked their way through the dark copse – their progress slowed by the low-hanging branches of stout pines. The rustle of birds was magnified, and their footsteps sounded impossibly loud. They shivered as squirrels scampered up trees and jumped when a dark form swooped overhead, hooting softly as it landed on a limb. The cold moonlight caught the horned owl's watchful eyes.

"Are you scared?" asked Augustus.

"No ... yes."

They crossed the meadow and circled behind the farmhouse keeping a good distance. The Zaltana's hound barked and loped up to them, wagging its tail and jumping on them.

"Go back, Bear, go back," Everett whispered. He pushed the dog toward the house. After a few pushes, Bear gave up and trotted back to the porch. The boys took up a position in a clump of trees about 50 yards east of the house and ten yards in from the road. They would be able to see any riders that came along the road from either direction, although they were fairly certain that these men would come from the south and east. They had figured correctly. The Jenkins farm lay at the southern end of the valley, on a road that branched off the Forshay Road just before the latter started climbing up the ridge.

Kneeling, they watched the road, which came over a hillock about forty yards away. Augustus gripped the .22. Everett gathered a pile of stones, putting a few in his pockets. The sky was now teeming with stars, and the moon cast a frightening glow on the woods and fields.

"We're going to get whipped again," Augustus said.

"It doesn't matter."

Everett gripped Augustus's arm. The boys stood up. Four barely visible riders had stopped at the top of the hill. They stayed still for a minute, and then a light flared – and another and another. Torches lit, the riders moved forward. Everett picked up two stones. When they were halfway to the clump of trees, Everett squeezed Augustus's arm and whispered, "Now." The boys stepped out of the clump of trees. Augustus fired a shot into the air. The riders stopped.

"You fellows better get on home," he called out in as deep a voice as he could muster. He fired another shot in the air.

Derek rode forward. "It's those kids," he snarled holding out his torch in front of him; his voice had liquor on it.

"Kids," bellowed Cody Murphy drunkenly. "No kids is getting between me and those dirty savages."

"Besides, they seen us," shouted the fourth man, Wesley Owens, who had lent Cody a horse for the night's work.

The hulking lumberjack carried a wood-splitting hammer with which he planned to smash windows and break down the front door while his friends fired into the house and threw in kerosene soaked torches. He spurred forward, the hammer held high.

"What are you doing?" screamed Aaron. "Are you crazy?"

Augustus raised his rifle, but before he could fire, a stone hit the lumberjack square in the forehead. He bellowed as blood trickled into his eye. He let his hammer drop, and his horse veered to one side of the road.

"Filthy rich bastards," cursed Derek raising his rifle.

A shot rang out. Derek screamed and dropped his rifle as a bullet tore into his shoulder. Another shot skimmed Wesley's hat off his head. A third shot smashed his ankle. Wiley Fitzgerald calmly trotted his mule down the center of the road, firing as he rode. Cody turned his horse back toward Augustus who shot him in the shoulder. Everett threw a second stone, hitting Derek's horse in the chest. The horse shied and almost threw Derek. Wiley fired again, sending a bullet past Aaron's ear.

Two men came running from the farmhouse, rifles in hand. A man shouting and running could be heard behind Wiley and, a little further away, the pounding of hooves.

"They've got a damn army," hollered Derek. The four horses were milling and bumping into each other.

"Let's get out of here," screamed Aaron, who turned his horse and started booting him. The workhorse lumbered off. The other three followed him. Wiley sent a parting shot whizzing past Owen's ear. The four riders disappeared over the crest of the hill as Hugh, Carl, and Robertson ran up. Dean Scudder galloped up a couple of minutes later. They were all brandishing rifles.

1896 - 1899

It was not until his seventeenth birthday party that Everett Scudder realized he was in love with Tehya Zaltana, who preferred her Indian name to Helen. She was sixteen, with black, glossy hair that she wore in a long braid. She had the highest russet cheekbones that could be imagined. Her eyes flashed fire when any of the three boys – who considered themselves men now – made her angry, but she reserved her greatest scorn for Everett.

Augustus and Everett considered themselves men from the time of the shoot-out, as they called it. In later years, whenever they mentioned the shoot-out, Tehya would say something about the Earp brothers and ask Everett if he thought Wyatt used stones instead of a six-shooter.

The event had several consequences. First, Thomas was angry with his friends for not including him and the Springfield.

"How could we protect you," asked Augustus with irrefutable logic, "if you were there doing part of the protecting?" Thomas suggested that Augustus might be spending too much time in that schoolhouse.

"And we saved you from a whipping," added Everett, something of an overstatement since the whipping had been mild in the extreme and more for form's sake than anything like a real whipping.

Second, Sheriff Benson, after talking privately to Everett and Augustus, drove out in his buggy to the Jenkins farm and had a word with Adam. They sat on the porch of the weather-beaten farmhouse. A few scraggly chickens scratched in the dirt yard. Aaron and Derek were nowhere to be seen. The day after the shooting, Dean Scudder had asked Dr. Grayson to see to Derek's shoulder.

No charges would be preferred against his boys, but their future behavior would be exemplary. The sheriff spoke softly but let his voice linger on the last word. Adam nodded and thanked him. He stopped by the Scudder farm one morning to thank Dean for sending the doctor. The Sheriff also spoke quietly to Cody Murphy and Wesley Owen. Both men left town and did not return. Their wounds were treated before they left.

Third, the Scudder and Baxter families were invited to a dinner at the Zaltana farm. Wiley Fitzgerald was also a guest that evening, and although he said little, he beamed when Mattie Zaltana presented him with a doeskin vest. Augustus and Everett proudly wore their embroidered vests throughout dinner.

Finally, it was made clear to Wiley that there would always be a place set for him at any of the three homes.

And since there is often no end to the consequences of such events, it was at that dinner that Hugh was persuaded to send Thomas and Tehya to school in the fall.

A fierce depression raged in 1896, and most of the farmers in the valley were having a difficult time. Robertson told Dean that he would probably have to sell his farm or let the bank take it in settlement of the mortgage. He knew of a badly neglected, unoccupied place on the western edge of the valley that he could have for a song. He thought he could do something with it.

Kate told Everett that he could invite a few friends over for a modest seventeenth birthday party. She would serve refreshments, and Frieda had volunteered to play the piano so they could dance in the parlor. Seven youngsters, including four girls, came from nearby farms while three lads drove from town in a buggy that had seen better days.

Dean and Everett pushed the furniture against the wall and rolled up the rugs. The guests stood around awkwardly, uncomfortable in their close-fitting church clothes. They talked about farming, who had left town to go to high school, and the latest Sears, Roebuck, and Co. catalogue. The party livened up when Kate announced that cake and fruit punch were being served in the dining room. Soon Frieda began to play a waltz, and Dean invited Kate to dance. Two boys followed suit, leading partners into the cleared space. Everett asked Tehya, who looked surprised and then took his arm.

The parlor was cramped as a dance floor; but spirits soared, and the boys took turns asking the girls – who were soon out of breath. Everett danced with Tehya as often as he dared.

After the warm parlor, the partygoers shivered as they stepped into the chill of an exquisite October night. Augustus brought the Baxter's buggy to the front door to pick up Thomas and Tehya. Looking up at the blanket of stars in the sky, Tehya said, "I'd like to walk, even though it's cold." She turned to Everett: "Will you escort me?"

She took his arm, and they started down the road. As the buggy passed them, Augustus leaned over and said, "If she's not home in twenty minutes, we're coming after you … with the Springfield."

They walked a ways in silence. Then Tehya asked, "Do you like being a farmer? I mean do you ever think of doing something else?"

"I've never really thought about it. We've been farmers for generations."

"But you like to read. You and Augustus have always got your noses in books when you're not working or hunting. Don't those books make you think about leaving Scudder's Gorge and doing something different?"

"No, not really. I love to read, but I guess farming's in my blood."

"Well, I want to be more than a farmer's wife. For one thing, I want to keep on with school."

"Even if it means leaving the valley?"

"Even if it does," she said softly.

Everett felt his knees go weak and his stomach constrict. He wanted to change the subject.

"Thomas doesn't like to read, does he?"

"He started too late and couldn't catch up. He won't do anything unless he's as good at it as you and Augustus."

"Or better – like shooting and hunting."

"Or better."

They had passed the Baxter's and stopped just short of her house. She looked up at him.

"It was a wonderful party, Everett. I like to dance, even with boys who have two left feet." She took his hand. "I think you want to … so you may kiss me."

He was stunned. He bent his gangly frame toward her awkwardly and kissed her quickly on the cheek.

"No, like this," she said. She stood on her tiptoes, put her arms around his neck, and kissed him firmly on the mouth. He started to pull back, but she held him tight, and then he leaned into the kiss.

"Good night," he said breathlessly.

"Good night, Everett, and thank you for walking me home. It's a beautiful night."

"I think … I think I love you."

"I know, and I love you. But," she added softly, "I have ambitions."

In November, the bank foreclosed on the Baxter farm and put it up for auction on a fittingly raw day. Clouds and mist enfolded the valley, and a chill seeped through sweaters and coats as the auctioneer – a man from Burlington - called out prices. Knots of surly farmers from Scudder's Gorge stood mutely listening to the rapid patter and glared menacingly if one of the ten or so outsiders seemed about to make a bid. Several men carried rifles. Two farmers in tattered work clothes (who never thought Robertson much of a farmer but just lucky enough to inherit prime land) looked on with poorly concealed satisfaction.

After a couple of low bids were greeted with profane murmurs and something about the farm making a nice fire. Mr. Timothy Duffin, the vice president of the First Bank of Scudder's Gorge, climbed onto the platform.

"Folks," he declared in a loud, but wavering voice. "I've lived in Scudder's Gorge all my life and I don't like this any better than you do. I know most of you here, and I can tell you that this is not helping the Baxters one bit. If we can at least secure enough to pay part of the mortgage, the bank will carry the balance; and Robertson can buy another place. So please, stop this."

"What do you want us to do, Tim," asked a man who was leaning on a Winchester, "throw the bank a party?"

"No, just let the bidding proceed peacefully."

"Timothy is right," said Dean Scudder.

He walked to the base of the platform and faced the crowd.

"The Baxters cannot keep this farm. Robertson is my friend, and it pains me to say this. If anyone here can lend him the money to pay off the bank, let him step forward. I would myself if I could. But these past three years have been gut-wrenching, and we are all just scraping by. We best encourage the bidding so that Robertson can start again. So please, let us show some courtesy to anyone – from the valley or not – who wishes to buy this excellent farm. And remember, we all came from someplace else."

The crowd murmured assent, and rifles were put back into leather sheaths or stowed under wagon seats. The Farrells, a couple in their twenties, whose families owned property near Montpelier, bought the farm and some equipment. Their fathers counter-signed the loan. In a last ditch effort, Robertson had six months earlier sold part of his herd, the Rockaway Carriage and his beloved bays – the horses and carriage to a funeral parlor operator in Barre.

"It seems," he commented to Dean, "that his business is steady no matter how harsh the times."

"Maybe better," Dean replied. "People at least want to make a graceful exit."

Helped by loans from Dean Scudder and Albert Forshay, Robertson bought the farm on the west side. The proceeds from the auction repaid eighty percent of his bank loan. Joshua Taylor, the bank's president, agreed to extend the balance and to provide a new loan for repairs and seed. The bank also allowed him to keep two horses, a few cows, the wagon, farm implements, and the buggy.

At the base of the ridge, enclosed by woods on three sides, the property had a view across the valley. A couple of miles beyond the farm, the dirt road became a track that wound up the ridge and into the next valley. Wayne Kennedy's widow had tried to make a go of the place with some help from an elderly neighbor. Her two married daughters pleaded with her to live with one of them. She said it would be the death of her not to work the farm, but the reverse proved true.

A rooster, chickens, a vegetable garden, and a potato field clinging to a hillside came with the place. The widow had used most of the farm produce herself and had generated very little cash. Consequently, great swaths of paint had flaked off the house, the chimney had loose masonry, three porch steps were rotten and the floorboards inside were cracked and separated in many places. Two other buildings shared the barren yard: a barn and large storage shed. While unpainted, these buildings were solidly built, although both needed new roof shingles, and the barn door tilted at a crazy angle.

Robertson moved his family the week before Thanksgiving. He and the boys started immediately on the most urgent repairs. He bought hay to carry his cows until spring. Grace and the girls cleaned the house of six months' worth of dust and grime. The family drove to the Scudder's for Thanksgiving dinner. Afterwards, Everett and Augustus walked down to the Zaltana's.

After Thanksgiving, Everett and Thomas saw much less of Augustus. It took a grinding effort from all the Baxters to improve the farm. They acquired an old bull in exchange for day labor, and in a year, they were able to sell milk and a couple of calves.

Exhausted, Robertson died two years after the move. Ogden was twenty-two and despised farming although he had never said as much. He let Augustus take over the place and he moved to Barre where he got a job in a granite quarry, married and raised a family.

With no relief from the depression in sight, Dean let the hired man go. He and Everett did the heaviest work alone while Frieda minded the chickens, helped milk and churned butter. She took weekly piano lessons from Elvira Grayson, who had performed in Boston before marrying Howard – a medical student at the time. Elvira said that Frieda was talented, and when times improved, she ought to study in Burlington or Boston. Frieda practiced for hours with hope, like her fingers, dancing along the keys.

Everett spent his free time with Tehya. He and Thomas continued hunting together, but it was not the same without Augustus. He and Tehya went for long walks and to socials at neighboring farms. They held hands and kissed ardently, but it went no further. He never tried. Just before his eighteenth birthday, he asked her to marry him. She reminded him of their conversation of a year ago.

"I love you, but I haven't changed my mind about being a farmer's wife." Her kiss did nothing to settle his churning stomach.

Despite the depression, through hard work and astute purchases of cows, Hugh and his sons had made something of their farm. The colt had brought a price sufficient to buy a young bull, whose services he offered in Scudder's Gorge and neighboring valleys. In the spring of 1898, a client told him about a large farm for sale east of St. Albans. It needed work but had great promise. He left the bull and wagon with his client and rode four hours to inspect the property. He reached an agreement, which he finalized the following week when he brought Carl and Thomas to see the farm.

Tehya had progressed rapidly through the grades in the one-room schoolhouse, and had been studying independently for the last three years. Mr. Dillard, who had replaced Mr. Osborne, upon the latter's well-deserved retirement, took a great interest in the social progress of Indians. Without charge, he tutored Tehya once a week and outlined study programs. He corrected her essays. Hugh had agreed that she could apply for admission to the university in Burlington.

The depression was finally ending. Hugh had bought the Macleod farm from Jessie three years earlier and sold it to the Farrells at a handsome profit. The Zaltanas moved in early June.

Everett and Tehya continued to kiss; and he hoped that a miracle would occur, but he sensed her drifting away. She was ecstatic about applying to the university. He thought of suggesting that she come back to teach at Scudder's Gorge, but he was too proud to risk another rejection. He let his last chance slip away the night before they left.

She promised to write often, and did for seven months. She was thrilled with the farm, new friends, and her studies. Devouring each letter, he replied immediately. By the following year, the letters came less frequently, and then stopped completely.

Dean Scudder died of a sudden stroke in 1899, and Everett took over running the farm. Kate died ten years later.

Chapter Five

February 1916

From the time she was a little girl, Roseanne had wanted to be a teacher. Sitting raptly in the first grade classroom, she observed everything Mrs. Evans did. She answered questions precisely but never volunteered to speak. At home, she lined up her rag dolls on the pine table she used as a desk, and gave them lessons. Whenever Lizzie and Esther Forshay came over, she insisted they play school. She read to them and asked questions. She gave them words to spell and arithmetic problems to solve.

"If my Daddy gives me a dime to spend at Tyrell's," she quizzed them one snowy Saturday afternoon, "And I buy hard candies for four cents, how much money will I have left over?"

"No fair," pouted Esther, who was a year younger than Roseanne. "That's much too hard."

Lizzie, who, like Roseanne, was seven and in second grade, smiled slyly, and said with confidence, "That's easy. Seven."

Lizzie and Esther laughed gaily and clapped their hands. They ran around Roseanne's narrow bedroom, jumping up and down, and poked each other in the ribs. Roseanne rapped on the table with an old, wooden ruler.

"Pay attention," she snapped. "The answer is wrong, Lizzie Forshay, and you will have to stay after school. The correct answer is five. Now repeat after me, two plus two equals ..."

Heat and the odor of baking dough rose from the wood stove in the kitchen and spread through the five bedrooms on the second floor. The bedrooms were grouped around an oblong hall at the top of the broad stairs, and each of the three Scudder children had their own small bedroom. The fifth one had stayed vacant since the death of little Melissa last winter from influenza.

"Excuse me, teacher," said May Scudder as she pushed open the door with her toe and carried in a tray stocked with a plate of cookies and three glasses of warm milk. "But could you briefly interrupt your class for a snack? You know students need nourishment if they are to learn properly."

The girls promptly abandoned their lesson, and even Roseanne forgot her duties while they nibbled cookies and drank milk.

Since noon, the sky had been thick with flakes as heavy snow smothered the countryside and piled up in great drifts against farmhouses and barns. Trees seemed to dissolve in a snowy haze. There was no wind, and silence wrapped the valley. There was no sign that the weather would let up anytime soon. Roseanne looked out her window and saw a white-tailed buck, still as a statue under a bare maple. "Look," she said to her friends, and they pressed their noses to the glass. The buck surveyed the farm with magisterial calm, then turned and bounded in great leaps over the snow-blanketed fields to disappear into the woods. The light faded, leaving the snow pale in the dimness of late afternoon. A fire crackled downstairs in the parlor. Roseanne felt safe in her warm, snug room. In France, young men shivered in the trenches.

In the early stages of the European conflict, Everett had stoutly argued around the stove at Tyrell's that neither side was right and that the United States should remain neutral. While still arguing for U.S. neutrality, his tone softened when a German submarine, in May 1915, sank the Lusitania, an unarmed British liner, with great loss of life, including one hundred and twenty-eight Americans. As the conflict intensified, questions about the war arose sporadically at the Scudder table. Howie, at twelve, the oldest of Everett and May's three children, was curious about submarines and machine guns. He once repeated the fulminations of his teacher, a descendant of Scots immigrants, that the Germans bayoneted babies and disobeyed the rules of war. Everett took exception with the teacher expressing such views in front of impressionable youngsters.

"The Germans fight much the same as the Allies," he patiently explained to Howie. "A lot of what we hear could be propaganda. This is a useless war. The United States should stay out of it, contrary to what Teddy Roosevelt, that traitor to the Republican Party, bellows."

"What is pro ... pro ... propaganda?" Roseanne asked.

"That's a tough one," said Everett, rubbing his chin. "It's things people say to make other people believe what they want them to."

"You mean like the advertisements in the newspapers?"

"You will make quite a teacher," said Everett with a smile.

Roseanne and Damon, ten, mostly listened quietly at the dinner table or teased each other until May put a stop to it. Rosanne knew that men were fighting each other in a far off land, but she didn't understand why. She had overheard her father telling her mother that Tommy Locke had joined the Canadian army. Tommy had just finished high school in Montpelier. Both Canada and high school seemed like distant, exotic places, and Roseanne knew that she would never leave Scudder's Gorge. Her parents and friends would miss her too much.

What the adults did talk a lot about was the farm, how much milk certain cows were yielding, the characteristics of Holsteins compared to Brown Swiss, how to speed up the milking process and the improvements in hay quality that could be obtained from different grasses. The two hired men ate with the family. One evening, Otis asked

Everett if he thought a tractor-propelled hay mower would ever replace the horse-drawn variety.

"Most likely."

May generally commented on how her chickens were laying and the price Tyrell was paying for a dozen. She used most of her eggs for breakfast and cakes, but sold a couple of dozen every week for pin money. The conversation ultimately turned to hunting, fishing, and by summer, speculation as to whether the Boston Red Sox would win the World Series. Nineteen-sixteen would make two in a row.

Though no Scudder had yet been to college, Everett, like his father, was a reader; and May had been the town librarian at the time of their wedding. As such, the conversation also turned to politics, history and literature, about all of which Everett had firm opinions. He could quote passages from Longfellow and doted on Twain and Dickens. While thinking of himself as a rock-ribbed Republican, he nevertheless had a Progressive's faith in man's ability to perfect himself, as well as the notion that America should be a land of boundless opportunity for all. In this, not all of his neighbors agreed, which cost him, more than once, the "Scudder seat" on the town council.

May's reading was wide-ranging, but favored the classics. She could read and re-read Chaucer and Shakespeare, but nonetheless greatly admired modern giants like Whitman or the more esoteric, Henry James. As librarian, she had arranged readings of great poetry, which Everett and Augustus, whom May commented they saw all too rarely, assiduously attended. Augustus shared her love of Shakespeare and the Greeks. She relished his visits with Onatah, his Indian wife, and their children, Jason and Marcus. While the boys would ask to be excused to play cards or go throw a baseball in nice weather, Roseanne always stayed at the table and listened to the conversation.

The snow was still tumbling and swirling when Howie and Damon tramped through the deep powder to help with the evening milking. Damon swept the barn while Jacob, the second hired man, shoveled manure into a cart to take to the spreader. The cows stamped in the cold. Roseanne had gathered eggs and completed her indoor chores before Richard Forshay brought his daughters in the horse-drawn sled, in which he had also stacked cans of maple syrup to deliver to Tyrell's.

They finished the cookies and milk, and began a new game with the dollhouse that Everett had built for Roseanne. The telephone in the kitchen rang three times—the Scudder ring on the party line. May picked up the pear-shaped receiver.

"Hello," she shouted into the mouthpiece that protruded from a wooden box attached to the wall of the passageway that led from the kitchen to the dining room. The pine-paneled passageway was gloomy in contrast to the airy kitchen. Across the front hall from the dining room was the parlor, with deep armchairs and chintz curtains. Beyond the parlor was a small room that served as library and farm office. Everett kept the accounts in two large wooden filing cabinets. At the back of the front hall, broad, oak-planked stairs led to the second floor. The old nails in the floors had distinctive square heads, unlike the round-headed variety that had come into use about twenty-five years ago.

"Yes, I can hear you, Richard, but just barely. You could be on the moon. Better I guess than shouting out the window, but not much."

The telephone crackled with static, and May grimaced in concentration. Large-boned, but neither heavy nor tall, she had a round florid face, reddish hair that hung to her shoulders, and blazing blue eyes. Her grandfather was born in a sod hut in County Kildare and left Ireland in 1848 after two successive failures of his potato crop. He was a great believer in Saint Bridget (called Mary of the Gael - Patroness of charity and justice) and named his first-born after her. He sailed from Dublin Bay in the filthy, dark steerage of a creaking, four-masted schooner that was jammed with half-starved families fleeing the blight. He was twenty-eight and brought along his wife and baby Mary. They barely washed for the six weeks of the crossing and ate watery soup laced with vermin. Mary died from diarrhea and dehydration. She was buried at sea, wrapped in an old shawl of her mother's. He settled in Boston, where he found work in a shipyard. Blaming them for the famine that followed the potato blight, he despised the English his entire life.

May's father was a police detective. He married a French Huguenot and moved his wife and six children to Montpelier because he couldn't get along with the Boston Irish, especially his own father, whom he considered narrow-minded in the extreme. May was twelve at the time, a studious child with her grandfather's stubbornness. May's father did not believe in these new women's colleges so, after high school, May took correspondence courses in library science while working in the Montpelier library. She was twenty in 1899 when an opening occurred in the small town of Scudder's Gorge about thirty miles northeast of Montpelier.

Roseanne inherited her reddish hair and quiet determination from both sides of her family, but her blue eyes came from her mother and her height from her father.

"You think the snow's too deep even for the sled? Then don't risk it. Of course, they can spend the night. Roseanne will be thrilled. If it clears up by tomorrow, we can all go to church in our sled and meet you there. Otherwise, they can stay until the road is passable."

May was hoarse from shouting into the mouthpiece. The girls screamed and jumped up and down when told the news. They hugged each other and insisted on going outside even if it was almost dark.

"Please, mama," begged Roseanne. "Just for a few minutes? We'll stay close to the house."

Dressed in heavy coats, thick wool trousers, mittens, and boots that came almost to their knees, the three laughing girls frolicked and floundered in knee-deep, white dunes. The girls each made a snow angel, waving their arms in broad arcs. Coming back with the boys from milking, Everett lifted them to their feet.

"Daddy," asked Roseanne, "when will I be old enough to help with the milking?"

"Next year, when you're eight."

Damon threw a fistful of powdery snow at Lizzie. Roseanne pelted Howie, and a melee began with the children shoveling armfuls of snow at each other. Esther, the youngest, snuck up behind Everett and, grinning mischievously, threw a loosely packed snowball at his broad back. Everett growled ferociously, his mouth wide open to bare his teeth, and leaned down to pick up giggling Esther, tossing her high in the air. As he put her gently back on the ground, the other kids wrestled him into a snowdrift. Laughing uproariously, he rolled over and flung each one carefully into the snow.

"That will do," called May good-humoredly. "Ev, you and Damon bring some wood from the shed. Roseanne, take Lizzie and Esther to feed the chickens. Howie, go with them, please."

Everybody brushed the snow off his or her clothes. Roseanne glanced petulantly at her Mother.

"But Mama, we don't need any help. I always feed them by myself."

"I know but we've got a storm. So please do as you're told and no more back talk."

After dinner, they settled by the fire in the parlor, the children lying on rugs, and everyone else, including Otis and Jacob, sinking comfortably into the sofa and armchairs. Everett took a book from the mantel and explained the story "so far" to Esther and Lizzie, starting with Aunt Polly, a fight in the street, and whitewashing a fence. He began reading at the point where the pirates planned on attending their own funerals.

"That was Tom's great secret, the scheme to return home with his brother pirates, and attend his own funeral. They had paddled over to the Missouri shore on a log, at dusk on Saturday, landing five or six miles below the village. They slept in the woods at the edge of town 'till nearly daylight, and then crept through back lanes and alleys before finishing their sleep in the gallery of the church among a slew of benches."

Everett's sonorous voice filled the room. He took almost as much pleasure from the sounds of the words as the events in the story. The fire glowed, and drowsiness spread around the parlor. May rubbed her temples, thinking that the heat had given her a headache.

Roseanne listened to her father's voice. The fire was comforting and peaceful—the crackle of the pine logs making her think of Christmas and strings of popcorn. Her eyelids drooped. Try as she did to pay attention to Tom's adventures, wisps of sleep, like smoke from the fire, curled around her head, and whisked her off.

Everett and May carried the three girls upstairs and put them to bed, Lizzie and Roseanne in her bed, and Esther in the trundle bed.

Roseanne, in later years, often thought back on that night. The comfort of family and the security of youth are often fleeting and not appreciated until recalled later in life. A simple snowball fight can bring a tear when unexpectedly remembered.

1918

It was a brittle, sunny day in mid-November. The war in Europe was finally over, with about ten million dead. The woods were aflame with color, although many of the leaves had fallen and created a multihued carpet on the forest floor. Up in the gorge, two hikers rested on a boulder overlooking the cascading water. The woman, tall and lithe with a freckled face, climbed down to the stream and cupped some water in her hand. "It's frigid," she said.

"It's always icy, even in summer," he replied, wriggling to get off the boulder while bracing himself with his only hand. His other sleeve was pinned to his shoulder. He scrambled down the bank to join her and put his arm around her shoulders, pulling her close to kiss her on the lips. She kissed him back, before drawling in a coquettish tone.

"Why, Tommy Locke, you presumptuous devil. Being a sergeant in that Canadian army has given you a high opinion of yourself."

Charlotte Fielding laughed softly and stepped close to him. He felt her warm breath on his face and smelt a hint of rose water. Their deep breathing sent wisps of steam into the cold air.

"All right," Charlotte said archly. "Kiss me again."

He did and then took her hand. "We'd better get going if we're going to make it up to the ridge and back before it gets dark. It'll take us several hours."

"If you insist," she said teasingly.

Four days later, a large group of people stood bareheaded in the bright sunshine along one side of an open grave. They had filed out of the First Congregational Church and walked in mute pairs and threesomes to the graveyard behind the church.

The earliest headstone was dated 1796 and read:

Emma McPherson
1788 – 1796
Beloved of God
R.I.P.

The worn stone was small and tilted slightly to one side. The face of an angel set against a pair of delicate wings was carved above the name. Generations of Scudders lay buried in the graveyard.

The service had been moving. Friends and family members, fighting back tears, had spoken of the deceased's fine qualities and accomplishments. They had told poignant and sometimes humorous stories illustrating her charm, her warmth, her courage and good sense. The Reverend Phidias Morgan had spoken of the dearly departed's many contributions to the church and community. Many present were noticeably shaken. The final illness had been sudden, striking at an early age.

Everett Scudder followed his wife's coffin down the steps and along the brick path by the side of the church. He stared straight ahead, his eyes seemingly impassive and hard as granite. But his gaunt cheeks were streaked with tears, and despite his outward calm, despair wracked his body. His lips were bloodless and his hair neatly combed, except for a cowlick in the back. He held Damon and Roseanne, each by the hand. Howie walked directly behind them. The boys wore black trousers and white shirts. Roseanne had on a dark, navy jumper with a white blouse. They all wore heavy dark overcoats.

May's father and mother had come from Montpelier, and walked on either side of Howie. Logan, Lizzie, and Esther Forshay were there with their parents. Lizzie and Esther gently hugged Roseanne before the service.

May had started experiencing frequent minor headaches about a year ago. She could not remember when they started getting worse because she had always been susceptible to headaches. The heat of a blazing fire or intense, dry cold seemed to bring them on. Over the last six months, the pain gradually became more intense, and aspirin was increasingly ineffective. As her agony became severe and persistent, Dr. Lawrence was at his wits' end. He advised Everett to send May to a specialist in Burlington.

The recently developed x-ray machine did not reveal the tumor, but showed enough distension in the membranes to convince the specialist, in conjunction with May's headaches and growing disequilibrium, of the accuracy of his diagnosis. He wrote Dr. Lawrence that nothing could be done except to keep the patient's discomfort at a minimum. The suspected tumor had most probably grown to the point where an operation, even if she survived, would likely leave May a vegetable. Toward the end, no amount of morphine would relieve her pain, and May's screams could be heard throughout the house.

Roseanne stood by the grave, paralyzed with fear. She did not want her mother to disappear into that hole in the ground. She was sure her mother would come back, but not if she were in that dark hole covered with dirt. Roseanne looked up toward the eastern ridge and gritted her teeth. She knew what she had to do.

Reverend Morgan intoned a prayer. He had known May well. She had helped with numerous church functions, chairing the committee to collect clothes and toys for American and Canadian war orphans. His voice was steady, but choked. He finished the prayer, and Everett stepped forward to place a single white lily on the coffin. The undertaker's assistants moved the coffin forward and, with a rope, began to lower it into the grave.

Roseanne screamed, "Mommy!" and rushed at one of the assistants, knocking him off balance. She tugged at the rope. No one moved. She screamed a second time, and then Everett picked her up, holding her to his chest. Her screams subsided into violent sobs, and then she was quiet. Everett held her tightly, her face hidden in his coat, while the coffin was lowered.

The next week, she got into a fight with Lizzie at school.

1924

A young girl climbs alone, up the faint, twisting path in the gorge. It is early afternoon on a late summer day, and she wants to see the view from the ridge. Although her father doesn't like it, she often hikes by herself. She relishes the solitude, the deep quiet of the woods, interrupted infrequently by the rustle of birds in a thicket or the rasping call of a hawk. She likes not having to talk to anyone. Talk is constant in her home, with a voluble housekeeper plus a father, a brother, and two hired men who will debate farming matters until she feels like screaming. She is reflective. She reads constantly, anything she can get her hands on.

She wants to go to college like her oldest brother who is finishing next year. He is the first of the family to attend college. Despite her despair, anger, and lashing out at all around her, the determination to become a teacher actually increased with her mother's death six years ago.

She climbs steadily, pulling herself up over rocks when the path is at its steepest. It is a perfect day: warm, dry, and late enough in the summer so that the persistent, whining mosquitoes have almost disappeared. She hates the whine and constant nuisance of slapping at them. Lost in thought, she thinks about her part-time job in the library, and the high school boy, Hawk Baxter, who is paying attention to her. His given name is Marcus, but his skill at hunting earned him a nickname that has stuck for years. He is more accepting than proud of it. She has known him since childhood.

His father, Augustus Baxter, works a scraggly farm to the west although he spends about as much time reading as he does farming. Hawk's older brother, Jason, is not much good. He runs whiskey from Canada in a beat-up truck, delivering some locally, but most of it goes to Montpelier, Burlington, and Boston.

Hawk, on the other hand, plans to go to college and medical school. He told her that his father is wonderfully entertaining but that he intends to amount to something more. She likes that, and the way his dark hair falls over his forehead. His mother is a full-blooded Abenaki. A number of years ago, two boys taunted him in the schoolyard and were very sorry for it. They found it exceedingly awkward to explain their cut lips and black eyes to their parents.

Her father and Augustus are still close friends, but they don't seem to have much time to get together these days. She realizes that since her mother's death, Everett has wrapped himself up in running the farm and raising children. She has not always made it easy.

Absorbed in her thoughts, Roseanne doesn't hear the slight rustle and low, dry rattle as she clambers up a narrow stretch between a leaning pine and a boulder. She steps into a wide, open area and, this time, hears the warning as the timber rattler coils and pulls back its head. She freezes about eight feet from the snake. A silent scream rises in her throat. She takes a step backward as quietly as she can. The snake raises the tip of its tail, and the rattles buzz more loudly. Roseanne takes another step backwards. As the snake senses the danger receding, the rattles slow down. The thick, mottled body stretches out and slithers slowly into the brush. Roseanne loses her footing and slides back down the hillside. A scream escapes from her dry lips.

Roseanne was not hurt by the short slide, except for a few scratches on her legs. Dirt and pebbles spilled over the tops of her ankle-high boots. She rests against a boulder to catch her breath and compose her thoughts.

"Dear God: that was a close thing. I wonder where it is. I have to pay closer attention to what I'm doing."

Slowly, she rises to her feet and, giving a wide berth to the ledge and surrounding brush, scrambles up the steep incline toward a point where she picks up the trail again. She stops every few feet, stomping the ground and clapping her hands. She finds a stout stick to carry. Her heart is still racing as she reaches the trail and follows it toward the crest.

She has seen the view from the ridge before, and it awes her every time. The stream rushes through the gorge sending plumes of icy water into the air. The valley spreads out below her with fields of hay and corn, pastures dotted with grazing cows, scattered farmhouses with trim vegetable gardens, and the town nestled against the river that, spilling from the gorge, winds through the valley from north to south. A red-tailed hawk, riding the currents, soars over the fields and meadows. Thick woods line the edges of the valley like fur trimmings on an expensive overcoat.

Roseanne is a big, strong girl. Her cheeks glow from the outside work she does on the farm and the time she spends rambling in the woods. She sits absorbed in the view before starting back down. She moves quickly but warily, watching where she puts her feet.

About half way down the slope, the trail dips close to the stream and follows it past a few grassy ledges before cascading into a pool. The ledges are partly hidden by thickets of holly, mistletoe, and wild roses. Below the pool, the path stays close to the stream until, near the rotted floors of some abandoned cabins; it runs into the North Valley Road where Roseanne left her bicycle leaning against a tree.

Nearing one of the ledges, Rosanne hears noises above the sound of the stream. She stops cold. Recognizing human voices, she steps forward a few paces. She bends down and peers through a thicket. She stands up quickly, her broad cheeks reddening. Tommy Locke and his wife,

Charlotte, are lying on the ledge, completely naked, and making love. He is moving vigorously and kissing her. She holds him in her arms with her legs clamped around his waist. Roseanne speeds down the path, making as little noise as possible. They are too caught up in their lovemaking to hear her. Her surprised expression changes into a grin. Tommy Locke is her science teacher.

After losing an arm in the second battle of the Marne, and being discharged from the Canadian army with distinction, Tommy had returned to Scudder's Gorge to a hero's welcome. Everett Scudder organized a collection to send him to the University of Vermont. Everett raised enough for Tommy to study science for two years. He returned to Scudder's Gorge in 1921 to teach at the new regional high school. Short on teachers, Principal O'Day was delighted to get him. Tommy continued studying for his bachelor's degree during the summer holidays and married his long-time sweetheart, Charlotte Fielding, in 1922. They planned on raising a large family. In the meantime, she was the secretary at the First Congregational Church.

After her mother's death, Roseanne became withdrawn and sullen, fighting with Damon and her friends at school. She was furious with her mother.

"How could you go away?" she angrily asked. "When are you coming back?"

Gradually, she accepted that May was not coming back but, except for brief interludes, her anger only intensified. When it did, she conducted conversations with her mother.

"I milked April, Violet, and Fanny today. You remember them, don't you? I'm the tallest girl in the class. Yes, I know the others will catch up, but it doesn't help. I don't want to be so tall. Why does Daddy have to be so tall? I got an A minus in spelling. Thank you. Howie is playing football. I don't know what position. A calf was born the other night. I wanted to stay up and help, but Daddy made me go to bed. I was mad at him. I don't care what you say. I hate school, but I have to go to be a teacher. I always get in fights. Lizzie hates me. How do you know? You're not here. What would you know about it? I need help tonight with my arithmetic. Why can't you? What kind of mother are you?"

She was shouting. Everett heard her and opened the door.

"Leave me alone!"

Everett sat on her bed. Roseanne glanced at him angrily and then stared at her textbook. Everett started to speak. Before he could say anything, she burst into tears and pounded his chest with her fists. He stroked her hair over and over.

"I know," he said in his softest voice. "It's hard on all of us, but it's hardest on you."

Roseanne cried and cried—her chest heaving and her breath coming in big gasps.

One night at dinner, she slammed her spoon in a bowl of tomato soup, spraying soup all over the table. She hissed at her father, "Why didn't you save her? Why didn't the doctors save her?" Howie and Damon looked down at their plates. The hired men went into the kitchen. Sally, the housekeeper that Everett had hired in Montpelier, stood stock still in the doorway, holding a bowl of potatoes.

"That's enough," he replied in a tone that was stern but gentle. "No one could save her as much as they tried. It was no one's fault, especially not yours."

Roseanne jumped up and ran to her room.

The explosions frightened Everett, but he was even more disturbed by her long silences. At dinner, more often than not, she ate quickly and kept her thoughts to herself. Her face looked drained. Lizzie and Esther stopped coming over. Reverend Morgan offered to counsel her, but when Everett took her to the pastor's office, she answered his questions in sullen monosyllables.

Dr. Lawrence recommended a specialist in mental disorders in Burlington, but Everett resisted. Doctors treated illnesses of the body and rarely did a good job of that. Individuals sorted out their own spiritual problems with the help of the family or a pastor. In the late spring of 1921, after Roseanne had suffered for over two years with no improvement, he finally took her to the specialist. She had turned twelve in January.

The psychiatrist spent an hour alone with Roseanne. He asked her about her school, her friends, her dreams, her feelings for her father and brothers, her physical longings and her feelings about her mother's death. He was a pleasant young man with a moustache, high, narrow cheekbones, and an earnest voice. He sat behind a massive oak desk and took notes while Roseanne answered his questions. There was a couch in the office, but he referred to it only in passing, saying that he was sure she would be more comfortable in the chair across from his desk.

She answered his questions more fully than she had answered the pastor. He had a soothing voice and didn't tell her how to think or respond. She told him a lot, but left out the conversations with her mother. She felt more at ease by the end of the hour.

Dr. Rankin spent a few private minutes with Everett. He began by explaining that, in America, psychiatric, or Freudian, analysis was a somewhat new method of treating mental and emotional problems. He added, however, that it had been used for a number of years in Europe, and that he had studied for several years with one of the pupils of Dr. Freud, the father of psychiatry. Dr. Rankin emphasized that one session was insufficient for an in-depth diagnosis of Roseanne's behavior, but that his preliminary findings showed an acute sense of guilt brought on by her mother's death.

Roseanne could have been undergoing a delayed or vestigial oedipal development phase at the time of May's death, in which she had subconscious sexual feelings toward her father and hostility toward her mother. She wished for her mother's death so that she could marry her father, taking the place of the dead mother in her father's affections. The actual death and now possible fulfillment of her subconscious wishes could have made her see herself as a powerful and dangerous figure. She could have felt responsible for the death, and since she loved her mother deeply, she now felt (all at the same time) guilty, terrified and devastated by the loss.

She also felt herself unworthy, a bad person for having caused this catastrophe through her evil desires. She would display this anguish, both internally and externally, through alternating periods of withdrawal and anger. It would not surprise him if she created a mother substitute, such as a favorite doll, and actually treated this doll as her mother. Going through puberty with this psychological burden could make this intense time especially difficult. If left untreated, the guilt could stunt her sexual growth and her ability to consummate a healthy relationship with a man, since she might view her sexual feelings and longings as dangerous and destructive.

Dr. Rankin apologized for the dry, technical language of his diagnosis, and recommended a year's course of treatment. Everett thanked the doctor politely, paid the fee, and took Roseanne back to Scudder's Gorge. He neither could afford, nor was he inclined to continue, the treatment. He didn't see how taking Roseanne to Burlington once a week to talk about her sexual feelings would improve her condition.

Nothing changed for several months, but in the fall, something unexpected happened. Tommy Locke had begun teaching that fall. He lived with his widowed mother, and drove her temperamental, black Model T. His father, who had worked as a supervisor in the granite quarry, had bought the car on credit seven years ago. He got some pleasure from the purchase before he was killed a few months later by a piece of falling machinery. With his two sisters still at home, Tommy's mother scraped by on a small pension and meager earnings as a bank teller. During the war, Tommy sent home almost his entire paycheck.

It was a fine, warm day and the leaves were just starting to turn. Haze hung over the ridges. The smell of wood chips drifted up from the sawmill. After school, Roseanne sat reading on a wall in front of the two buildings that housed both the lower grades and the new high school. A neighboring farmer would give her a lift. If none came by, she would wait until Richard Forshay picked up Lizzie and Esther from music, or until her father fetched the boys after football.

Tommy Locke pulled up to the curb and shouted, "Get in. I'll give you a ride."

He grinned at her as she settled herself. He jerked the car into first gear, throwing Roseanne back into her seat.

"Hold on," he called gleefully. "I'll get the hang of this yet."

Tommy was considered a menace on the road since he had to let go of the steering wheel to shift. As he shifted through the gears, the swaying car zigzagged down Cedar toward Mill. They followed Mill past St. Agnes and turned onto the Forshay Road. Not a mile out of town, Tommy careened onto a side road and quickly downshifted. The driver behind him, in a sleek Chevy, angrily honked his horn.

Roseanne practically jumped out of her seat and shouted, "Where are we going?"

Tommy said nothing. Leaving a trail of dust, he drove quickly past a couple of houses and stopped in a clearing overlooking the river. Young couples came here in the evening. Maples and spruce surrounded the clearing, and a willow drooped its feathery branches to the water's edge. He turned a steady gaze on her but said nothing, as though collecting his thoughts. He put his one hand on the dashboard. He lifted the hand and scratched the back of his neck.

"You've become a real nuisance. You're making everyone miserable, especially your friends and family."

"Mind your own business!"

"Ah well, I thought I would make it my business. You're too young to spoil your life now. There'll be plenty of time for that later."

"What would you know about it? Take me home."

"Not until we've had a little talk, and yes, I would know something about it. I know something about loss, about losing something precious."

She looked into his steady eyes, the color of cornflowers. He sported a sandy-colored moustache, which he had started when he left the army. Charlotte said it tickled. Roseanne dropped her eyes.

"I had a good buddy in the army, a fellow from Nova Scotia. He always said the best salmon fishing was in Nova Scotia, in the streams along the coast above Halifax. He said we would go fishing after the war. We would eat fresh lobster for dinner and catch brook trout for breakfast.

"'Fried eggs and trout, the best breakfast in the world,' he always said.

"During the second battle of the Marne, in the summer of 1918, we got the order to go over the top in the morning. Just before dawn, the artillery started. The noise was deafening. The sky exploded in starbursts of light. Clouds of dirt sprayed up all around us. Shells whistled overhead and detonated in the trenches behind us. At first light, the signal came to attack. No matter how many times I went over, my stomach turned to liquid when order came down. The first wave went over. The machine guns started their 'rat-a-tat-tat'. We were in the second wave. There were bodies all around us. You could smell the blood. We had to splash through shell craters filled with foul water. A machine gun burst hit my buddy and ripped open his stomach. I grabbed him around the chest and screamed his name. My uniform was soaked in his blood. He died fast.

"I was dragging his body back to the trench when a shell burst a few feet away. It sent me flying backwards. I woke up in the field hospital two days later, missing an arm. I never knew who pulled me into the trench, and I never saw my friend's body again."

Roseanne looked in shock at the empty sleeve pinned to his shoulder. She started to cry. Her breath came in huge sobs. She tried, but couldn't stop. Her shoulders shook. Tommy put his one arm around her and pulled her to his chest.

"Yes," he said. "Just keep on crying."

When she stopped, he continued.

"My father died in an accident when I was sixteen. I felt like a hole had opened in the earth to swallow me up. I was in a daze for longer than I can remember. I loved my father, and now I wanted to hate him. I wanted to beat on him with my fists. I wanted to fight every kid in school and nearly succeeded. I had been getting top grades, but I almost didn't graduate."

"But you're a teacher now," she said. "What happened?"

"The Canadian army," he replied. He paused as if to be sure of his footing. "So tell me, what did it feel like to lose your mother?"

Roseanne could not stop grinning as she headed down the path, past the pool where the most daring boys in town came to show off, diving from the rocks and swimming in the frigid water. Growing up in farm country, she had seen dogs and cattle rutting, but never people. Except for her brothers, she had never seen a naked man. She was not shocked, only amused to wonder what others would think. Her father would have shrugged and smiled tolerantly, especially since it was Tommy.

Tommy Locke held a special place in Everett's affections. After all, he had returned his daughter to him.

Richard Forshay, on the other hand, would be outraged, being the narrow-minded old fart that he was. Esther would have giggled, but Lizzie had become a bit of a prude. She was always complaining about the boys in her grade.

"They're always fooling around and always up to something," she griped frequently. "Always trying to see how far they can go."

Funny how life goes; Lizzie would get pregnant the following year and have to marry Cyrus Markham, whose father owned the Ford dealership in town. Her parents thought she was marrying beneath her station.

Roseanne's grin faded as she thought back to that first car ride two years earlier. After that, Tommy frequently picked her up after school, and they always stopped to talk. She came to relish and look forward to those times. She poured her heart out to him. She even told him about her conversations with May. She was not sure why, but she trusted him. Perhaps because, while he generally spoke little during those times, he never hesitated to speak his mind if he felt the need.

"Ah, that was a vulgar thing to do," he commented when she told him about spitting at Damon. "But I'll bet it felt good. I would have loved to see his face."

Perhaps it was because he never judged her, only what she did, and because he could see the humor in some of her most outrageous behavior, while also showing her how difficult she was making life for herself and everyone else. But most of all, it was because he taught her that loss was universal—while it might be tragic and heartbreaking, people must take responsibility for what they do, and not for what God has done. To make others pay for her sufferings would diminish, not ennoble, her mother's death. To go on living as a proud, decent human being would honor May's memory.

Over the course of a year, her anger and sense of shame diminished. She rejoined her family's laughter at the dinner table. One night, she jumped up from the table and ran to hug her father. "I love you," she whispered. She hugged each of her brothers in turn, then went into the kitchen, and hugged Sally, who looked as if the roof had fallen in. A smile spread across Everett's face, and a tear dropped from his eye.

In the spring of 1925, the Lockes had the first of their three children, a healthy pink girl weighing seven pounds and nine ounces. A week after the birth, a letter arrived containing a bond for two hundred dollars and a brief note, "For baby Clara's college education."

1931

An icy wind blew off the lake as Roseanne walked along the curving path in Battery Park, thinking about how she would approach the subject. It was late March, and the crusty snow was a foot high in the garden overlooking the lake. To be contrary, she walked a few steps off the path. At first, the crust held her weight, but then she sank in with snow tumbling over the tops of her boots. She hitched up her skirt and overcoat, and struggled back to the path. In spots, it was icy, and she was careful of her footing. She slipped anyway, and her arms gyrated backwards as she started to fall but managed to catch herself.

"Damn," she cursed, and stopped to catch her breath. Her heart was beating fast.

She looked out over the lake and saw mares' tails scudding over the far Adirondacks ranges. Waves whipped against the islands scattered across the lake. A steamer nosed its way into the harbor, puffs of smoke rising from its tall stack. She glanced down at the railroad tracks, and Union Station, and then back toward downtown. Chunks of ice floated in the lake, and the wind cut through her heavy overcoat. Her cheeks tingled and glowed with rugged good health. But she felt slower now, heavy and clumsy.

She liked Burlington and was happy living in this friendly city that was small enough to get to know people. She would have felt lost in a big city like Boston. As valedictorian, she had been offered scholarships by several colleges including Boston University and the University of Vermont. But Burlington was not so small that everyone knew her business – a good thing at the moment.

She had flourished at the university, concentrating in English but also taking education and history courses. She found a part-time job in a store to help with expenses. The scholarship covered her tuition and part of the room and board. Everett paid the balance; and she earned enough for incidentals and movies with friends at the Strong or Majestic, followed by dinner at the Star where she acquired a taste for Chinese food.

She wrote to Esther, saying that her first bite had been something of an epiphany and had confirmed the severing of her Scudder's Gorge umbilical cord. Esther came to the university a year later, and they shared a dormitory room.

She dated infrequently but relished long hikes with friends. She also thrived on the debates, often on the proper role of women in society, which erupted like a live volcano in the dormitory lounge. Roseanne argued that the woman of the future would have two roles: professional careerist and homemaker, and that the stress to be expected from this development would lead to an enormous increase in the demand for psychiatric therapy. Few agreed with her.

"If you're right," said Alice McNair, whose father owned a mansion on South Willard, "you should become a psychiatrist and make a fortune."

"I'm not interested in a fortune. I just want to be a teacher, maybe in a poor community. They could use good teachers."

"How about out West among the Indians? I'll bet they don't have many good teachers."

"We have Indians right here in Vermont that could do with some help," Roseanne replied.

For a while in her junior year, she dated a serious young man but backed off when he wanted to sleep with her. She and Kirk still went out from time to time, for a movie or a meal at Gianni's, a cheap Italian place that served family style dinners at long tables. She loved the noise of the loud conversations and clattering dishes, and the big families that spread out along the tables. She always talked with the other people at their table. She was interested in their lives and asked questions but never in a way that would make them feel awkward.

"You have a knack for making people comfortable," said Kirk. "I could never do it."

They graduated in June 1930. Kirk took a job as a junior accountant with the telephone company in Rutland, his hometown. With the economy slipping, it had been difficult for him to find something. He wrote a few times and then announced at the end of the summer that he was engaged to his high school sweetheart.

In September, Roseanne started a job as a second grade teacher. For the first year, she would be closely supervised by Forest Tucker, an experienced third grade teacher. She spent the summer working in the city library, and preparing for her teaching assignment. She read textbooks and wrote lesson plans. Just before classes started, she took a week's vacation at the farm.

She was renting a room in the home of a widow for ten dollars a week. She shared a bathroom with another woman, who worked in a large pharmacy. For an additional ten dollars a week, the widow provided breakfast and dinner. The widow shared the roomy Victorian on Monroe with her sister, a spinster who gave piano lessons. On summer evenings, Roseanne sat on the veranda watching the lake, the sky turning rose above the Adirondacks, and couples strolling through Battery Park.

She and Consuela (a fellow lodger) walked in the park or took excursions up Pearl and along South Winooski to the Miss Burlington Diner for a dish of Fro-joy ice cream. When Consuela was a teenager, her family had emigrated from Cuba. She told Roseanne about Cuba at the turn of the century while Roseanne described growing up on a Vermont dairy farm.

When Esther came to dinner, the widow charged an extra dollar and insisted on being advised two days in advance.

The widow also had a male lodger, Mr. Meeker, who had retired five years earlier after forty years as a sales rep for a women's shoe manufacturer. He had covered all manner of retailers from Rutland north. Located in another state, his employer (despite keeping an eye on changing fashions) had fallen victim a month ago to the slumping economy; and Mr. Meeker thanked his lucky stars for his timely retirement.

A sprightly woman in her sixties, the widow fancied a bluish tint to her gray hair, to which she added a bit of a curl every few weeks. She indulged in a glass of bootleg Canadian whiskey every evening, but offered none to her lodgers, unless they cared to pay. She kept a strict house. Women tenants were not allowed male visitors except in the parlor on Saturday and Sunday afternoons.

"Do you think she's got her eye on Mr. Meeker?" Roseanne asked Consuela playfully.

She started along the path again, taking short steps on the icy parts. She tucked her head down and pushed against the wind. It was growing late on a Saturday afternoon, and the pale sun was setting across the lake. She was going to meet Forest Tucker for dinner and possibly a movie. She intended to tell him that she was pregnant.

They had first gone out, quite accidentally, toward the end of the previous September, her first month on the job. She had wanted to talk about the problems a couple of her students were having in reading and arithmetic.

"How about a walk down to Battery Park?" he suggested. "It seems a shame to stay inside."

It was Friday, a fall afternoon full of warm sunshine, and she had an empty weekend ahead so she said yes. A breeze off the lake rustled the leaves in the sugar maples. A few orange leaves skittered across the path. She picked one up and crumpled it between her fingers. Sitting on a bench, they discussed her students and then whether the Hoover Administration's leave-it-alone policies would end the recession. Both, it turned out, were Republicans, but Forest insisted that stronger medicine was needed.

"This could turn into a full-blown Depression."

He was not ready to vote for a Democrat, but he was worried.

Thirty-four, tall and ungainly, he had thick eyebrows that arched over steel grey eyes. His ears were too big for his head, and he walked with a slight stoop. He told her about the year he had spent teaching on a Navajo reservation in Arizona. He had volunteered through his church. There were Navajo children, he commented incredulously, who spoke no English.

"What a wonderful experience. I envy you."

He took her arm as they walked up the hill toward the University. It was growing dark, and he asked if she would like to have dinner. He knew a good Italian place near the university. She laughed when they approached Gianni's. He was surprised when all the waiters knew her. She seemed like part of the large family seated at their table, even ruffling the hair of a six-year-old boy.

"It seems that you've been here before," he said petulantly.

"Oh yes, but I'm so pleased that you chose it. It shows what a down-to-earth person you are."

They walked to the park again the following Friday, and he called at the widow's on Saturday. The widow charged her fifty cents for the tea and petit fours in the parlor. He took her to see Greta Garbo in Anna Christie. At the Star, he showed her how to use chopsticks. She did not let on that she had learned years ago.

"I loved Garbo's accent," Roseanne said. "'Gif me a viskey ... and don't be stingy, baby.' Good beginning for her first talking role."

"How about that comeback? 'Well, shall I serve it in a pail?'" Forest squared his shoulders as if the line had been his. "I had tears in my eyes at the ending. Even if a woman starts out wrong, like being a prostitute, through a man's love..." Forest's eyes went distant.

Rosanne felt something odd but shook it off.

"What were you going to say?" she asked quietly.

"Oh, nothing."

"I'm not convinced," she said, "that O'Neill meant the ending to be happy. Mat needs to be so sure that she loves only him, never any of her customers. He's thinking of himself. Maybe she doesn't need forgiving. Maybe she just did what she had to do. But he cannot accept her as she is, or was. I don't think they're going to be so happy. This will gnaw at him."

"She was a woman of the night," Forest retorted with an edge to his voice, "and his love saved her. At least, it cured her of that hatred for men. I felt so uplifted."

"'Fog, fog, fog ... you can't see where you're going.' It's what her father says at the end and I don't think it's positive."

On Fridays, they went for walks. On Saturdays, it was dinner and a movie or concert. He came to the house occasionally but was annoyed at the widow constantly popping in and out and her sister practicing the piano.

"Don't mind me, I just have a few scales to run through."

"For God's sake, she teaches the piano. It's her snot-nosed pupils that should be practicing."

She found it awkward that he was her supervisor, but since they were only good friends, she was not overly concerned. When he took to kissing her goodnight, she thought nothing of it since it was always on the cheek.

She took a creaking bus home for Thanksgiving. Howie came up from Montpelier where he had been working ever since finishing law school in Albany, and Damon invited his fiancée, Jeannie Mitchell. Brent, one of the two hired men, had gone to visit his sister's family. Jacob had no family except the Scudders. Around the table, they talked of nothing but the falling level of prices for farm products.

"There's not a farmer in the valley that's not worried," said Everett.

"The Baxters seem to be getting along," said Damon, "what with the extra income Jason brings in."

"Damn foolish law," snapped Everett. "A good drop of cider or whiskey never hurt a man ... nor a woman." He winked at Roseanne.

"His kind," responded Damon, "never did take to working for a living."

Everett's eyes flashed.

"I'll have none of that talk in this house."

Damon looked sullenly at his plate. Sally, with exquisite timing, brought in the turkey. The skin was a perfect, crackling brown.

"I just hope I'll have one to burn next year," she laughed, setting the platter in front of Everett.

The rest of the holiday was gloomy, with everyone nervous about the recession, and Everett angry with Damon, not that he didn't deserve it for making a nasty crack about Jason. Regardless of Jason's employment, he was Augustus's son. Roseanne rode the bus back on

Saturday morning and, that evening, hurried through a cold drizzle to meet Forest at the Majestic. She had told him on the phone that he shouldn't bother stopping by for her. Closing the front door, she realized that she had forgotten her umbrella. She was impatient to see Forest and didn't want him to miss the beginning of the film so she decided not to go back upstairs.

Wet leaves blew along the sidewalk, and puddles had formed at the curbs. She was shivering when she reached the theater, and her hair was plastered against her damp cheeks.

"Forget the movie. You'll catch pneumonia. I'm getting you in front of a fire. Then we can go to dinner."

"Hardy farm girls don't catch pneumonia, or colds for that matter. But I guess I should dry off. I forgot my umbrella and was running late so I foolishly didn't go back for it. It would have just taken a minute. Silly, huh?"

"Not at all. It's the bane of our civilization, the preoccupation with the hands of a clock."

The stone facings on his building consisted of elegant swirls and intertwined ivy vines, but the lobby was tired-looking. The sallow yellow walls needed painting, and the marble tiles showed the wear of forty years' footsteps. They rode to the fourth floor in a swaying elevator. He handed her a towel before taking kindling and three logs from a copper bucket. She stood with her back to the fire, vigorously rubbing her hair and repeating how foolish she had been.

"I still feel awful that I made you miss the movie."

"Don't think twice about it. Listen, it's so ugly out, why don't we have dinner here. I'll make spaghetti.

The backs of her legs were warm, and heat spread through her body.

"What a wonderful idea. I've never seen a man cook. I should have guessed you'd be one."

He put a scratchy Beethoven recording on the phonograph, a gift from his mother. He chopped onions and peppers for the sauce. She stirred while he warmed bread and set the round table in an alcove off the living room. After dinner, he put on a big band record and led her by the hand to a bare space behind the sofa. He was a good dancer and held her close as they glided around the confined area. She placed her cheek next to his while he caressed the back of her neck. He kissed her, and she kissed him back.

They sat on the sofa, watching the fire burn low while rain lashed at the windows. Forest brushed a curl away from her forehead. His hair was combed back to cover the balding spot on top. She slid a fingertip down his cheek, and he put an arm around her shoulder. She snuggled up against his chest and raised her face to his. As they kissed, he pushed his tongue against her lips. She hesitated for only the briefest instant and then opened her mouth. He undid the top buttons of her blouse, cupped her breast in his hand, and reached inside her bra. A shiver ran down her spine. She slowly unbuttoned his shirt.

During the night, the sky cleared. Roseanne slept deeply, her arm draped lightly over Forest's bare chest. She woke with sunlight flooding the room. She pushed her buttocks up against Forest's hips, luxuriating in his warmth and wondering if she were in love. She felt happy and warm. Was this love? Or was it something altogether different? Unable to answer the question, she listened, half asleep, to Forest snoring. He was the most wonderful man she had ever met. She rolled over and nibbled his earlobe. She ran her hand over his chest. He woke and leaned on his elbow.

"You were wonderful, especially for your first time." He studied her reaction. "It was your first time?"

She nodded, and they made love again.

Forest made scrambled eggs and toast for breakfast. They went to church, and then she went home. The widow asked her, suspiciously, where she had spent the night.

"I was out late with Esther," she said, "so I slept on a spare bed in her dorm. Then we went to church this morning."

The next few weeks went by in a blur. They couldn't see enough of each other. They splurged on dinners, did their Christmas shopping together and then, feeling broke and uneasy, hunted for free concerts and cheap dance parties. She slept over on Saturday nights and, hurrying to Monroe Street before the widow got up, changed to meet Forest for church. She missed her timing one Sunday morning and endured an icy glare as she climbed the stairs to her room. Sometimes they were so anxious to make love that they met at his place after work. At school, he was as formal as ever.

"Miss Scudder, could we please review your lesson plans for next week, when you have a spare moment."

"Certainly, Mr. Tucker, whenever you like."

She always risked a shy smile that spoke volumes.

She could not remember ever having been so happy. Even a cold, wet December could not dampen her spirits. She was astonished that such a wonderful, mature man loved her. As she walked to school one bitter morning, she recalled the afternoon she had seen Tommy and Charlotte making love in the woods. She smiled. Now she knew what they were experiencing.

She spent Christmas on the farm and wrote Forest a long, chatty letter, which she mailed to him at his mother's house in Middlebury. Everett was delighted to hear about her job, but it was otherwise a bitter holiday. The mood in the valley was sour. Prices had only gone lower. Worst of all for the Scudders, Jacob, who had been part of the family for eighteen years, contracted pneumonia and died two weeks before Christmas. Like the exhalation of a breath, he had gone that fast.

"He was only fifty-two," said Everett, and then turned to the other subject on his mind, "I just hope things don't get much worse." He thought back to Augustus's father losing his farm over thirty years ago. Roseanne had never seen her father like this, except when May died.

"The government certainly isn't helping," complained Damon. "Hoover is spouting nonsense. How is raising tariffs or interest rates going to help the farmer? Mellon rants about 'purging the rottenness out of the system'. I'd like to purge him, the rich bastard. Like to see him without his millions. Treasury Secretary, my rear end."

"I don't know," said Everett. "We don't want the government butting into our business and regulating the devil out of everything. We've got enough already with the Department of Agriculture. Not that I object, mind you, to these Vermont fellows inspecting the creamery. It keeps us honest."

When she got back to Burlington, she rushed over to Forest's apartment. They fell into each other's arms as if they had been apart for years, not just a week. They celebrated New Year's Eve at a party given by a friend of Forest's who lived in a small house near the university. Forest knew most of the guests. Roseanne had asked if Consuela and Esther could be invited, and Forest's friend had enthusiastically replied, "The more the merrier—especially beautiful young women!"

Forest's friend hugged Roseanne at the door and introduced her to his wife, a short, middle-aged woman in a satin, sequined dress that was too tight for her. Her hips bulged, and her fleshy arms hung loosely at her sides. She was red-faced and effusive.

"Come in. Come in. Welcome. Forest has talked about you so often. He really is in love this time. Oh dear, what am I saying? But you are so beautiful and young. How I envy you," she giggled.

"Adele has had a nip of the bootleg," explained her husband with a knowing grin. "It goes straight to her head. God only knows what trouble she'll get into this evening." His wink made Roseanne blush.

They wandered around the party. Forest greeted friends and introduced Roseanne. Neither Consuela nor Esther had arrived yet. Roseanne was surprised that so many of the guests seemed on the verge of middle age. Several couples had brought children.

"Oh dear," she whispered to Forest. "I feel a little out of place." She didn't like how that sounded, and added, "You have so many sophisticated friends."

"If you're out of place," he whispered back, "it's only by being the most beautiful and wonderful woman here."

She kissed his ear and squeezed his hand.

"You are so grand," she said.

Intent on introducing her to everyone, he moved quickly around the living room and dining room. The men firmly shook her hand while the women kissed her on both cheeks. She sipped at a glass of bootleg whiskey and relaxed. She liked the warm feel in her stomach. A woman with streaky blonde hair approached and hugged Forest tightly. She smiled queerly at Rosanne and shook her hand.

"So nice to meet you. Take good care of him; he's such a little boy." She

132

melted into the crowd.

"Who was that?" Roseanne asked incredulously.

"Just an old friend," smiled Forest. "Look, here's Esther and Consuela."

The host and a few guests pushed the living room furniture against the wall and turned on an upright radio. The dancing spilled into the hallway. Roseanne and Forest ate cheese sandwiches, drank more whiskey, and danced wrapped in each other's arms. They kissed for a long moment at midnight and sang Auld Lang Syne. Consuela and Esther hugged them both. Walking home, the freezing air stung her cheeks and cleared her head. She breathed in deeply and sang out.

"Happy New Year, my darling."

They made love until three in the morning. 1931 had arrived.

The widow became increasingly hostile and suspicious. In early February, she suggested that Roseanne seek other accommodations. Since she was spending so much time with her women friends, perhaps she could move in with one of them.

At first, she was upset at the prospect of a change in her routine, but quickly realized how nice it would be to have the freedom of her own place. She could sleep late on Sunday mornings and make love without having to rush back to the widow's accommodations. If they occasionally missed church, it would not be so serious. Rents were cheap now. Forest was hesitant though. This was a big step in these times, but he came around when she mentioned Sunday mornings. She scanned the classified section and looked at two tiny apartments, but found neither of them suitable. In early March, her doctor confirmed that she was indeed pregnant.

She decided how she would begin. She walked up Pearl to Pine and then over to College. They would get married as soon as possible and live in his apartment until they could afford a larger place. She would have to request a different supervisor, or possibly even change schools. Her heart was singing, and her breath came in quick gulps. Her body felt awkward, but so far, she had only experienced minor morning sickness.

Forest would be surprised but happy. They were so much in love and so right for each other. After hearing the news, he would want to get married quickly. It was more than time for him to settle down and raise a family. A wave of anticipation swept over her. She had been worried when the doctor confirmed her suspicions. Now she was sure of herself and feeling bubbly, like champagne. She would start off with a little joke.

"Forest," she would ask demurely. "Do you think I'm gaining weight? Am I still thin enough for you?"

He would vociferously deny it, and then she would tell him.

He stared at her in shock and disbelief. He felt the well-ordered structure of his life crumbling. His narrow shoulders sagged, and his mouth gaped. Anger and fear crept into his eyes. He tried to speak but could only stutter. Seeing his expression struck her like a freight train. Where she had expected surprise, astonishment, and then rapture, she found dismay. She walked to the window and stared out at the dirty snow.

Forest struggled to find his voice. "Tell me this isn't happening," he finally blurted out in a quivering voice. "Please tell me you're joking."

She turned to face him, a look of anguish spreading across her broad features. "I thought you would be happy," she said. "I thought we would get married."

"Married!" he gasped. "I can't get married." He repeated himself in a daze, "I can't get married."

"But why not?" she asked plaintively. "Why can't you marry me? You love me, don't you?"

"Love you?" His distracted voice trailed off. "Love you? ... Yes, I suppose I do."

Her face froze in an outraged grimace. She glared at him without moving. Her expression jarred him.

"Of course, I love you. I just can't get married, not to you, not to anyone."

She thought she saw an opening, and her expression softened.

"What is it? Why can't you get married? Do you have some dreadful sickness? Is there some dark family secret? I don't care. I just want to marry you and have our child."

His face contorted with rage. Purplish blotches appeared on his cheeks.

"You can't make me! I won't! How do I know you're pregnant? How do I know the baby's mine? You're trying to trap me," he practically screamed.

She couldn't speak. Her lips moved in silent sputters. She turned and walked to the window again. She looked out for a moment and then buried her face in her hands. She started to cry.

"Look," he said, trying to calm down. "Don't cry. We can fix this. You don't need to have the baby. I have some money saved up. I'll give it to you. We can fix this. It will be all right."

He took a step toward her.

"Then we can go on the way it was. Only we'll have to be more careful."
He took another step toward her, his face hopeful. "It will be all right,"
he repeated.

"It will never be all right," she sneered and walked past him to the door.

Consuela went with her to Canada three days later. Just before she left,
an envelope arrived. She took it with her.

Chapter Six

July 1920

Damon was big for his age. He had sweated all morning cleaning the barn, shoveling manure and weeding the vegetable garden so Everett told him he had the afternoon to himself. Right after lunch, he jumped on Noah, the bay gelding, and rode bareback to the Forshays to see if Logan wanted to go swimming. It had not rained in a week, and the road was dusty as they trotted toward the river. They tied Noah to a tree and headed for the swimming hole. About a dozen kids were swimming, watched over by two men leaning against a truck and smoking cigarettes.

"Hey Damon, tell your father I got a new fishing rod I want him to see."

"Yes sir, Mr. Howell."

They swam for over an hour, and then lay on the bank looking up into the hazy sky. Around four, Damon sat up.

"I've got to ride into town. Daddy asked me to pick up some nails at Tyrell's. Want to come? We can get some caramels and baseball cards."

"Nah. I've got to weed the strawberries. I'll walk or maybe Mr. Howell will give me a lift. It's almost milking time so they're probably fixin' to go."

On his way home, Damon heard someone holler his name just as he passed the bridge south of town. The sun shone in his face when he turned to look, and it took him a second to recognize Jason Baxter trotting across the bridge on Augustus's old mule. Jason slapped the

137

stubborn mule's rear, hurrying to catch up with Damon, who reined in.

"Where ya going?" asked Jason.

"Home."

"Been to town?"

"Yup."

They rode side by side in silence. A vulture circled lazily overhead. They passed two small farmhouses built close to the road, one on each side. Maples shaded the houses. In a field, a farmer and his hired hand forked hay onto a wagon. The draft horse waited patiently.

"What are you doing way over here?" Damon ventured.

"My Pa asked me to take some money over to Mr. Schmidt to pay a debt."

They rode again in silence. Jason leered at Damon, his eyes glistening with anticipation.

"So, rich boy," he chuckled, "I hear you're sweet on the principal's daughter."

"Who says?" Damon demanded. He pulled Noah up sharply.

Jason shrugged.

"Oh, it's going around. It's not a big town – especially for Scudders."

"It's none of your fu... none of your business."

Damon kicked Noah, and the bay broke into a trot. Jason caught up.

They were approaching the big curve where the Forshay Road turns east.

"I saw her tits once. She was showing us behind St. Agnes. Nice tits."

"You're lying, you son-of-a bitch. She never did."

Jason eyed Damon coldly, his eyes hard and emotionless. His tongue flicked out and licked his upper lip.

"Watch your tongue, rich boy," Jason smirked. He laughed and drew himself up. Then he leaned toward Damon.

"Now look, don't get all worked up about it. She's kind of common property, ain't she? Everybody gets a share. Who'd have thought Lara O'Day would be so good?"

Damon leapt off Noah, screaming, "You bastard." He started pulling Jason off the mule. Jason reached down with both hands and grabbed Damon around the throat.

"Listen, rich boy, if you want to get the shit kicked out of you, okay; but let's do it private like."

He released Damon and nodded toward a large, weeping willow near the river.

"No one will see us over there."

Dancing backwards, Jason let Damon take the first swing. He laughed and let Damon swing again. This time Damon caught him on the chin. Jason rubbed his chin, darted forward, and slammed Damon in the stomach. Damon fell to one knee. Jason stood over him laughing.

"Wanna' keep going, rich boy"?

Damon grabbed Jason's ankle and threw him to the ground. He leapt on him as both boys punched at each other. They rolled over, still punching. Damon landed a hard blow on Jason's ribs and rolled away. He staggered to his feet.

"Yeah, I wanna' keep going," Damon snarled.

Jason stood up. They circled around each other in the confined space under the willow branches. Sweat dripped from Damon's forehead and stung his eyes. He wiped them with the back of his hand. They continued to circle, jabbing and feinting. Jason leered at him.

"Not much good at this are you, rich boy?"

Damon pulled back and shot his fist out, hitting Jason on the shoulder. Jason stumbled back but quickly straightened up.

"Is it possible that you're so mad because you ain't seen her tits, that she didn't give you what she gave the rest of us?"

Damon lunged punching with both fists. Jason caught him, held him with one arm, and hit him hard repeatedly in the side and stomach with his other fist. He pushed him back and slugged him twice in the chest just below his throat, being careful not to hit him in the face. Then he grabbed Damon by the shoulders, pulled him forward, and slammed his knee into Damon's groin. Damon howled with pain and slumped to the ground. Jason took hold of Damon's hair and lifted him slightly. He slapped Damon across the cheek.

"Listen and listen good, rich boy. Don't ever start a fight you can't finish, especially not with me."

He let go of Damon and strode back to his mule.

Damon lay doubled up on the ground clutching his groin. A few minutes later, he got to his knees. As he stood up, he swore out loud.

"Goddamn half-breed."

From that day forward, Damon's hatred for anything Indian grew like a cancer.

Chapter Seven

Jason Baxter
(1904 -)

November 1924

Jason leaned heavily on the steering wheel and strained to see the dark, winding road. The creaking wipers on the truck barely cleared the driving rain off the windshield, which contained a tiny hole, parallel to and just above Jason's left temple. A maze of tiny cracks radiated from the hole, and drops of water squeezed through to slither down the glass. The truck slipped coming out of a corner, and Jason gripped the steering wheel with his left hand while quickly shifting with his right. The soaked, hard-packed dirt road was slick; and the truck slid sideways. Jason spun the wheel; the truck's rear end fishtailed, and Jason hit the brake. He pumped it rhythmically, and the truck straightened itself.

"That was close," said Hawk. "Top-notch driving, brother." It was his first trip with Jason, and Augustus had been none too happy about his going.

"Yeah," said Jason, glancing quickly at Hawk. "You'll be pushing her through mud holes if this fucking rain keeps up. Good thing you got muscles."

Hawk stretched his right leg to ease a cramp. He leaned back in the seat and rubbed his eyes. They had left the farm at dawn, followed back roads into Canada, and made the pickup not far from Montreal. Coming back, the officials at both sides of the border smiled sarcastically as Jason handed out the two envelopes. It was almost eight in the evening. It had started to rain when they bypassed Montpelier an hour ago. Jason planned to cross into New Hampshire at White River Junction, and then stop a couple of hours later at the house of a business associate. They would bed down for a while, but it would still be dark when they started again. He expected to make his destination – a warehouse in Lawrence outside Boston – by late morning. The rain was making the driving difficult and wearing him down.

"I just hope water don't get underneath that damned tarp," Jason added. "My friends don't like soggy cartons."

The road skirted a river. In the headlights, Hawk dimly saw the swirling water careening over boulders. He stared in exhausted fascination at the river and the rain glancing off the windshield. In Canada, he had loaded most of the almost forty cases onto the truck's wooden bed. He had also driven several hours while Jason napped, waking only when Hawk needed directions. He wished he could sleep, but he was either too tired or too excited. He was a bootlegger now. The idea thrilled him. They rounded a bend, and a single lit sign – "Café" - loomed in the dark like a Cyclops eye. They had not seen any buildings, not even a farmhouse, for several miles.

"Looks like something out of a ghost story," said Hawk, grinning.

"Yeah, probably haunted. Good thing ghosts don't take to whiskey," Jason laughed, pulling off the road in front of the building. The windows were shuttered, but a few cars and trucks were parked haphazardly in the dirt yard. The rain let up.

"I could use something to eat," said Jason. "Looks to be safe here. Doubt any cops are in the neighborhood, especially on a night like this. They're all tucked in tight with their fat wives."

They parked at the far end of the lot and hurried around the puddles that had formed in hollows and tire ruts. The cafe stood on a slight bluff overlooking the river. As they crossed the yard, Hawk looked at the pinewoods crowding the opposite bank and heard the rushing water swollen by the heavy rain. The front door had at one time been a canary yellow, but the paint had faded and cracked leaving dark veins slanting across the surface. A diamond-shaped window was centered in the upper half. The rest of the building was brown weathered clapboard. As they passed into the vestibule, the lights from another car pulling into the lot cut across their backs.

Entering the dimly lit cafe, they faced a counter and a row of revolving stools. Two men were hunched over their dinners. A red and black woolen shirt stretched tight over the broad back of one while the second man's denim shirt hung loosely on his hungry body. They swiveled as one and stared at Jason and Hawk. A shadow crossed the heavy man's face.

"Funny looking pair," thought Hawk.

Four booths lined the wall opposite the counter. At the far end of the room, an open space was surrounded by tables. Two of the booths and a couple of tables were occupied. A waitress with pitted cheeks and dishwater brown hair falling over her shoulders stood at the end of the counter adding up a check. A phonograph played dance music from an Isham Jones record.

Jason and Hawk waited by the cash register. A woman in her thirties with curly blond hair squeezed past them on the way back to her booth from the rest room. Gathered at a slim waist, her flowery dress hugged the contours of her fashionably small breasts. She eyed Hawk, and he smelled brash perfume. She sat down across from an older woman who ground a cigarette into an ashtray. A middle-aged couple entered the cafe and paused behind Jason and Hawk. The husband had fat cheeks and wisps of hair combed neatly over an otherwise baldhead. He looked around as if hoping to see a familiar face.

The waitress headed toward a table where three men were talking loudly. An empty whiskey bottle surrounded by overflowing ashtrays stood like a lighthouse in the center of the table. A gaunt farmer in frayed bib overalls tilted back in his chair and tamped tobacco into a pipe. He lit a match and held it to the worn bowl. His cheeks were wind-burned and hollow. The skin on his hands was leathery and cracked. He dragged deeply on the pipe, and blew a cloud of smoke over the heads of his companions. He took the pipe from his mouth and jabbed the stem at the man next to him as he made a point. He then picked up a glass of amber whiskey and drained it. The second man wore a crimson, pullover sweater darned at the elbows. Crescents of black grime had accumulated under his fingernails. He scratched the back of his head and was about to respond to the man with the pipe when the waitress reached their table. The third man, in white shirt and suspenders, was not someone who worked with his hands. Without a glance at the check, he handed the waitress a bill and told her to keep the change.

She smiled and went back to the counter. She looked around the room and then seemed to notice Jason and Hawk for the first time. She approached them warily, studying their faces as if they had sprung from the bowels of the earth. Hoping they would return there without a fuss, she asked tartly, "Is there something I can do for you?"

Jason forced his voice into a softer tone than its usual harsh, guttural pitch and said with a little shrug: "A table, please."

"You'll have to wait a minute."

She looked past Jason and addressed the middle-aged man:

"May I help you, sir?"

He blushed and said hesitantly, "We'd also like a table for dinner."

He took his wife's fleshy hand. Neither his pinstriped suit nor her beaded velvet dress was cut to the latest style, but their outfits were neatly pressed and almost new. The purple of her cloche hat didn't quite fit with the navy blue of her dress. They smiled awkwardly.

"Right this way please," said the waitress.

Whispering, "excuse me," the couple edged past the two young men. Hawk gritted his teeth. Seeing anger suffuse his brother's face, Jason placed a hand on his arm.

"We don't want any trouble."

The waitress returned and showed them to a table in the far corner. As they passed by, the men at the counter mumbled something about not seeing their kind before in a nice place like this.

"Wonder what they're up to," said the skinny one. He forked a load of mashed potatoes spackled with gravy into his mouth.

Seated at the table, Hawk glared at the two men.

"Did you hear what that ugly bastard said?"

"I didn't hear a thing."

Hawk looked at his brother in shock.

"What are you talking about, Jason? You must have heard the bastard. Are we going to put up with this shit?"

"I already told you," Jason muttered, clipping each word as if he were cutting the loose ends off a string, "that we don't want trouble. We got more important things in hand. Now shut up and look at the menu. Besides he didn't mean me."

When the waitress finally came to their table, they each ordered fried chicken with mashed potatoes and string beans. The three men finished their coffee, scraped back their chairs and, laughing loudly, walked to the door. The man in the pinstriped suit escorted his wife to the empty space between the tables and counter. They danced cheek to fleshy cheek. A slowly spinning globe cast shards of light on the chunky pair, making them appear to be glowworms in a cave. When the music stopped, the waitress started the record again.

Jason and Hawk had not eaten since breakfast, and they wasted no time in polishing off two chicken legs apiece. Augustus liked leisurely meals, with discussions of literature or politics; but Jason always ate quickly and left the table, saying he had more important things to do than talk.

Hawk was concentrating on a chicken breast and didn't notice the blond woman approach their table.

"Hey handsome," she said, her voice unsteady, "wanna' dance?"

Jason had been watching her. Hawk looked up.

"Not you," she said to Jason. "The one with the copper skin, well, you both got copper skin, but the one with the eyes."

She looked straight at Hawk. Jason put a hand on his arm, but Hawk grinned and stood up. She took his hand and led him to the dance floor. He felt a ring on her third finger. She spun around and put both arms around his chest. Hawk didn't know how to dance. They shuffled to a bluesy number.

"I never danced with an Indian before. It feels ... unique. You certainly are handsome."

She snuggled closer. The heavy-set man at the counter watched, an expression of disgust displayed openly on his beefy features.

"You're married, aren't you?" Hawk asked.

"If you can call it that."

"If you were married to me, you wouldn't be dancing with a white man, or anyone else for that matter."

"I don't believe I would," she giggled and rubbed her body against his.

The skinny man at the counter whispered to his companion. They paid their check and left. Watching them intently, Jason signaled the waitress and gave her a ten-dollar bill.

"It's all yours," he said tightly.

"Why, thank you ... sugar. Come again."

Jason walked over and touched Hawk on the arm.

"Let's go."

Hawk turned around: "But ..."

"Move."

The rain had turned to a steady drizzle. A chill breeze sliced through their jackets. The light from the "Cafe" sign dimly picked out their truck. Blocking it was a battered truck with slatted, wooden sides. The heavy-set man was pulling a carton from under the tarp in Jason's truck while the scrawny one anxiously watched the door. Jason broke into a run followed closely by Hawk.

"Sid," whispered the lookout. "They're coming."

Sid turned around and picked up a hoe that he had leaned against Jason's truck. He took a step toward the running men and brandished the implement. Jason stopped a few feet away.

"We're not looking for trouble," Jason said.

"Funny thing," said Sid, "Neither are we, especially not with any Indians."

Hawk took a step forward. Sid raised the hoe higher.

"Easy," said Jason. "Now just get in your truck and head on home. Take that carton for your next party."

"We'll take more than a carton. Why don't you just go back and finish your dinner. Your brother here, or whatever, can dance some more with that nigger-loving blond whore."

Head lowered, Hawk moved so fast that Sid only got in a half swing with the hoe. The handle thumped harmlessly against Hawk's shoulder. Hawk butted Sid in the chest and punched him in the pit of the stomach. Sid just managed to clip Hawk in the side before Hawk pushed him back against the truck and, swinging widely, hit him square in the mouth. Blood squirted from Sid's lip and a tooth hung loosely. He dropped the hoe and crumpled to the ground.

When Hawk charged Sid, his friend started to run toward the café, but Jason tripped him. The man cried out and fell face forward to the ground. Jason kicked him in the side several times before Hawk pulled him away.

"Leave him; he's down," Hawk hissed. "Let's go; they won't cause us any more trouble."

Jason stared at Hawk, his eyes cold. "Not a chance. Got to finish it."

Jason stepped quickly to where Sid crouched, moaning and gasping. He picked up the hoe by the blade and, lifting it high, brought the handle down with a sickening crack on Sid's head. Sid rolled over and lay curled up like a fetus.

Hawk snapped, "What the ..."

"Shut up."

Jason hit Sid once more with the handle and then reversed the hoe. The blade sliced into the motionless man's skull. Hawk turned away and fought to control his stomach. The other man was struggling to his knees. He looked around in a daze. In that instant, Jason swung the hoe and smashed him in the face. He fell sideways. Jason slammed his head with the blade and then the handle. Jason knelt by the men and searched their pockets. He found two wallets and some loose change. He stood up and spun Hawk around.

"Now they really won't cause us any more trouble."

He glanced toward the cafe.

"Quick. Let's get them into the river. It'll be miles before their bodies come to shore. If we take their truck, no one is likely to make the connection. With any luck, they'll sink and never be found. The rain will wash away the blood on the ground. Anyway, no one here knows us, and there were no witnesses. You drive their truck. We'll head straight to Lawrence, no stopping. My friends will know what to do with their truck."

Jason tossed the hoe into his truck and picked up the heavy man's feet.

"C'mon," he said to Hawk. "Move!"

Chapter Eight

1931 – 1932

When Roseanne returned from Canada after her abortion, she asked Miss Grant for a change of supervisor. She explained that, while she greatly admired Mr. Tucker as a teacher, some differences in style had arisen; and she thought her students would be best served if she could work with someone else.

The assistant principal gave Roseanne a stony look but acknowledged that Miss Crenshaw was available to be assigned as her supervisor. She would agree to this unprecedented procedure because of the consistently favorable reports that she had received from Mr. Tucker in recent months. Furthermore, little time remained in the school year, after which Roseanne would work independently.

In the interest of thoroughness, Miss Grant checked with Mr. Tucker who expressed no objections. He reiterated that Miss Scudder was an excellent, if sometimes headstrong, teacher who would be a credit to the profession.

Roseanne began to work with Miss Crenshaw, a spidery lady with gray hair, sunken cheeks, and a termagant's reputation. She turned out, however, to be a cordial woman with an offbeat sense of humor who taught Roseanne a thing or two about working with second graders. Now teaching fourth grade, she maintained a firm discipline but encouraged her students to tell jokes, no matter how silly, as long as they were not hurtful to others.

Miss Crenshaw, who insisted that Roseanne call her Julie, also had nicknames for most of the teachers, especially the stuffy ones. She referred to Forest Tucker as "Sherwood." Louisa Barton, a Kentuckian who dragged out each syllable further than Roseanne thought possible, was called "Mint Julep." Mort Gershon, who often stood rubbing his left foot against his right calf, was "Stork." Some nicknames were not easy to follow. She explained Mr. Fogarty's moniker of *Bogey*: "He plays golf badly; he wears checked sweaters, and it rhymes with "Fogey." Need I say more?

"How do you know his golf is bad?" asked Roseanne.

"Look at him," said Miss Crenshaw.

The teachers were unaware of the honor accorded them as Miss Crenshaw refrained from using the nicknames except with Roseanne and a few privileged friends outside the school. Roseanne avoided Forest. If he entered the Faculty Room, she returned to her classroom. She passed him in the halls without speaking. She spent most of her free time in her room. She tried to read but generally found herself staring out the window. Occasionally, she cried. The widow had agreed that she could stay for the balance of the school year. She didn't visit Esther but instead went for silent walks with Consuela. In late April, Miss Crenshaw suggested the two of them go out for dinner on Saturday.

"Unless you have other plans."

"Not at all. That would be very nice."

It was drizzling when they met at a café that catered to a young crowd. They sat at a round table with a candle in a dish. Rosanne ordered a chicken fricassee with potatoes au gratin. Miss Crenshaw had a breaded veal cutlet with buttered carrots. They talked about the students, and how some of the families were having a hard time. Quite a few fathers were out of work. Some had abandoned their families to take to the rails. The women had gone to whatever jobs they could find. Miss Crenshaw abruptly changed the topic.

"You may be fooling the others, but don't think you can fool me. You can talk about it or not as you wish, but something happened between you and Forest Tucker, and I have a pretty damn good idea what."

Roseanne froze, her fork halfway to her mouth, cream sauce dripping onto the tablecloth. She quickly put her fork down and rubbed the tablecloth with her napkin. Miss Crenshaw waited patiently. Finally, Roseanne shrugged. Tears came to her eyes.

"We had an affair, and I stupidly got pregnant. I thought he would want to get married, but he didn't."

"Ah," said Miss Crenshaw with a nod. "I remember you're being sick for a few days last month. You don't have to talk about it."

"It helps. It was awful. I'll never do it again. But the doctor was kind and sympathetic. I went to Canada."

"By yourself?"

"No, a friend went with me."

"I see. What else would you have expected from a man like Forest Tucker? He is totally concerned with himself. I believe these psychiatrist fellows would call it 'egotism' or 'narcissism.' Why do you think he's not married at his age? Next time you feel inclined to have an affair, let me inspect the fellow first. I've had my share of experiences."

Roseanne studied Miss Crenshaw, wondering if she would elaborate. Miss Crenshaw noticed her look.

"So, like the others, you think I'm a withered old maid?"

"Oh, no, Miss Crenshaw, I mean Julie, I didn't think anything of the kind. I didn't think anything at all. I mean I was a bit curious about ...

well you know I was thinking..."

"About my past, or rather if I had a past to be curious about?"

"I guess so. I know it's rude to be curious, but I couldn't help wondering. You are such a compassionate, intelligent person that..."

"That you asked yourself why is there no one, or more specifically, no man in her life. Is that it, more or less?"

"Well, that's a bit blunt, but yes, that's more or less it."

"What are friends for, if not to be blunt with each other? And yes, I do have a past, and yes there have been men in my life, two to be quite precise. One is still in my life. Since it may be instructive for you, and since instructing others is not only a way of life, but also an obsession for me, I'll tell you about them. You might want a cup of coffee while you listen. In fact, we could both do with a cup of coffee. Excuse me, waiter, two cups of black coffee please."

Miss Crenshaw sat silently until the waiter brought the coffee. Then she reached into a large, navy blue pocket book and brought out a small metal flask engraved with a heart entwined with the initials: JMC. She opened the flask, sniffed the contents, said "Ah," and poured a little into each cup.

"Good for what ails you," she winked. "Smuggler's Best. Now, settle back and listen to the lurid tale of Julie Crenshaw.

"The year is 1896; the country has been in a devastating depression for three years. Conditions were not dissimilar to our present glorious times, except a gentleman could get a proper drink in a saloon without looking over his shoulder and a lady could take a genteel glass of sherry in the privacy of her home. Not that there wasn't plenty of opposition to a good stiff drink. The infamous W.C.T.U. was active in town, and the misguided Anti-Saloon League had been founded in 1893, the same year that the depression began. So you see, temperance inevitably leads to a depression. I'm not an inveterate tippler, but I do think that a glass of something does a man – or woman – good every once in a while."

Miss Crenshaw took a sip of coffee, and Roseanne did the same.

"Times were exceedingly hard, but fortunately, my father still made a good living selling life insurance. I had been teaching for two years and paid for my own incidental expenses. I, of course, lived at home. Young ladies thirty-five years ago did not take a room, not for licit purposes anyway. We had a spacious house not far from the lake.

"I loved that house. It was full of nooks and crannies where you could hide for hours and lose yourself in a book. My favorite spot was a settee built into an alcove with a tall window facing south and west. On a sunny day in winter, it would be deliciously warm all afternoon. It was at the end of a hallway on the second floor. I would tuck myself into the cushions and read, drowsing off from time to time.

"As a family of some position, we had two carriages: a small brougham that my father liked to drive and a larger, but rather old, landau that the gardener, who also served as coachman and butler, drove when we went to church or town. We were not exceedingly wealthy and had only two servants, including the gardener. They were a couple and lived in rooms off the kitchen. I had great fun as a child riding in the open landau, jumping up and down and pointing out the sights. My two older brothers were much more sedate.

"I am not absolutely certain, but I don't remember any automobiles in Burlington at that time. I think the first autos arrived a few years later."

Roseanne drank some coffee.

"Does perk it up," Roseanne said with a grin. "Sorry for the interruption. Go on."

"It was spring, a ravishing spring, and I was in love—engaged to be married in June to an upstanding, and very handsome, I might add, young man named Harold Lockhart, who had a fine career ahead of him in a prominent bank. He had been promoted a year earlier to senior clerk and was studying nights for a better position, something to do with loans. You know, my dear, I never had a head for financial matters and could barely understand what Harold was saying when he would go on about the bank. I have always been more interested in teaching those little imps.

"May was a pure delight. The gardens in Battery Park literally burst with colors; there were flowers everywhere. The sun had never shone so brilliantly nor had the lake sparkled so like cut crystal, or so it seemed to me. I was beautiful, carefree, and deliriously happy. Hard to believe, looking at me now, but I was truly beautiful that spring."

"Julie," pleaded Roseanne. "Don't talk that way about yourself. You are..."

"Hush up and let me continue. Harold and I had known each other forever, since college where we met in 1892 during my sophomore year. He was a senior. We both knew from that very first moment. We talked only to each other during the entire afternoon tea. I think some of the other girls were annoyed, but I didn't care. He started calling at our house, and soon we were going to dances and concerts. Two years later, we got engaged. We agreed on a long engagement because of the depression and Harold's desire to reach a more secure position.

"Harold was promoted to senior clerk a year later. That would have been 1895. We set the date for the following June. My best friend, Minnie Sheldon, was to be maid of honor; one of Harold's closest friends would be best man. I could not have been more excited.

"I was only sorry that Minnie had no beau. Two weddings in the same month would have been grand.

"The year rushed by in a whirl of parties, dances, teas and suppers. Since both our families were still well off, we kept up an active social calendar despite the depression, a bit insensitive I guess. Father, however, did want to economize, so the previous summer we hadn't taken our usual holiday at a lake resort. I preferred, in any case, to be with Harold.

"One afternoon in late winter, we were sitting on the settee in my favorite nook. There had been a blizzard two days ago, and snow was piled thickly around the house with glittering icicles hanging from the eaves. The sun had come out, and it was hot in the nook. You could hardly look out the window, for the sunlight glancing off the snow was blinding. We were holding hands as we always did. Harold kissed me on the lips. I kissed him back – a long, lingering kiss – and held him in my arms. He startled me then by saying that we needn't wait to be married, that he was on fire with his love for me and wanted me now. He was sure he could find a hotel where we could get a room. We could register as man and wife. No questions would be asked."

Roseanne laughed and said, "Times have certainly changed."

"Maybe ... maybe not," said Miss Crenshaw.

"Nevertheless," Miss Crenshaw went on, "I was shocked but stayed calm. I said no—that while I burned for him as much as he desired me, I wanted to be a virgin on my wedding night. He let the matter drop then but brought it up on two other occasions, pressing me to his breast and saying that, loving me so intensely, it was almost impossible for him to wait. I was firm, and Harold bowed – albeit after some cajoling, which included fervent kissing – to my insistence on first night virginity. I never thought to wonder – or ask – if he was a virgin.

"June finally arrived – and was just as glorious as May. The wedding took place in the Methodist church that my family attended. I wanted to be a traditional bride and wore a sweeping silk dress with a long train. My hair was piled high on my head and an antique lace veil rested lightly on my face. The silk rustled as my father walked me down the aisle. Harold stood there, handsome and smiling. I was so nervous; and he seemed so calm, so at ease. I remember little of the ceremony; it went by so quickly. He lifted the veil and kissed me. I was transported.

"The reception took place at the American House; after all, my father said, he only had one daughter. At that, Tad, my oldest brother, poked me in the ribs. My brothers and I had always roughhoused with each other and have an incredible bond to this day. Poor Tad, a grandfather now, is not well. The ballroom was decorated with silver and gold ribbons, and one of those mirrored spheres circled lazily overhead creating a shimmering pattern on the floor. In keeping with the hard times, there was only a small orchestra; but they played beautifully - all the latest waltzes and polkas.

"The food was sumptuous, although I ate practically nothing except the smoked salmon and the strawberries and cream. My father made a very funny – and a little risqué - toast. Something about time's winged chariot, grandchildren on his knee and, oh damn, I can't remember, for the life of me, what else. Do you think it's because I'm getting old or just don't want to remember?"

"Maybe it's what you put in the coffee," said Roseanne.

"Oh no, that would help my memory," said Miss Crenshaw.

She took a sip and looked past Roseanne as if struggling with her memory. She sighed and continued: "My father was very literary and well-spoken. That's why he was so good at selling life insurance. His customers looked up to him although he was never condescending.

"My father was the first to dance with me, whirling me around the polished floor in a waltz. Then I was in Harold's arms. We danced and danced. Of course, I also danced with all the men - and Harold with all the women, starting with Minnie. I beamed at him.

"The party went on until late in the evening. My father had taken a room in the hotel for us. We were to catch a train to New York the next morning and then a ship to Bermuda for our honeymoon. At one point, I couldn't find Harold and thought he might have gone up to the room to change out of his morning coat. The ballroom had gotten warm, and his shirt was soaked with perspiration. I was damp myself and realized it would be a good idea to change into another dress before saying good-bye to our guests and spending a little time with our families. I was absolutely thrilled and excited as I rode up in the gilt-edged, mirrored elevator.

"I opened the door to our room. There stood Harold and Minnie naked in each other's arms. I stared in disbelief for a few seconds – I don't know how long - then slammed the door and ran down five flights of stairs. My brother, Phil, was in the lobby smoking a cigarette, and he saw me run out of the hotel. Barely conscious of what I was doing, I ran all the way back to our house – I must have looked a sight – and up to my room. I locked the door, tore off my wedding dress, and began cutting it up with a pair of scissors."

"My God," said Roseanne. "I would've gone for the shotgun."

"Didn't think of it," said Miss Crenshaw, "or I might have."

Miss Crenshaw laughed.

"I can laugh now," she said.

"Phil told my father and then raced after me. I was long gone. His only hope was to try the house. My father presumed that Harold and I had had some awful argument although he could not imagine what sort of argument would cause me to run away. He was too decent a man to suspect the truth. He went up to the room thinking he could sort things out. He got out of the elevator just as Harold and Minnie were leaving the room. Harold pushed Minnie behind him, and the truth struck my father full in the face."

"He walked up to Harold and pulled back his arm. He paused for a moment before erupting. 'You're not worth it,' he said and spat in his face. He left Harold with spit running down his nose and chin."

The guests were quietly told, and presents returned. My father reasoned that any story that would hide the truth would only make me seem unbalanced. He refused to do that. Tad and my mother followed Phil to the house to look for me while my father did the dirty work. Harold's parents were outraged and did not speak to their son for several years.

"I never saw either Harold or Minnie again. They got married and moved away. I heard that they had three children and ultimately divorced."

Roseanne said nothing. She stared at Miss Crenshaw. She took a big gulp of coffee.

"I think," blurted Roseanne finally, "that I would like some more of what's in that flask."

Miss Crenshaw smiled obligingly and reached inside her purse. She opened the flask and started to tip it into Roseanne's cup.

"Not in the coffee," said Roseanne. "Straight up, if you don't mind."

She took a large slug and handed the flask back to Miss Crenshaw, who took a delicate sip.

"My God," said Roseanne. "How ... how absolutely awful! I can think of nothing else to say except how did you ever recover?"

"Slowly."

"The second man? I take it that was different."

"Ah, Lincoln," Miss Crenshaw sighed dreamily. "That is indeed a horse of a different color. I love him – and will for the rest of my life. And he loves me – of that I'm sure."

"Then why aren't you married – or at least together? Why does no one seem to know about him?"

"Because, you see, Linc is married - just not to me."

"Oh."

Roseanne noticed the waiter approaching their table and shook her head. The waiter turned and left the room.

"Not that we don't see each other. And act like a married couple, complete with fights and passionate make-ups. We just do it all in private. We are not seen together in public. Well, that's not totally true. Very, and I mean very, occasionally, we will risk going to dinner in some dark, obscure restaurant. But we don't hold hands. We act like the most casual of acquaintances."

"This is all a little hard to take in at one sitting. How did this – uh – situation come about?"

"That takes some telling. Let me start at the beginning, as the Red Queen said.

"For years after the annulment, I would have nothing to do with men, although there were a few suitors. After all, my family was prosperous.

But I ignored them all despite long talks with my mother and harangues from my father. At one time, he even said that I was enjoying the self-pity – wallowing in it, I believe, was the cliché that he used. Mother was subtler, but no less insistent. She said that I should not let one experience – no matter how devastating – completely dominate my perspective. She said that one rotten apple didn't mean the whole barrel was bad. She said that I would end up a lonely, old woman. In that, she was probably right; but then who doesn't?

"At the end, we're all alone. The point is to live until you get there.

"I don't know if I enjoyed my misery; but I couldn't bear the thought of another courtship. It was not so much the pain; but you know how, when you have an upset stomach, the very thought of food makes you ill. Well, the thought of falling in love again made me physically ill. Maybe it was an instinctive reaction to protect my sanity. I'm not much on this psychoanalysis, but I guess the term "defense mechanism" might have properly applied.

"I lived at home and worked hard at my job. I became a very good teacher and loved it. I adore the kids and regret never having had any. They are so endearing – most of the time. I saved most of my earnings and had a pretty good nest egg. I was well on my way to prosperous old-maid hood. I was happy with my family and had a nice circle of friends. My brothers each had two kids, and I was close to my niece and nephews. Christmas was always a wonderful time. The whole family gathered in the old house. We gave each other such superb, if simple, gifts—sometimes only a book or a small Chinese porcelain vase, but always something special.

"The first big change came when my father died of a stroke in 1912. Fortunately, he went quickly and did not suffer. My mother decided – rightly – to sell the house and move in with Tad, who was always her favorite. With my savings and inheritance, I bought the cottage where I now live. You must come visit sometime – and perhaps meet Linc."

"I think that I would like that," said Roseanne. "In fact, I would be honored."

"Oh pshaw! Honored indeed!" said Miss Crenshaw. "It's just that it's about time someone knew us as a couple.

"I was thirty-nine in 1912 and living on my own for the first time in my life. At first, I was scared – petrified more like it. Gradually, I came to love it. I even cooked dinner for friends – and washed up afterwards. Of course, I had a woman do the cleaning once a week, which was often enough for a spinster, and about what I could afford.

"My friends invited me to dinner. While they were mostly couples - I knew a few other single women - they didn't seem to mind having an odd number at the table. It was at a friend's house about two years later that I met Linc and his wife, Dorothy. I could tell almost immediately that something was not quite right with Dorothy. She was incredibly beautiful - with thick, wavy chestnut hair and skin the color of a pale peach – and talented. She had been in the theater at the university and was a huge success. She had tried various things after college but never lasted long in any one job or interest.

"That night, she seemed brittle, as if about to burst into a thousand shards of glass. She talked but was not really part of the conversation. She was in her own world. I learned subsequently that she experienced wild shifts of mood, going from being almost giddily joyful one day to the deepest depression the next. Furthermore, there was no predicting the nature or shifting of her moods. Nothing obvious or logical seemed to trigger them. Linc told me later that, in the early years of her illness, she had seen a couple of local neurological specialists. They could not find anything wrong physically and did her virtually no good.

"He also took her to New York to see two noted alienists. They did no better - not that they didn't have their pet theories: female hysteria; nutritional imbalance; sexual aversion; or, and I like this one best of all, penis envy. The only one that ever made any sense to me was "manic depressive," meaning – as I understand it – a person with an uncontrollable and irrational pattern of mood swings from absurdly delirious joy to unfathomable despair. The sufferer is generally unaware of what causes the mood swings and has no ability to moderate them."

Roseanne shook her head: "It must be terrifying to lose control of your emotional balance."

"I imagine so. No, in truth, I cannot imagine it. Except for that moment of shock when I saw Harold with Minnie, I have never lost control of my feelings – which doesn't make them any less intense."

"I know what you mean," said Roseanne.

Miss Crenshaw took a long pull on the flask and handed it to Roseanne.

"Not right now."

"So to continue," said Miss Crenshaw. "They had been deeply in love at one time, and the first years of their marriage seemed pure bliss. Then, about six years before Linc and I met, her moods started. It was imperceptible at first. She would sometimes pick a fight for no apparent reason. Then suddenly, for no better reason, she would fall into his arms crying, apologizing profusely, and begging him to make love to her. These incidents resulted in white-hot passion, which was for Linc more disturbing than satisfying. Afterward, he would lie in bed feeling agitated and uneasy while Dorothy was euphoric, saying how good it had been. Often, she continued to be aroused and insisted on more.

"Their fights began happening more and more frequently – sometimes as often as once or twice in a week. In between the fights, she had no interest in making love, though she would comply if Linc made the overture. Then the fighting stopped and Linc was hopeful.

"Dorothy seemed happy, almost giddy, for a time. It took a while for Linc to realize that bouts of depression accompanied the happy moods with frightening regularity. Gradually, the mood swings grew more extreme and the depressions deeper. They terrified Linc, especially as Dorothy took longer to recover from them. She seemed in another world – even during her giddy times. She refused to make love at all.

"Realizing that she desperately needed help, Linc not only took her to neurologists and psychiatrists; but he finally had her hospitalized at the Lake View Sanatorium where a new phase developed. She sat mutely in her room, sewing, or reading - sometimes the same novel two or three times. She barely walked on the grounds and spoke to no one when she did. The doctors were at a loss. Linc brought her home, arranging for her to have a separate bedroom and hiring a specially trained live-in companion.

"Dorothy stayed in her room for hours. Sometimes she played cards with Miss Braddock but rarely spoke. When Linc visited, she did little more than acknowledge his presence. The violent mood swings were gone, but she was like a zombie. When she periodically regained her vitality, she would accompany Linc to restaurants, parties and the theater but had no interest in a marital relationship. The manic-depressive cycle, however, always returned, and she would retreat to her bedroom.

"Linc decided that withdrawing was Dorothy's only means of controlling her condition when she sensed the moods approaching. By keeping her activities and emotions limited, she was able to hold her exaggerated moods at bay and maintain some kind of emotional balance. She would resume a somewhat normal life when she felt the moods abate, if only temporarily.

"Such was the situation when Linc and I met at that dinner party – during one of Dorothy's so-called good periods. It was in October 1914. War had engulfed Europe. Certain voices were clamoring for us to join the Allies, but most people I knew wanted us to keep out of it and let the Europeans suffer the consequences of their madness. Conversations were intense, to say the least. All the talk that night was about the war, and I weighed in with my opinions. I've never been one to take a backseat – as you know. I think that's what Linc first noticed.

"He was in his late forties and not much to look at: short, a paunch, and going bald. But he had a way of looking at you - with clear hazel eyes - that made you feel that you were the most interesting person in the world. We had a spirited argument that evening, with Linc contending that, since we would join the war sooner or later, it would be better to do it sooner and put an end to the bloody mess. Linc fancied himself a man of action and was a great admirer of Teddy Roosevelt. I responded that American boys should not lose their lives in a war that ought not to have started in the first place. It got a bit rancorous. Dorothy sat smiling like a porcelain doll.

"I could not have been more surprised when he called me a few days later and asked me to lunch. What surprised me even more was that I accepted. Linc had inherited a real estate business from his father; he owned and managed office buildings around the state. He took me to an elegant restaurant and, in the way of explaining his somewhat unusual invitation, described a little of Dorothy's condition. He said that he enjoyed – and sorely missed – the conversation of an intelligent and attractive woman.

"We went to lunch a few times and then he asked me to dinner. You are thinking, 'I know what he's after.' Well, you would be wrong."

"And you would be wrong," said Roseanne. "I wasn't assuming anything. But I am very curious about what comes next."

"What comes next is this: I relished these occasions and had to admit that, despite his homeliness, I was attracted to him - not in love, at least not yet, but attracted. One morning, I woke up realizing that I no longer wanted to die a virgin and that, at forty-one, Linc might be my one and only chance. So, I seduced him – with no better idea about how to go about it than what I had read in certain novels. It was pretty awkward – and comical.

"I invited him to dinner at my cottage. I arranged everything just so: down to the fire, candles, and a bottle of claret."

Miss Crenshaw gazed for an instant into space.

"I prepared a wonderful meal - if I do say so myself: saddle of lamb with roast potatoes followed by a tomato salad. I served stuffed mushrooms for appetizers. I prayed that I looked my best. After dinner, we sat on the couch. I edged close to him. He fidgeted. I touched his arm. He virtually bolted off the couch. I stood up and took his hand. For the first time in our acquaintance, he was speechless. He gaped at me. An absolute disaster was coming on fast. I could think of only one thing to do.

"'Will you make love to me?' I asked in what I thought was my calmest voice but which, Linc later told me, was shaking so violently he thought I might have a seizure.

"Which he almost did. He stared at me briefly and then walked over to the window. Why, at times like these, do we always need to stare out a window? I was too scared to say a word. Finally, he came over to me, put his hands on my shoulders, and said, 'Yes.'

"It wasn't fireworks that first night. I had no clue. It took me awhile to get the hang of it, but I did – eventually. I guess God gives us the equipment and lets us stumble around learning how to use it. After a while, we realized that we were in love – and we have been ever since. It's been sixteen years, and I think we'll love each other forever.

"Yes, yes, I know–Dorothy. Her condition has not changed much in all this time. Sometimes she is better, sometimes worse. The psychiatrists seem to have gotten a little more adept, but she generally refuses to go. Twice, her mood swings became quite wild. Linc was so frightened he sent her back to the sanatorium – once for five months.

"He no longer loves her, but he cares deeply about her and will never leave her. Nor do I ask him to.

"Am I a shameless hussy? An evil temptress? I ask myself that question from time to time, but I have no answer. I've come to the conclusion that I will let God decide that one."

Roseanne took a sip from her coffee cup and looked steadily at Miss Crenshaw.

"I hope I'm not sounding like too much of a dim-wit, but all I can think of saying is that I am deeply touched."

"That is nice to hear. I must admit to having planned to tell you. It seemed that you needed a little bucking up. Based on my own experience with Harold, and what I guessed to be yours with Forest, I was worried that you might be tempted to give up on love. I wanted you to see that love often comes unexpectedly and in odd guises and that the best, most enduring love is not always the one that our society has taught us to anticipate."

Miss Crenshaw winked and lifted her coffee cup. Roseanne clinked her cup against Miss Crenshaw's.

"Thank you, Julie."

"I also had a more selfish motive. I wanted one other person besides Linc to know that I'm not a shriveled up old maid."

Roseanne looked around the room and signaled the waiter over.

"Dessert?" he asked.

Roseanne returned home in June. She had accepted a position teaching third grade and moved back into her old room at the farm. She didn't miss passing Forest silently in the halls. Having worked summers at a girl's camp in New Hampshire, she had seen little of Scudder's Gorge the past five years. Except for Esther, she had not kept up with her friends.

She looked forward to teaching in a small town – even if she was nervous about it being her hometown. She loved her room, and the valley was beautiful. She walked along the roads and helped with the chores. Everett had not replaced Jacob, even though a plethora of good men were begging for almost any kind of work. Struggling to keep up, they were glad to have her pitch in.

Damon's wedding to Jeannie Mitchell was scheduled for late in the month. Roseanne planned to help with the preparations. She knew that she was lucky. Esther had just graduated with no prospect of a job. She was down in the dumps when she and Lizzie came to visit. While the women talked on the porch, Lizzie's two boys, Francis (five) and Scott (four) played cowboys and Indians in the yard.

"Lizzie fancies herself a writer these days," Damon had told Roseanne at breakfast.

"Rubbish," Lizzie blushed. "It's just a hobby."

"Sis," Esther laughed, "you wear modesty like a bull in heat."

"Is that what they taught you girls over in Burlington? I think I'll keep my two down on the farm."

"Keep 'em dumb and proud of it," quipped Roseanne. "Like some others we know."

They all laughed – without worrying if they had the same person in mind.

"Seriously, I love the writing, and what's better, the stories annoy the hell out of Daddy."

The Gazette, which the First Congregational Ladies' Auxiliary printed on a mimeograph machine, had published a series of her stories. Tyrell's, Sellick's Hardware and other stores sold the paper for a penny. Lizzie created tales of women who struggle with harsh lives. Her heroines were often Southern since Lizzie imagined the South as a dark region where women were even more constrained than in Scudder's Gorge.

In her latest story, a young woman flees her family's dirt farm in the North Carolina hills and settles in New York City where she takes a position as a sales clerk in a large department store. In her one-room flat in Queens, she can hardly sleep for the ear-splitting rumble of the el. To her surprise, she longs for the pine-clad, southern hills where she can at least see the stars at night. She is shocked by the rudeness of her customers, to whom she is unfailingly polite. She feels invisible. Another clerk in her department, women's sweaters, has been dismissed. She has only one friend. They can barely afford to go to the movies and a greasy Chinese restaurant once a week. She takes a walk one raw November day. She kicks the scraps of newspaper eddying along the sidewalk. She can smell garbage rotting and the fumes of trucks. Black puffs of smoke belch from tenement incinerators; soot dusts her overcoat. She hates her life and determines to go back home. She stops for a cup of hot chocolate in a delicatessen and sees a flyer for nighttime business courses. She shrugs and takes the brochure. It cannot get any worse.

Years later, she takes a minute to look out her corner office window. She is sad never to have married, but relishes her many friends and – until recently - a long-time lover. Married to a wealthy shrew whom he would divorce – or murder – if he dared, her lover cheats on her with the same insouciance as on his wife. When she gives him an ultimatum (that two women is the house limit), he follows the manly course and dumps her.

Did she make the right choice so long ago? She is successful beyond her wildest dreams but something nags. She sighs and turns back to her desk, with its neat piles of sales reports. At least she had paid off the mortgage on the family farm.

"Where does she come up with these ideas?" asked Augustus Baxter, scanning the Gazette in Tyrell's. "She doesn't write too badly, but where would a Forshay learn about people like this?"

"Maybe from her own experiences," chuckled his neighbor, Ross Caruthers.

"Men," sniffed Mavis Tyrell. "The small amount you do learn, you make precious little use of. That girl has not had it easy with that damn fool father-in-law forced to close the dealership and then shooting himself to top things off. Cyrus ain't too bad for a husband, and I hear he works hard over at the creamery, but life's not what she was taught to expect. Her tightwad father is no help at all. So she don't have to imagine but half of it. I think she tells a good story. I don't know where she finds the time - what with two kids at home and working at the Bijou. Are you going to pay for that paper, Augustus, or just read it?"

The Gazette reported valley news including the results of the boys' baseball team against Marysville and Roseanne Scudder's appointment as third grade teacher, replacing Mrs. Shay who was retiring after thirty-seven years of dedicated service.

"I like this story, Lizzie," said Roseanne. "Why don't you write one that I could read to my class next fall?"

"It would have to be considerably different from the kind that has 'shocked' Scudder's Gorge," sniffed Esther.

"Are people really shocked by your stories?" asked Roseanne. "This one is so interesting and well-written."

"You've been away too long," said Lizzie. "In our backwater paradise, a woman's place is in the kitchen or the chicken coop. My stories show women as too independent – not to mention aspiring to something other than agricultural bliss."

"Are the men here aspiring to so much? It seems we're all just trying to get by. But it's true, I haven't been around much – not even summers."

"Just come on over to the Forshays for dinner, and you can catch up on all the dirt," Lizzie said angrily.

"Speaking of aspirations," Esther quickly asked Roseanne, "wasn't Hawk Baxter a bit taken with you at one time?"

Esther knew about the break-up with Forest, but not the cause. Consuela had managed everything through a friend who knew a doctor in Montreal. While abortions were also illegal in Canada, this doctor was willing to make the arrangements.

"Oh, he paid a little attention to me in high school, but I've not seen him since. He wanted to do something he could be proud of. He was talking about medical school back then."

Rosanne leaned back and took in the view across the fields: the green corn stalks, the hay and the Holsteins (with a few Guernsey and Brown Swiss mixed in for good measure) grazing or lying chewing their cuds in the shade of a maple. Major, the old bull, watched over the herd. Everett wanted to buy a younger bull, but times were too difficult.

Gleaming ten-gallon milk cans waited by the barn door to be filled, left overnight in the milk house and picked up by the creamery truck in the morning.

She helped with the milking most afternoons although she'd had precious little practice since high school. She loved the swishing and splashing sounds and the heavy dung smell of the barn. She patted each cow on the rump. The barn needed painting; it was starting to peel. Maybe next year things would get better.

"He never made it to medical school - or college for that matter," said Lizzie.

"He was gone for a few years. He served an apprenticeship in a forge and then worked in a factory in …," she chewed her lip "… Buffalo, if I remember correctly. Anyway, a couple of years ago, he and another fellow set up a forge in that old shed on Augustus's place. They make grill work - mostly for railings and windows. Also decorative items when they get the chance. Nice looking work. They sell all over the county. They're not doing badly, considering. He's as handsome as ever with that black hair and high cheeks. And those eyes that look right through you."

"You seem to know a lot about his business," said Roseanne.

"Oh, he and Cyrus were buddies back in high school so he drops by every once in a while. He's so different from Jason."

"I see." Roseanne shifted in her chair to face Esther. "What a tough time to step out into the world. What are you going to do?"

"You mean apart from enjoying my father's hospitality?"

"Humph," snorted Lizzie.

"I'm sorry, Lizzie. That was thoughtless. I honestly don't know, Roseanne; there don't seem to be any jobs anywhere. Logan says that, in these times, a woman working just takes a job away from a man. Maybe he's right."

"Humph," said Lizzie again. "Like father like son."

"Lizzie, enough – please." Esther pushed on: "I studied chemistry because I want to work in a laboratory, but I've tried all over New England, and no one's hiring. It's discouraging to say the least."

"Let's turn our minds to something else. We've got a wedding coming up, and I'm going to need both of you to help."

"Just like when we were kids," said Esther. "Remember the day of the big storm and we had to stay over?"

"Yes," Roseanne smiled. "I remember. We rolled around in the snow with my father."

"After dinner, he read to us from Tom Sawyer, and your mother..."

"And my mother had a headache."

"Oh God, I'm sorry, dear. I didn't mean..." Esther reached out and took Roseanne's hand.

"That's all right, I know you didn't." She squeezed Esther's hand.

"Bang, you're dead," shouted Francis, pointing a finger at his brother. "You're a dead Injun!"

"Francis," snapped his mother. "How often have I told you about that?"

For the next two weeks, the three young women and Sally worked feverishly making decorations. The service would be held at the First Congregational, but the reception was planned for the Scudder farm – in deference to May's memory and because the Mitchells lived in town and had a small yard. Everett planned to set up long tables in the space between the house and the barn. He, Damon and Brent had been building the tables in their spare time for the last two months. They also laid down interlocking planks for a dance floor and anchored them to four poles hammered into the soft ground. Howie came up on weekends to help out.

The women fringed tablecloths with colored bunting. They built a trellised arch to place next to the dance floor, decorated it with bright ribbons, and dried flowers. Roseanne planned to add fresh flowers on the wedding day. It would be a great spot for wedding photos. They nailed colored bows to trees and potted wildflowers to place around the dance floor. Esther painted "DAMON and JEANNIE" on a sheet to be hung on the barn.

Below the words, Sally depicted a cupid shooting an arrow through a pink heart while on the chicken coop; she did a strutting rooster followed by a hen and chicks. Roseanne painted "THE DAMON STRUT" in bold letters below the rooster.

Real chickens scratched in the yard, and the women laughed giddily as they worked.

"You have a hidden talent," Esther commented to Sally.

"Nice of you to say so. My father had me take drawing lessons. He hoped I would be an artist."

"Maybe it's not too late," said Roseanne. "It's never too late for anything."

"I think that rooster looks just like Damon," chuckled Esther.

"Yes, like most men," giggled Roseanne, "he thinks he's bossing the show."

"That had better wash off or get painted over someday," growled Damon.

The women jumped.

"Damon," shrieked Esther. "What are you doing sneaking around like that? You could scare the wits out of a person."

The chickens scattered.

"Wits is it? You mean like these chickens here who are bossing the show?"

"Isn't Sally marvelous?" asked Roseanne.

"Yes," smiled Damon. "That is a mighty handsome rooster."

Jeannie made her own wedding dress - of white satin adorned with white silk roses. Roseanne and Esther helped her finish the two bridesmaid dresses, one for Roseanne and the second for Jeannie's younger sister, Katie. These were of pink satin and also adorned with silk roses.

"They are so beautiful," said Roseanne, hugging Jeannie. "You will be such a gorgeous bride."

Starting two days before the wedding, the Scudder, Mitchell, and Forshay kitchens were a hive of activity. Sampling dough as they worked, Sally, Roseanne and Lizzie baked breads and cakes in the large Scudder oven.

"Oh, this bread is good," exclaimed Roseanne.

"Sally, would you please hand me that blue bowl?" asked Lizzie.

"I think Damon should run to Tyrell's for more flour and sugar."

"Roseanne, we have plenty," said Sally, "but have him go if you're nervous."

"How many guests did you say are coming?" asked Lizzie.

"About a hundred and ten at last count."

"Are the Baxters coming?"

"I don't know," said Roseanne. "Daddy insisted that Damon invite them. He grumbled but gave in. My brother has his blind spots. He doesn't like Jason's bootlegging."

"He's in good company," said Lizzie. "Speaking of the Baxters, I recall my father saying some time ago that they didn't always have that farm over on the west side. Augustus grew up on what's now the Farrell place. His father had to sell out back in the Nineties."

"Something else struck me," Lizzie continued. "Father said an Indian family was farming next to the Baxter property. A story went around that some drunks tried to run them out, but your father and Augustus intervened."

"But they would have been boys at the time. How could they have confronted grown men – even drunks?"

"It does seem improbable," said Lizzie, forming dough into a loaf. "Maybe your father will tell you. What my father knows is hearsay."

"I don't know. He can be pretty close-mouthed at times, especially about himself. He talks about Mother but never his feelings for her."

"You've got to catch him at the right time," said Sally, who had been listening quietly. She smoothed chocolate icing on a cake. "I wonder if that's how Augustus met his wife. I mean was she part of that family?"

"No," said Lizzie. "Onatah comes from North Marysville. Her family has a small farm. Hawk doesn't know how his parents met."

"Did your father say what happened to the Indian family?" asked Roseanne.

"I asked. All he could remember was that they moved a few years after the incident. He didn't know the circumstances."

"Funny," mused Roseanne, "that there aren't more Indians living in the valley."

She wiped her floury hands on her apron and lifted an edge to her eyes. She had suddenly thought of her mother missing the first of her children's weddings.

Esther spent the morning before the wedding baking cookies. At eleven, her mother finished her cleaning and came in to help.

"Try this," said Esther, handing her a hot oatmeal raisin cookie.

"Mmm," sighed Lucille, "delicious. What can I do?"

"Mix this batter please. Then roll out the dough. There are some animal shapes by the sink. We'll make a batch of cookies just for the younger children."

Trays of hot cookies were cooling on the big table. Mixing bowls cluttered the counters. Three jars filled to the brim stood by the door.

"After the cookies, we need to do bean casseroles. We'll reheat them in the morning and take everything over before going to church."

"I imagine that will be fine, but let me ask your father."

Esther stopped kneading dough and looked at her mother. Lucille was forty-eight and appeared older. Her dark hair was streaked with gray and knotted in a bun at the back. Her cheeks were shallow, and she had the beginnings of crows' feet at the corners of her eyes. She took care of the house by herself and spent long hours helping weed the berry patches.

Esther wondered what she would look like at her mother's age. She was a wisp of a girl with a tiny waist of which she was proud and pointed breasts, which she feared were too small. She wanted a life different from her mother's – or Lizzie's.

"Momma, why is Daddy so hard on Lizzie? Cyrus is a decent fellow and works hard to provide. It wasn't his fault about the dealership. Is it because she had to get married?"

"My, where did that question come from?" Lucille stirred the batter.

"No, I don't think it's that. It's just that your father expected more of Lizzie. He expects more of all of you. He doesn't understand the way young people are today." She fumbled for her words: "Your father is ... can be ... a ... hard man sometimes."

Esther started to say something but refrained. She opened the oven door and felt the heat hit her face.

"I almost forgot," Esther said casually. "We need to roast one of the four turkeys tonight."

"Four? Let's see: ourselves, the Scudders and the Mitchells. Who's doing the fourth?"

"The Farrells."

"My, what a lot of excitement. The Scudders certainly know how to do things."

Katie Mitchell had taken Lizzie's boys berry picking; and that afternoon, the aroma of hot raspberry, blackberry and elderberry pies wafted through the Mitchell's house.

The Mitchells had come to Scudder's Gorge four years ago, in the spring of 1927, when Jeannie's father, Phil, took a job as foreman at the granite quarry, having lost his prior job as a result of a corporate merger. He now had an uneasy feeling about Northern Vermont Granite. He was glad that Jeannie was marrying a well-off farmer. Although, who was well off these days? Not wanting to spoil the big day, he kept his fears to himself. Northern Vermont Granite closed the following spring.

Phil had huge, muscled arms, a thick moustache, and sandy hair that was thinning in the back. He strode into the kitchen, tracking dirt onto the black and white linoleum floor, and wrapped Jeannie in a bear hug. Jeannie pushed him away, brushed herself off, and laughed:

"Oh Daddy, now look what you've done!"

Pretending to be abashed, Phil examined his boots and clothes, then pulled Jeannie into his arms again, and whirled her around the kitchen singing: '*She'll Be Coming 'Round the Mountain*' at the top of his lungs. Jeannie shrieked, and Katie smacked him on the rear with a rolling pin crusted with soggy pie dough. Francis and Scott watched, their gaping mouths showing the spaces between their teeth. Phil's husky wife Sharon, her hands caked with flour, barked in mock anger, "Stop it this instant, Philip Mitchell! In case you haven't heard, there's a wedding tomorrow; and we've got pies yet to bake, a turkey to roast and potatoes to boil for the potato salad. Not to mention fixing dinner for tonight's company."

Phil looked Sharon in the eye and saluted. He grabbed her around the waist and pulled her to his chest. Breaking into a laugh, she put her hands on his cheeks and kissed him loudly on the lips. When she stepped back, there were two white handprints on his cheeks. Jeannie and Katie giggled; the boys joined in, and soon everyone was laughing uproariously.

"That will do," said Sharon. "Phil, ride these boys home. It will be time for their supper before long."

She bent down and touched each of the boys on the cheek with a fingertip, leaving a faint white mark.

"Thank you, young gentlemen, for your help. We could not have done it without you."

Francis and Scott grinned proudly.

Earlier that afternoon, a battered truck had clattered up to the Scudder farm. A thin man in worn overalls and a bloodstained, checked shirt got out to deliver four freshly killed turkeys. His thin hair was wind-blown, and he was smoking a pipe. He spoke briefly with Everett.

"These are nice turkeys, Everett. Picked 'em out myself. They're a mite over twenty pounds each."

"Thank you, Hiram. Appreciate it."

"I reckon you'll have enough."

"Yes, I think so."

Hiram shaded his eyes and surveyed the farm and the valley. The afternoon sun highlighted the deep creases and sharp cheekbones in his burned face. He scratched the back of his neck and knocked his pipe against a tree.

"Looks like the weather will hold for tomorrow," he observed carefully.

As in a time-honored ritual, Everett looked to the western horizon and said, "Yes, I believe it will."

"Appears like your farm is holding up nicely." Hiram stared hard at the grazing cows. "Your cows look sleek. Grass must be rich."

"We're scraping by. Milk prices are down a third from two years ago. Hardly worth selling the extra hay and corn. But we've got food on the table." Everett nodded at the pasture. "Major's getting old, but he'll have to keep it up a while longer."

Both men laughed softly. Everett asked quietly,

"Can you hang on?"

"Wish I could say so." Hiram scuffed the toe of his boot in the dirt. "May have to let the bank take the place. After almost eighty years in the family. God knows what they'll do with it. Who's going to buy a damned turkey farm?" He scraped his boot harder and coughed, clearing his throat. "You couldn't use an extra hand, could you? Maybe part-time? Me or my oldest boy would be glad of some work. I heard you hadn't replaced Jacob."

Everett sighed, "I couldn't afford to replace him." He put a hand on

Hiram's shoulder: "Let me think on it. I can't promise..."

"I know, but I would appreciate it. And I appreciate your paying what you did for these turkeys. Haven't sold more than four or five a month this year, and those few fetched miserable prices. Used to sell a good ten a month – fifteen, sixteen at Thanksgiving and Christmas. My potatoes and vegetables go for a song."

He put the pipe in his mouth and walked to his truck. It started with a sputter. He leaned out the window.

"Wish Damon good luck for me. Tell him I don't know how such an ugly dope got such a beautiful and intelligent bride."

Everett watched Hiram drive off toward the county road, his tires kicking up eddies of dust. He had dipped into his savings for this wedding. He didn't like it, but it was the first, and he owed it to May.

At five, the Scudders piled into the Ford and drove to the Mitchells for dinner. Phil hugged Damon and sat him next to Jeannie. The young couple beamed at everyone around the table. Sharon put a pot roast surrounded by crisped roast potatoes on the table. Then she brought out a silver gravy boat brimming with dark, thick gravy and an immense bowl of wax beans from her garden. Phil carved and served the roast. The room grew quiet as everyone began to eat. Grinning slyly, Phil reached into the sideboard for a bottle of wine that he had acquired from Jason Baxter.

"Katie, would you please fetch some glasses from the kitchen?"

He uncorked the wine and filled the dime store glasses.

"I would like to welcome our guests and wish long life and happiness to the intendeds. Here's to the union of industry and agriculture!"

Phil winked at Everett and kissed Sharon resoundingly on the cheek. He walked around the table, pulled his daughter to her feet, and hugged her. He did the same to Damon.

"Welcome to our family."

Everett rose and raised his glass.

"Many thanks. And Jeannie, welcome to the Scudder family. May God bless the two of you, and in this time of trial, may God bless our country and guide President Hoover in the struggle for recovery."

A few stars still glimmered as the first pale streaks of dawn crept over the dark ridge. The serried ranks of pines stood on the hills like soldiers on parade while broad maples spread their leafy branches over weathered farmhouses. By the river, a willow formed a shelter where generations had kissed and touched inquisitively. A hawk hunted high above the valley.

Everett and Brent led a fat hog from the pen to the back of the barn. The hog squealed in desperation as they tied its rear legs and hoisted it in the air with the help of a pulley. They slit its throat and let the blood pour into a pail. They built a low fire in an open pit, which they had dug a few days earlier. They skewered the hog on a sharp, stout pole and hung it over the fire. Fat dripped and sizzled.

Roseanne and Sally also rose just before dawn to pick and shell an enormous bowl of peas. Sally brought up a basket of carrots from the root cellar, and the two women washed and sliced them. Mixing in the peas, they set a cauldron on the stove to boil.

Brent held the ladder while Roseanne nailed the painted sheet to the barn. In the meadow, she cut daisies and dandelions for the arch. The sun felt delicious on her back and shoulders. She stood up, stretched out her arms, and let out a shriek. She felt clean again.

At ten, Joseph Trochino, who owned Napoli, the Italian restaurant in town, delivered platters of olives, spicy peppers, and pickles.

"I will bring the spaghetti and the salad after the ceremony," he explained to Sally and Roseanne.

"That will be fine," said Sally. "Most everybody is bringing things then."

Phil Mitchell arrived with four large bowls of potato salad. "Pies and turkey after the ceremony."

"Wonderful," said Roseanne, "but before you go, let me try this potato salad." She dipped in a spoon. "Oh, that is scrumptious."

Lucille and Esther, gaily honking the horn of their Buick, bounced to a stop and started carrying trays of cookies into the kitchen. "We'll ..."

"Bring the turkey after the ceremony." laughed Roseanne. She hugged a bemused Lucille and shouted, "What a perfect day for a wedding!"

Just before eleven, Roseanne drove the Ford into town while others bathed and dressed. She parked at Tyrell's and sat in the car. Ten minutes later, a Vermont Transit bus stopped in front of the store and two passengers climbed out.

"Consuela," called Roseanne running up to hug her. "It's so good to see you and so nice that you could come. Let me take your bag."

They climbed into the car.

"You're staying in Damon's room since he won't be needing it. Daddy's treating the lovers to three days in the big city."

Chaos reigned at the normally well-organized Scudder farm as everyone bustled to use the two bathrooms. Everett showed Consuela into the parlor and took her bag up to Damon's room. Roseanne hurried upstairs to dress. In his room, Damon struggled with his tie.

"Relax," said Howie. "It's only twelve. You have an hour."

"You relax, you lummox. I'll never get it right. I can't remember the last time I wore one of these things."

"Your high school graduation in ... 1924. Let me do it. I wear one every day. I hope you do better taking it off. Otherwise, Father will never have grandchildren. Or you'll have to go to bed wearing only a tie."

Damon socked his brother on the arm and then stood, his arms hanging heavily at his side, while Howie knotted the navy tie resplendent with red polka dots. Howie held Damon at arm's length.

"Very elegant – for a farmer."

Everett poked his head into the parlor and asked Consuela,

"Can I get you a glass of water – or anything else?"

"A glass of water would be nice, thank you, and then you just ignore me. I brought a book and will sit here reading."

Damon came downstairs and introduced himself. He tried to make conversation, but he kept looking at the Grandfather clock. The pendulum mesmerized him, but he soon jumped up to pace nervously.

"I must be driving you crazy."

"Not at all," said Consuela. "I know how you must feel." She glanced at the book resting in her lap. "I was married once." She had not meant to say that.

Damon stopped pacing. "What happened?"

"It's not a story for a wedding day."

Howie joined them followed shortly by Everett and Brent, looking particularly uncomfortable in one of Howie's suits. Roseanne came in wearing her pink bridesmaid's dress. The conversation stopped.

"How beautiful you look!" exclaimed Consuela.

"Have you seen my sister?" Damon asked Roseanne.

Howie poked Damon in the ribs, then went over and hugged Roseanne, careful not to muss her dress.

"You're gorgeous," he said and winked.

Sally hurried into the parlor in a slightly faded navy blue dress with loose fitting sleeves and a straight skirt. She carried a large navy purse and wore a small, round hat with a tiny veil that covered her forehead.

"My word, Sally," said Roseanne. "Aren't you smart?"

"I always said it would be a miracle if everything happened as planned. We may just have a miracle." She crossed herself.

The Grandfather clock struck one. Howie and Brent got in the truck while everyone else piled into the Ford. The crowded church buzzed with greetings and small talk. Cynthia Staunton, the church organist, played a few hymns and selections from Bach. Reverend Lloyd McHenry, who had replaced Reverend Morgan on his retirement, nodded to Cynthia up in the balcony and she broke into Wagner. Everyone stood. Jeannie walked slowly down the aisle on her father's arm, her veil covering her delicately molded face. Phil kissed his daughter on the cheek and joined Sharon in the first pew. Reverend McHenry asked the congregation to be seated.

"Dearly beloved, we are gathered here..." Reverend McHenry spoke briefly about the sanctity of marriage and added a few homilies about how to build a loving home and family.

"I wonder," thought Roseanne, "how he would know about that." And more maliciously, whether he was a virgin. "Probably unless he had gone to a ... stop it. Cynicism is not pretty." She hardly knew Lloyd McHenry so what right did she have to make assumptions?

Reverend McHenry led Damon and Jeannie through their vows and concluded the ceremony. "I now pronounce you man and wife. You may kiss the bride."

Everett and Roseanne walked arm in arm toward the open door of the simple clapboard church where the Scudders had worshipped for over a hundred years. Memorial plaques lined the walls. Two stained glass windows - installed ten years ago - cast a roseate glow on the altar. The other windows contained the original rippling glass from 1827.

"Mama would have been very happy and proud," Roseanne said - a catch in her voice.

The musicians - a fiddler, a guitarist, and a banjo player – had already started when the Ford pulled into the farmyard. Everett shepherded Sharon Mitchell and the newly-weds into a reception line while Roseanne and Sally organized setting out the food. Phil joined his wife after hurrying home for the turkey and pies. Other guests had also stopped at home to pick up dishes of scalloped potatoes, creamed corn, string bean salad, and devilled eggs. Parked cars and trucks lined the Forshay Road, and the back yard was soon crowded with guests admiring the array of dishes and the decorations – especially Sally's art. The children played tag in a pasture while the adults salivated and commented on how nice it was to have such a wedding in these times.

Following the odor of roasting meat, a crowd moved around the barn and gathered at the pit where the hog had slowly cooked. Brent tested a piece and then layered thick slices on platters, which Sally and Lizzie carried to the buffet - where eager guests were already filling their plates. The creamery had sent over a huge wheel of cheddar with a red ribbon tied around it in a bow. Everett put his arm around Roseanne.

"You know a good part of that cheese consists of our milk."

Tommy Locke strolled across the yard, holding hands with Charlotte and preceded by three neatly dressed children.

"Tommy," Roseanne shouted and ran up to throw her arms around his neck. "I'm sorry I haven't been over. We've been so busy with the preparations, but that will change now." Charlotte beamed as Roseanne squatted down in front of the children to ask their names and ages.

"Clara. Six."

"So you're going into first grade. In two years, I'll be your teacher. And you, young man?"

"Douglas. I'm almost five."

"My father's name was Douglas," said Tommy.

"And this strapping fellow?"

"I'm Everett, and I'm..."

Surprised, Roseanne rocked backward and quickly put her hand on the ground to catch herself.

"Tommy, I didn't know. Daddy must be very proud."

"Your father's not the most expressive man alive."

Roseanne stood up, brushed off her bridesmaid's dress, and said to Charlotte, "They are so lovely."

An open truck clattered up to the house and Jason Baxter stepped down from the driver's side. A spare, angular woman clutching a baby to her chest wiggled out from the passenger's seat. A wiry four-year-old boy climbed down behind her. Augustus, Onatah, and Hawk pulled up in an old Chevy. Jason hefted two large jugs from the truck and presented them to Everett.

"What's a party without a touch of cider?"

Smirking at Lloyd McHenry, he proclaimed, "There are a few more jugs in the truck and a couple of cases of whiskey. Perhaps those who are not afraid of the devil – or the federal government – will help me unload the goods."

The pastor turned pale and coughed. Several men unloaded the truck, and glasses were soon being clinked.

"This is mighty thoughtful, Jason." said Everett.

"Think nothing of it. Consider it a wedding gift."

Damon was sitting with Jeannie and Toby Farrell. He was telling Toby about the Extensions Service agent's comments concerning developments in milking machines when he saw Jason hand Everett the jugs.

"Goddamn half-breed." he muttered softly and got to his feet.

Jeannie lay a hand on his arm. Damon sat down again.

"I was just going to thank him."

"I think your father's already done that," she said quietly.

Hawk drifted aimlessly through the crowd. A few people greeted him, and he returned their interest with a polite smile. He glanced at Jason opening bottles of whiskey and pouring drinks into outstretched glasses.

"Goddamn him," he said to no one in particular.

"What's that you said?" asked Roseanne behind him.

Hawk started and turned around. "Roseanne! I've been looking for you."

"Was I that hard to find?"

"No, of course not ... I meant..."

"You meant that you didn't recognize me among all these beautiful women."

"That's not what I meant at all." He studied her. "You've changed. You're not..."

"The child you played with or the fifteen-year-old girl that you flirted with in high school. No, I'm not. I'm a woman of the world. But what were you muttering about?"

"My rotten brother, if you must know. Does he always have to flaunt what he does?"

"I don't think most people object. They're glad to have the booze."

"What would you know about it?" He raised a hand involuntarily and held it in the air. She took a step toward him. He lowered his hand. "It's a dirty business ... and ... and just confirms the way people think about us."

"Oh..." She looked straight at him. "Chip on our shoulder, have we?"

They stared hard at each other; people swirled around them as if they were a boulder in a stream. They both started to laugh.

The musicians played a waltz, and Phil escorted Jeannie onto the floor for the first dance. He twirled her madly around the empty space and, when the music stopped, lifted her high off the ground. The crowd applauded while Jeannie shrieked, "Daddy, put me down this instant!" But she hugged him fiercely when he did. She danced a slow number with Damon and the applause grew louder. Other couples surged onto the dance floor. Roseanne took Hawk's arm.

"Will you dance with me?"

Everett, scanning the crowd and not finding Roseanne, asked Consuela to dance. They were walking onto the floor as Hawk and Roseanne whirled past to an Irish jig. Everett looked sheepish, but Roseanne smiled broadly at him – and winked at Consuela.

Older couples maneuvered slowly while younger ones skimmed past them. The smaller children, flinging their arms wildly, bounced up and down on the grass. The big ones imitated the adults, sliding across the slippery floor in exaggerated loops and dips – like larks flitting over a meadow.

"By the way, do you always talk to yourself in crowds?" Roseanne asked Hawk when they paused from dancing.

"Who else should I talk to in this crowd?"

"Me – for one."

"You're the only reason that I came. I wanted to see if you had turned out differently from your brother."

After slow waltzes, jigs, foxtrots, and a few contra dances (with the fiddler calling out the steps), Joseph Trochino asked for a tarantella, which the musicians awkwardly attempted. Joseph led Consuela onto the floor and implored others to join them. A few brave souls had enough liquor in them not to care how they looked.

Howie took the floor to propose a toast. He mentioned important incidents in Damon's life, including his short-lived career as a half back and his first belle, Daisy - who was as yet grazing peacefully in the pasture and taking in the proceedings without a hint of jealousy. The cider and whiskey having been served generously, Howie's remarks were received with enthusiastic applause and guffaws. Wiley Fitzgerald, now in his seventies and still eking out a living with a few cows, a vegetable garden and his rifle, beamed and called out, "Hooray". Wiley was no more able than ever to hold a drink, and Roseanne later saw him fast asleep – his head resting on an empty plate. She gently removed the plate.

Following Howie, Katie made a few kind remarks about her sister. She related how Jeannie also had a former suitor who was prevented from attending the festivities solely due to the regulations at the insane asylum where he was presently residing.

"Her sister," Katie said while struggling not to laugh, "would make a perfect wife and companion once she discovered that the kitchen was where food was prepared."

As the sun descended over the ridge, the first guests started to leave. Damon and Jeannie went to the house to change. They had planned to dash for the Ford, but Roseanne and Esther were ready for them. They passed around a bowl of rice while Lizzie had Francis, Scott, and several other children tie tin cans to the bumper. The couple was pelted with rice as they came out the front door. They ran to the Ford, suitcases banging against their legs, and waved as they sped off, tin cans and all.

Night fell. Stars hung in the black sky. A soft breeze blew across the valley. Roseanne and Consuela sat on the porch and kicked off their shoes.

"Thank you for inviting me. It was a wonderful wedding, and I had such a good time. They make a handsome couple."

"Don't they? I thought Howie and Katie were so funny. And poor old Wiley - asleep on the plate? I can't remember a time when Wiley wasn't around. He's not much of a farmer." Roseanne paused. "Father sends Brent over to help him out. I understand it's an old story."

"Who was the man who brought the booze?"

Roseanne hesitated for just an instant, and Consuela glanced at her curiously.

"Jason Baxter, our local rum runner. His brother is quite nice."

"I see. Is Jason a gangster?"

"Oh no, I think he's small potatoes. I've heard that most of what he's made he's already lost. I think the gangsters hang onto their money."

"He certainly livened up some peoples' party."

Roseanne contemplated the stars.

"I wonder if we'll ever know what's up there—such a mystery." She looked at Consuela. "Damon mentioned that you had been married. I hope it's all right that he told me."

"Of course, it's all right. It's not a happy story – and certainly not one for such a happy occasion."

"I'm sorry. I didn't mean to pry."

"It's fine. I don't know why I've never told you." Consuela lightly touched Roseanne's arm. "Actually, it is a very happy story; it's just the ending that's sad." Consuela imperceptibly lifted and dropped her shoulders. "In 1910, when I was in my early twenties, I married a wonderful man from Rutland. He was a stonecutter, like my father, at the Vermont Marble Company. He was from Italy. After four years, we had a baby, a little boy. We named him Giorgio after my husband's father. We were so happy."

Consuela started to cry; she put her face in her hands. Roseanne got up, knelt by Consuela's chair, and put an arm around her waist.

"Don't go on if you don't want to."

Consuela sobbed and choked back the tears. She lifted her tear-stained face.

"No, I want to. I almost never talk about it, but you are my best friend."

She wiped her eyes with the back of her hand. Roseanne sat down again.

"When Giorgio was four, Ridolfo bought us a two-seater bicycle. We decided to go for a ride one Sunday and leave Giorgio with a neighbor, but he wanted to go too. We said no, but he started to cry. We lived on a quiet street, so Ridolfo said he could ride on the handlebars once around the block. It was a sparkling fall day. The yards were covered with brilliantly colored leaves. We rode slowly around the block. Giorgio laughed and called to friends. He begged to go again, and I said okay - once more.

"We had gone halfway around when a speeding car suddenly loomed in front of us. I was told later that the driver was showing his son how fast he could go around a corner. I can still see the car in my mind, a silver Buick. I dream about it. But I remember nothing else, not even the impact. I woke up in the hospital two days later. Giorgio and Ridolfo were both dead."

"Oh Christ," gasped Roseanne, getting up and throwing her arms around her friend. They hugged for a minute. Consuela continued.

"For weeks everything, including the funerals, passed in a blur – like one of those fogs in northern Italy that Ridolfo used to describe – where you can hardly see to walk. That's what it felt like – as if I could not see where I was going. I remember so little of it. Maybe that's a blessing. I don't know."

She stopped, her brow furrowed.

"Except for one thing that stands out, I don't know why since it had so little to do with what I was feeling. A few days after the accident, I heard that the war had ended."

Roseanne sat immobile, like a marble statue, her mouth open but without making a sound.

"What is it, Roseanne? What's wrong?"

"My mother died that month."

Consuela stayed a few more days. She enjoyed helping around the farm. With Damon gone, Everett said they could use the extra hand. He added that she was a born farmer. She quickly learned how to milk. She borrowed rubber boots and slopped the pigs. She rose early to gather eggs and scatter grain for the chickens – with a little extra for her favorites. She was even prepared to shovel manure into the spreader.

The day before she left, Roseanne and Consuela drove north of town and parked at the end of North Valley Road. They walked along the path toward the gorge. Hobos had erected flimsy shacks on top of the old cabin ruins. Two anglers were wading in the river, casting silver flies in long arcs over the stream. They had wicker baskets on their hips. The two women paused to watch a trout flash in the air as it was being reeled in. The path started to climb. They heard the cascade thundering in the distance. They sat on a bank and dangled their feet in the cold, rushing stream. A dark form skimmed over the shining rocks.

"Trout," said Roseanne.

Consuela noticed a black water snake coiled in a hollow about ten yards away. She jumped.

"Harmless," laughed Roseanne. "Just an old water snake enjoying a bit of sun. Speaking of which, you've gotten so brown in just a few days here. All I do in the sun is burn."

"Must be my Cuban blood. You know, I've loved these few days. I'm going to miss the farm. Certainly beats ringing a cash register and keeping books. I'm going to miss you especially."

"Same here. We're all going to miss you – not least my father. I'm not sure I should say this, but I've been thinking about it a lot so what the hell. Nothing to lose and everything to gain."

"I have no idea what you are talking about."

"Shouldn't wonder since I hardly know myself. Well, here goes. My father's much too reserved to say anything, and he thinks he's past that sort of thing, but it's easy to see he's quite taken with you. It's been over twelve years ... since Mother died ... and the same with Ridolfo ... and well ... you know ... I thought ... I'm sure I'm turning beet red."

"You are indeed. What a wonderful daughter you are – and friend."

Consuela hugged Roseanne with arms strengthened from farm work and kissed her on both cheeks. Tears welled up in her eyes.

"Thank you, thank you. But I am past that. I have made my peace with myself and with my God. I could never love another man – even your father, who is truly a gift."

"How sad," thought Roseanne, and took Consuela's hand.

A few days after Consuela left, Roseanne drove out to the Baxter farm. In addition to her farm work, she had been busy preparing for the start of school. She especially loved working in the vegetable garden that not only provided for the family but also produced a surplus, which they sold in town or trucked to Montpelier. Along with Sally, and now Jeannie, she weeded the zucchini, yellow squash, and bell peppers.

She crossed the river on the old, stone bridge about a half mile past Tyrell's. The bridge south of town was more direct, but she liked this old one with its gentle arch and carvings of pioneers and Indians on the corner stones. There was a small sign that said the bridge had been built in 1829, replacing the original bridge built by the first settlers.

She drove past corn, potato, and hay fields and pastures with grazing cows. Although the farms were rattier over here, a vegetable garden flourished next to each house. A mile from town, the road turned to dirt and a billow of dust rose behind the car. She hoped Hawk would be glad to see her. At the wedding, he had briefly mentioned her visiting the forge, but she had not heard from him since.

The bottomland gave way to rolling hills dotted with clumps of spruce, maples, and hemlock. She rounded a wide curve and saw the Baxter farm. It was on a hilly lot set back in the woods. The side of the two-storied, unpainted house fronted the road, while the porch faced a dusty yard where the open-slatted truck and cadaverous Chevrolet were parked. About twenty yards from the house was a chicken coop with a dozen chickens scratching in a wire-enclosed dirt run. Next to the chicken coop stood an unpainted barn. The roof at the far end was sagging, and two planks along one side were missing. A ladder was set against the wall. Several pieces of sawn timber lay on the ground.

Across the yard from the house, a narrow hay field had been carved out of the woods. A meadow sloped down the hill toward a small stream that ran under the road through a culvert. A small herd of Holsteins and Guernseys grazed under the watchful eyes of a wan-looking bull. A vegetable garden, which needed weeding, and a small potato field grew in a clearing across the dirt road. Past the barn at the far end of the yard, a nondescript building was jammed against the woods. Also unpainted, it appeared better maintained than the other buildings. A Harley Davidson motorcycle with twin cylinders rested against the building - a leather helmet and goggles hanging from the handle bar. Roseanne could see a glow through the open sliding door as she drove into the yard. An equally nondescript dog lazily got up from the porch, stretched and barked at the car in an offhand way.

Hawk walked out into the sunshine, mopping his brow, as Roseanne stepped out of the car. "Hush up, Sophocles," he called to the dog in an easy voice and sauntered toward her.

"I didn't think you would come."

"You did mention it. Is it all right?"

He let his lips part in a hint of a smile. Sweat glistened on his forehead and copper cheeks.

"Yes, of course. We don't get many social visitors."

He took her arm and guided her toward the forge. The dog barked again and lay down as if to say his job was done.

"What a wonderful name for a dog!"

"It was Dad's idea. He thought it would encourage the mutt, unlike his sons, to go to college. You can see what good it did. All Sophocles does is lie on the porch."

As he led her past the barn, he cautioned, "It will be hot in there. I hope you can stand it."

"Hot I don't mind; it's cold that gets to me."

He introduced her to his partner, TJ, a tall man with dirty blonde hair that curled over his ears, powerful bare biceps, and a face red from the fire. TJ took off his goggles and extended a grimy, calloused hand. Hawk showed her the forge where they heated the iron until it glowed white, the heavy tables and vises where they shaped the glowing rods and the cooling tanks. He proudly displayed their most recent products: fire irons, a pair of tall candlesticks with petal decorations and a wrought iron gate with spikes and scrolls.

"The gate is a special order from a lady over in South Cabot. She saw some of our things in a hardware store in Montpelier. We also make railings, weather vanes, tables, or whatever people ask for." He held up a preening rooster that he was about to fasten on top of the arrows of a weather vane.

"Why that looks just like the rooster that Sally painted for the wedding."

"Where do you think I got the idea?" he laughed. "Do you think Damon would like to have it?"

Roseanne chuckled: "If not, the rest of us would."

"Then it's yours."

Roseanne nosed around the workroom picking up fire pokers and candlesticks. Hawk watched her while TJ held an iron rod over the fire. It was hot and close. She felt beads of sweat forming on her forehead and meandering from her armpits down her side. She enjoyed the sensation; and slowly wiped her forehead and pushed back her hair with her fingertips.

"These are so beautiful," she said holding up a triple candlestick with an ivy vine curling along the base. "You have real talent."

Hawk smiled and dipped his head at an angle. A thatch of black hair fell across his forehead. "Thank you. I must say I appreciate being complimented by a Scudder."

"My word! How that chip does appear when least expected."

"I could knock it off for you," laughed TJ. He spoke with an accent. "I've had some experience in that line."

Roseanne studied TJ's biceps and the gap between his front teeth.

"I imagine you have, but no thank you, perhaps another time. I would just like to know where it came from."

"Maybe someday you'll find out," Hawk said.

"And maybe someday I'll knock it off myself."

They all laughed, and TJ waved a fist at her.

"C'est une bonne femme. Prends ta garde, mon ami."

"Bien sur," agreed Roseanne. "Quelle bonne idée."

"Do you speak French?"

"Only enough to cause trouble."

TJ laughed. "Vraiment! I imagine you could be more trouble than mon ami here can handle."

Roseanne decided to change the subject.

"Tell me. How do you go about selling what you make?"

"That has been the toughest part," Hawk replied, "especially at first. We went to hardware and garden stores with samples and finally got a few orders. Now we have some regulars. We found a fellow to truck things to Burlington, Montpelier and Rutland. Sometimes we get special orders – like the gate – from individuals and small contractors with construction jobs."

"This is wonderful, Hawk. You're going to be a success. I can feel it in my bones."

"We're struggling now, but things will pick up again."

TJ pushed the goggles onto his grimy forehead. "Sans doute. Pas de question."

Hawk and Roseanne walked toward the house. Looking at the truck,

Hawk sighed. "Looks like Jason is still here."

"I don't mind. I want to say hello to your parents."

When they reached the porch steps, Roseanne stopped and surveyed the pasture. She looked back to the forge.

"Is that your motorcycle?"

"It's TJ's. He lives in a shack situated on a farm about a mile from here. We barely have room for the family, what with Jason and Shannon having two youngsters." He glanced thoughtfully at the motorcycle. "Would you like to go for a ride?"

Roseanne's eyes lit up. "Of course, I would."

"Wait here, then."

He dashed up the steps and into the house. Roseanne paced in front of the steps. Sophocles yawned and sidled off the porch to sniff carelessly at her legs. She reached down to scratch him between the ears and heard the screen door open.

"That was fast," she said, and stood up to see Jason coming down the steps. A thin woman holding a baby was watching him through the screen door. A boy was tugging at his shirt, saying, "Please Pa, let me go with you."

"Oh," said Roseanne, "I was..."

"Expecting someone else?"

He tugged the boy's hand loose and pushed him toward the house.

"I told you no, you can't come. Now go back to your Mother and leave me be."

With a sour look, the boy opened the screen door. The woman took him by the hand into the house, saying, "Your Father's got business to attend to."

Turning back to Roseanne just as Hawk opened the screen door, Jason asked, "Come to see how the half-breeds live?"

"Lay off, Jason," said Hawk.

Jason spun around. "Now listen here, sonny boy. You show some respect to your elders, or you'll be looking at the business end of something other than one of your fancy fire irons."

"No, Mr. Baxter. I came up to thank you for livening up the wedding."

Jason laughed. He looked Roseanne up and down.

"Miss Scudder," he said sardonically, "I think those third graders will learn something from you."

He walked to the truck, got in and drove off. Hawk clenched and unclenched his fists. Then he handed Roseanne a leather helmet and goggles.

"Oh my," she said, and put them on.

They drove up the hill, spitting up plumes of dust. Hawk leaned into the curves, and Roseanne gripped him tightly around the waist. She thrust her head to one side to feel the cool wind on her face. The road weaved back and forth through the forest as it climbed toward the ridge. She breathed in the fresh smell of the pines. Her dress billowed around her knees. She looked to the side and saw the trees clipping past like bowling pins being knocked over. Above the grinding din of the motor, she shouted in Hawk's ear, "I love it."

They stopped in a small clearing at the summit. The road continued across the ridge and into the next valley. Hawk leaned the motorcycle on its stand. They walked to the edge of the clearing. The valley spread out below them - a mosaic of rolling meadows, cultivated fields, white farmhouses, and red barns. Strung out along the river were the leafy streets of Scudder's Gorge lined with clapboard houses in disparate styles.

The slender steeple of the First Congregational stood out against the sky like a finger pointing toward God, while the squat mass of red bricks that was St. Agnes the Martyr looked like an impregnable island fortress set in the midst of a Protestant ocean. To the north was a crease in the woods that formed the gorge. They stood silently – wrapped in their own thoughts. He started back, but she took his hand, stood on her toes, and kissed him on the lips.

"That was unexpected."

"Precisely. I thought it would be a good start in knocking off that chip."

"In that case..." He took her in his arms, and they kissed long and eagerly.

"Why do you dislike Jason so?" she asked. "Is it because of the bootlegging?"

He looked at her and then over the valley. She noticed what Lizzie had said about his eyes. Looking through you was about right.

"It's not really the bootlegging, although he acts like it makes him something. It's that he's ashamed of who he is, and I hate that. His shame makes him bitter and vicious – a bully. I hate bullies – because they're cowards at heart. I may have a chip because I'm resentful of some things, but I'm proud of my Indian blood. I'll beat the hell out of any man who insults me – or my family."

"I seem to remember that you already did that once a while back."

He laughed.

"Yes, I remember—in the schoolyard. Were you there?"

She nodded.

"What were those things that you resent?"

"Another time."

Augustus was standing on the porch as they drove up. He watched them with a queer look in his eye. He extended a hand to Roseanne.

"Come in and have a cup of tea."

They sat in the weathered kitchen. The sink was worn, and the cabinets were cracked; but the counters and table were spotless. A large iron cauldron bubbled on the stove and steam rose to the ceiling. The odor of venison stew permeated the room. Onatah served Roseanne a homemade tea brewed from spearmint, blackberry, and elderberry leaves. She placed a plate of fresh, hot cookies on the table.

"How did you like riding on that evil-smelling, cacophonous contraption?" asked Augustus.

"It was marvelous. I can't remember the last time I had so much fun."

"I reckon they're a threat to the life, liberty, and pursuit of happiness of the ordinary citizen of this county and ought to be banned outright."

"Oh quit your babbling, Augustus," said Onatah. "You make as much sense as that hound out there – less mostly."

"Ah, the joys of connubial bliss." Augustus nibbled on a cookie. "I highly recommend the conjugal state, although I fully confess that it's not suitable for everyone. My eldest progeny..."

"Dad," said Hawk. "Quit now."

"So much for a man's castle. It was all a myth anyway – like blind Homer's Gods and Goddesses with their insatiable appetites running around mucking up the lives of mortals. It was not for nothing that Will left Anne back in Stratford. And now Dr. Freud has informed us that our misfortunes in this sphere begin all the way back in childhood."

"If you keep this up, Augustus," said Onatah, "Roseanne will never come back."

"Oh no, Mrs. Baxter. You needn't worry about that. I've had a grand afternoon." Roseanne sipped her tea. "Have you read Homer, Mr. Baxter?"

"Not in the original, no my dear, but we do have some books – and current magazines - over here on the west side of the valley."

"I didn't mean..."

"I know you didn't." He patted her hand. "But we don't get many visitors so we have to show off a bit when we do."

Shannon came into the kitchen, holding the baby while her four-year old clung to the back of her faded skirt. A cigarette, its long ash ready to fall off, dangled in her mouth.

"Ma, can I help?" she asked.

Augustus stood up.

"Roseanne, I don't recall if you met Jason's wife, Shannon, at the wedding - or my grandsons, Rory and Martin? Rory, come gladden an old man's heart – which means sit on my knee and I'll tell you a story about a dragon."

The boy peeked around his mother's skirt and then went to his grandfather who sat down and took him on his knee. Augustus began quietly.

"One fine morning in the month of May, in merry old England – which is far, far away from Scudder's Gorge - a young woman was riding through a forest. It was a terrible time in England because a fearsome dragon..."

"We hardly had a chance to speak at the wedding," Roseanne said to Shannon. "I hope you enjoyed yourself."

"Sure, it was a splendid party," said Shannon.

Roseanne looked surprised.

"Were you born in Ireland?" she asked. "Excuse me, if I'm being nosy."

"Oh, don't worry at all. Yes, my family came from Cork when I was a young girl and I never quite lost my accent – or manner of speaking. We settled in Boston, which is where I met Jason. He was on a business trip, and I was working in a ... well ... a restaurant."

"A speakeasy, you mean," smiled Roseanne. "What fun!"

Shannon was a lean, worn-looking woman with pale blond hair that hung in damp strands around her gaunt cheeks. She gave off an air of having been hard used.

"I know you mean it in a kind way, but it was not one of your grand sort of speakeasies. It was a low place and Jason was a step up, begging your pardon, Mrs. Baxter." She hugged the baby to her flat chest. "When my father died, I had to go to work young."

"I'm sorry," said Roseanne. "I sometimes don't know how lucky I've been."

"...The dragon had set whole villages on fire with a single blast of its fiery breath. It had ravished the golden fields of wheat and rye so hunger, with its terrible scythe, stalked the land. The bloodthirsty beast scooped up little children in its dripping claws and carried them off to its lair. The bravest and most skilled knights had fought the dragon and been slain one by one. No one could do a thing until this courageous, young woman determined to kill the dragon and free the cowering people - nobles, merchants, and serfs alike - from this awful terror. She issued forth on a heady spring morning from her father's castle, which rose majestically from the banks of a sparkling river full of silvery bream and salmon. Her armor gleamed in the sunlight like a burnished mirror, and a red plume on her helmet waved in the fresh breeze. She rode into the forest, and she had not gotten far when she heard a terrible commotion. Screaming in terror, a party of pilgrims – men, women, and children – raced past her and disappeared into the woods. She saw spouts of flames. A tree near her exploded into dust. She drew her sword just as the fearsome beast appeared - roaring, shaking its scaly head, and spewing jagged flames in every direction. She asked the Virgin Mary's blessing, pulled down her visor, shrilled a shattering war cry, and charged. The fighting was terrible as the dragon raked the air with its claws and the maiden swung her sword in broad, sweeping arcs. Her horse reared and pawed at the awful creature. It was finally over. The brave girl cleft the dragon's head in two and rode home with cheering crowds lining the high road. Raising her sword to acknowledge the accolades, she was tired but little the worse for wear – except for a few strands of singed hair."

Roseanne and Shannon clapped. Hawk prodded the boy and, with a wink at Shannon and a mock scowl, said in a Vermont brogue, "A powerful dragon killer sure the lady was, my fine lad?"

"I'm going to kill a dragon when I grow up," said Rory.

"You'd better be growing up quickly then," said Shannon, "for the woods around here are full of dragons."

"Sit down, Shannon," said Onatah, "and have a cup of tea." She spoke to Roseanne. "Won't you stay to dinner?"

"I wish I could, but I have my chores. Another time, the stew smells delicious."

She drove back across the valley thinking how wrong Damon was about the Baxters. While Hawk's explanation put it into perspective, Jason still seemed like a rough, nasty sort. But Augustus and Onatah were warm and funny. She liked how they kidded each other. She was drawn to Shannon, perhaps because her life had been a struggle - probably still was being married to Jason. And Hawk, well, she felt a little thrill.

She imagined that Damon looked down on the family because Augustus and Jason were not dedicated, sweat-of-the-brow farmers like the Scudders. On the other hand, Hawk pushed himself hard and Augustus had a range of remarkable interests. Damon should be more broad-minded. She wondered fleetingly if Damon's distaste had anything to do with the Indian business. She had assumed that the remark at Thanksgiving about "his kind" had related to Jason's livelihood – or Augustus's lackadaisical approach to farming, but perhaps it should be seen in a different light. It had certainly made her father angry.

As she was leaving, Hawk had asked her to go to the movies on Saturday. When Hawk drove up in the Chevrolet to pick her up, Damon and Jeannie were sitting on the porch.

"Good evening, Damon. Jeannie." said Hawk.

Damon rose from his chair, said "Good evening" and went inside.

"Good evening, Hawk," said Everett, coming out the front door. "Nice evening for a movie. What's playing? Would you like a glass of lemonade?"

"The Painted Desert with William Boyd and someone named Clark Gable," shouted Roseanne, as she rushed out the door, took Hawk by the arm, and hurried toward the dilapidated Chevy. "We don't have time for lemonade, but thank you anyway, Daddy."

"Got us out of that nicely," she said to Hawk as she settled next to him on the worn seat. "I apologize for Damon. I don't know what's bothering him. Maybe he can't tolerate his sister having grown up."

"Maybe he can't tolerate who she chooses to grow up with."

"Could be, but I think it has more to do with Jason than you. Let's forget Damon. We've each got a brother who's a pain."

After the movie, they went to Harvey's Café out on the new county road, which ran along the eastern edge of the valley.

"Nice to see you, Hawk," said Claudia, a thin waitress with her hair in tight curls. "You haven't been in for a good while."

She showed them to a booth and handed them menus.

"Seems like you're pretty popular here," said Roseanne.

"We come here for dinner if we have a little extra cash, but TJ's the one they really like. It's the accent. Drives them crazy – especially when he throws in a few words of French."

They left Harvey's and drove down to the river to the spot where, ten years ago, Tommy Locke had taken her to talk. A couple was kissing in a car so they walked beside the river. They sat on the bank and watched the moonlight rippling on the dark water. Hawk threw a stick, which floated for an instant before being pulled under. It reappeared a second later.

"We're all like that stick," said Roseanne. "We get dragged under but then we pop back up and go on our way."

"I like how you think – like you've seen more than most girls your age. Have you?"

"Another time. Oh hell, yes probably, but then Shannon has been through a lot more than I have."

"Jason was right about one thing. The third graders are going to learn a lot this year."

They were silent for a moment. She fidgeted on the grass. It was a soft night with a myriad of stars spread across the heavens. Across the valley, masses of pine trees were silhouetted against the purple ridge.

"Kiss me," she said.

They kissed for a long time, their mouths parted. He put his arm around her shoulders.

"Whew!" she said. And then, "Tell me about Buffalo."

His brow furrowed, and he examined his roughened hands as if they would guide him. He breathed deeply and adjusted his position.

"In my senior year, I asked Principal O'Day about college scholarships and told him that I wanted to do pre-med. He advised me against it.

Said I would have a difficult time trying to establish myself. He didn't say it directly, but I knew what he was talking about. I would be wasting my time. Who would go to an Indian, or half-breed, doctor?

"So I went to Rutland and learned to operate a lathe and turn metal. I was an apprentice for two years, earning a minimal wage and putting in extra time as a handyman. After finishing the apprenticeship, I wanted only to get out of there so I hit the road: hitched, slept in fields, cadged meals. The open road - it was a thrill. I saw a lot of places. I was on my own. I ended up in Buffalo after a few months and got a job in a metalworking shop. We made components for machine tool and construction companies.

"I worked there for a year and then found a job in a forge that made wrought iron furniture, railings, and decorative pieces. That's where I met TJ. When, after a year, we decided to go into business for ourselves, I convinced him to come back here so we could start off without paying rent – although I give Dad something when I can."

"So that's why you gave up medical school and where the chip comes from. I can hardly say I blame you."

"I hated O'Day back then and still feel resentful occasionally, but he was probably right. He was just trying to spare me from getting hurt."

She took his hand.

"It's still awful."

"There's something else. Maybe I shouldn't tell you, but I had a girl in Buffalo whose family was less than happy with her dating an Indian."

Hawk left out the part about her brother, Maurizio, threatening to blow his fucking head off and how Lina, a passionate young woman with waves of black hair and smoldering eyes, spent Saturday and Sunday afternoons in the steel-framed bed in his cramped room with water-stained walls.

But he did tell Roseanne how Lina came to him one morning, one cheek swollen and purple, to warn him that her brother and his friend had pistols and were working up the nerve to come for him. Hawk raced to TJ's and said: "Brother, it's time to start our new business." They left without resigning their jobs.

"I'm sorry," she said and squeezed his hand. "I had an awful experience also."

"Like that stick, you just have to keep bobbing back."

She put her hand on the back of his neck, ruffled his black hair, and pulled him close for a kiss.

"I like working in the forge, making things. It feels right. Another reason why I came back was that I thought you might also return home someday."

Damon bristled every time Hawk came by to pick up Roseanne, but Jeannie kept him from saying anything. Everett always seemed pleased.

Roseanne loved to go to the Baxter farm. Jason was seldom there and, apart from occasional jibes, left her alone when he was. Hawk and TJ showed her how to do basic tasks in the forge. The more she learned about shaping the molten rods, the more she enjoyed it. She took one astonished look at Hawk's record keeping and devised a simple set of books. Daunted at first, since she knew nothing about bookkeeping, she was amazed when she was finished at how easy it had been. She arranged her chores at the farm so she could stay at the Baxter's for dinner as often as possible. She was fascinated by Augustus's conversation. His knowledge of literature and politics was astounding.

"Which is why he's never been much good as a farmer," said Hawk one day as they walked along the road before supper.

"Before Jason lost most of his liquor money gambling and in the stock market, he used to give Father enough to keep the farm profitable. But now, what he gets from the milk, vegetables, and eggs is barely enough to keep the place going. I help around the farm and give him a few dollars from time to time, but we need our cash to buy materials. And TJ needs something. It's a good thing Daddy's a good shot so he can keep meat on the table."

When Hawk was extremely busy, Roseanne went for walks with Shannon, who carried the baby while Rory either tagged along or stayed on the porch pestering Sophocles.

"Do you think all that smoking is good for you?" Roseanne asked one day. "I know the magazine ads say that cigarettes help your digestion and what not, but you seem to cough a lot."

"Sure, and if you were married to Jason Baxter, you'd be smoking as well. Not that he's a completely bad man. I've seen my share of worse, mind you. I don't really care what he does for a living except that I thought we were going to be comfortably off and we're sure not."

She took a deep drag.

"But it's something else. He's cold inside, like a fish laid up on the bank of a river. He's got shame and anger, and he's always chewing at them. It makes me afraid. You can't really warm up to a man when you're afraid."

Although he was not an elementary school teacher, Roseanne talked to Tommy Locke about preparing for her first classes. Notwithstanding her year's experience, the other teachers might think her very young. Some had been at the school when she was a third grader. Knowing that she would have to establish her authority and credibility quickly, she prepared a detailed program for each day of the first three weeks. Tommy told her not to worry. She was as thoroughly prepared as any teacher he had ever seen with just one-year of experience. But she went over her plan again and again, making minute adjustments until she could hardly stand to look at it.

She visited the Locke's several times and delighted in family games in the back yard. Once, during hide and seek, Tommy and Roseanne made it to home base at the same time. While they chuckled at little Everett scampering from bush to bush, Roseanne touched Tommy's arm and said, "Thank you."

***

Toward the end of August, McFarlane and Thompson's Greatest Little Show on Earth came to town, arriving in a bus and two trucks – one with animals in cages – at midday on a broiling Friday. Huge American flags were painted on the bus while a bald eagle spread its wings the length of the larger truck. Watched closely by a crowd of youngsters, a stage crew worked all Friday afternoon and into the night setting up a tent and booths in a meadow by the river. The booths were arrayed in a semi-circle around the tent. Inside the tent, rows of hard benches faced a bare stage. The more delicately framed could rent cushions – never a brisk trade in farming communities. The employee canteen was in a small tent behind the booths. The performers had lined up their own tents nearby giving the meadow the appearance of a Civil War encampment.

Four muscled young men left handbills at Tyrell's, the Vermont Clothing Emporium, Napoli, Sellick's Hardware and the other businesses that lined Cedar Street. They tacked them to telephone poles and gave handfuls to kids. They could have saved their time. As

Vaughan Tyrell said, "Apart from the First Congregational choir's Christmas concert, old Liam Tierney's barbershop quartet songfests, and UVM's annual Shakespeare tour, nothing of this magnitude has come to Scudder's Gorge since the Crash."

Within an hour, everyone hooked up to a party line knew that a carnie would open in the morning. It took a few hours for the news to spread to outlying farms and homes without telephones; but by late afternoon, only the most isolated farmer was ignorant of the metamorphosis underway in Dale Royce's meadow. Everyone else was reaching under his or her mattresses. The young children were the most excited - pleading at supper tables throughout the valley to be allowed to go.

Augustus Baxter said to Rory, "I don't know what the fuss is all about. You can see monkeys and a jackass at Tyrell's any day of the week."

Richard Forshay, the current mayor, welcomed the carnival to Scudder's Gorge but advised Angus McFarlane that he would need a town permit – a matter of but a few minutes' arranging and the payment of a modest fee. Angus stopped by the town clerk's office that afternoon.

Saturday morning both ridges were hidden in mist, the sky was thick with clouds and a cold drizzle dripped from the booths and tents. The performers sullenly ate breakfast. Pacing in front of the main tent, Sylvester Thompson cast anxious glances at the sky. The thought of breakfast made him nauseous. The company's finances were trembling at the brink. While the dramatic and musical numbers were held under canvas, good weather was critical to success at the box office. The children, towing money-spending parents in their wake, came for the games and animals.

It was the devil wringing money out of these tight-assed farmers in the best of times. The cursed animals were too mangy for the big towns, and his performers were hardly "slick." So, he had to make it in these dirt bag hamlets or not at all – which was beginning to look like the more likely outcome.

"Hey boss, want me to open the box office same time as always?"

A middle-aged woman with bleached hair and rouged lips planted a kiss on Sylvester's cheek and pinched his butt. She wore a sequined dress that was too tight and had seen better days – as had her jiggling breasts and upper arms. Sylvester pushed her away.

"Cut it out. Can't you see I'm praying?"

"Praying for what? That I'll go to bed with you tonight?"

"No, you ditz. I'm praying for the sun to shine on this forgotten corner of the manure-soaked state of Vermont. Besides I slept with you last night."

Sylvester's wife never traveled with the show - having her own sources of entertainment. Frannie managed the box office and Sylvester's bed. She took occasional breaks from the box office to croon a few numbers in the big top while Sylvester filled in for her. He couldn't bear to hear her sing.

To allow for morning and afternoon milking, Sylvester normally opened from ten until four and then seven to eleven. He had to give his people some time to eat and rest. With fifteen-minute intermissions between shows, he managed six performances a day. In addition to Frannie's singing, Sylvester could no longer tolerate listening to the sallow man with a thick moustache who read from the most notable works of American literature. The juggler, acrobats and clowns were, at least, talented and, for the most part, silent. Sylvester cast a last pleading look at the sky, shook the raindrops off his battered fedora, and rubbed his hand over his gray wisps of hair.

"Open at the regular time – and pray."

By ten, a press of children was waiting near the box office, each with a fistful of pennies. Children under twelve were admitted to the grounds free. Older children and adults paid five cents each with another nickel for the big-top show. When Frannie rolled up the wooden slats, the children crowded forward, bought their tickets, and raced toward the booths. Adults followed more leisurely. Sylvester watched the steady stream of ticket buyers with silent approval. While some adults wandered toward the big top, the children explored the booths, spending precious pennies on tossing rings, firing corks at bobbing ducks and throwing leather balls at wooden milk bottles. The older boys measured their strength by squeezing a spring device or wielding a hammer. A privileged few won candy bars, stuffed animals, or packs of baseball cards.

An organ grinder played popular tunes while a monkey in a red vest and cap did somersaults, back flips, and cartwheels and then held out a dented tin cup to the admiring children. An immense woman with brightly rouged cheeks strolled past with a boa constrictor draped around her neck like a long strand of pearls. Stroking the indolent snake cost a penny. A wiry mongrel leapt through hoops and barked at anyone who failed to put a coin in his cigar box.

The attention of the excited children switched immediately when a gypsy led a small, skinny bear with matted fur from behind the truck. The monkey jumped up and down, chattering angrily as his audience dashed off. At a jerk of its chain, the bear stood on its hind legs and waved its paws. The children shrank back. The bear rolled over several times and then, lying on its back, spun a large, rubber ball on its paws. It finished by standing on its front paws and doing a back flip. The cheering children filled the gypsy's cup with pennies.

By midday, the drizzle had stopped; and the victorious sun was banishing the clouds when Hawk and Roseanne arrived at the carnival with Esther, Lizzie, Cyrus and the kids. TJ had told Hawk that he was going over to Harvey's to pick up Claudia and would meet everyone later. They wandered around the booths. Hawk knocked over a pyramid of milk bottles and won a candy bar that he split between Francis and Scott. Tommy Locke and Charlotte came up with their kids so he had to go for another candy bar – which took him three tries and three cents.

At the high striker, Tommy hefted the hammer one-handed and almost rang the bell. Roseanne insisted on trying and rang the bell once.

"See. A woman is every bit as good as a man."

Hawk laughed. When no one was looking, she blew him a kiss. Rubbing his hands together, Hawk stepped to the mark. He hit the bell two out of three times.

"Mon cher, let un vrai homme show you how."

TJ clapped Hawk on the back. Then he nudged Hawk aside, wiggled his arms to loosen them up, took the long-handled hammer, and stepped back. They gave him space. Claudia murmured when the iron weight shot up the shaft and smacked the bell three times in a row.

"Voila. Shall we go see the show?"

The children watched transfixed as the acrobats twisted their bodies into impossible shapes, built human pyramids, and leapt in vaulting turns from one shoulder to the next. Their mouths hung open in frightened disbelief as the juggler kept three razor sharp swords in the air – all the while telling jokes. Scott hid his head on his mother's shoulder when the juggler swallowed a fiery torch, and Francis kept asking how the magician did his tricks. Douglas Locke yelled "No" when the magician sawed his sister Clara in half. Everett pointed and giggled. The clowns brought all the kids on stage and soon had them running in circles and whooping madly. When a clown did a flip over two kids, Roseanne whispered to Hawk, "Looks suspiciously like an acrobat."

Hawk squeezed her hand.

"Hard times. A fellow's got to work two jobs to make ends meet."

The kids clapped fiercely when the show ended. Getting up, Roseanne saw Damon and Jeannie sitting off to one side. She smiled but Damon glared at her.

Except Claudia, who had to work, they all gathered after chores at Cyrus and Lizzie's for dinner. Hawk and TJ arrived with loaves of crusty bread and ice cream while Charlotte brought fresh coleslaw. Esther filled a basket of lettuce, tomatoes, and onions from the garden; and Roseanne contributed samples of prize Scudder zucchini and squash. While the kids played freeze tag, Lizzie and Roseanne fixed spaghetti with tomato sauce thickened with diced vegetables. TJ offered to help Esther make the salad.

With the sauce bubbling, the adults sat at the picnic table that Cyrus had built. They devoured crackers with thick slices of cheese from the creamery. Hawk uncorked a jug of hard cider and filled the jelly glasses lined up on the table. The conversation hummed and laughter rose into the darkening sky. Night fell and the cicadas' throaty song filled the air.

The children begged to go back to the carnival. Everyone squeezed into two cars - with children sitting on laps. Kerosene lanterns had been hung from poles, casting a mysterious glow over the meadow. More lanterns were placed on the stage and around the edges of the big top. Shadows flickered on the canvas. Wisps of acrid smoke drifted through the tent. The children went with their parents to play games. Esther and TJ, and Hawk and Roseanne wandered off in separate pairs. Hawk and Roseanne strolled past the arc of booths. The grass swished under their feet. A soft breeze disturbed the still air. The carnival sounds floated toward them. They glanced at the stars. Roseanne murmured, "I'm so happy. I love you."

Hawk took her in his arms.

"I love you, too. But I'm worried. I don't want trouble with Damon. It's clear that his feelings have as much to do with my skin color as with Jason's employment or our rundown farm. You haven't been willing to say so, but you know it just as well as I do."

"It's been slowly dawning on me. But this isn't Buffalo. I love you and my brother be damned."

"You are some woman."

"I'm not giving you up."

He took her in his arms again and kissed her tenderly.

When Roseanne got home, Damon was waiting in the parlor. He stood up as she came through the front door. His mouth was set in a thin line; his eyes had narrowed to angry points. He held his fists at his side, clenched, his fingernails biting into his palms.

"I want to talk to you," he said, forcing himself to speak calmly and softly.

She stopped in the hallway, thought a second, then entered the parlor.

"What if I don't want to speak with you? At least, not on the subject I expect you want to talk about?"

She started back toward the hall. He took her arm and spun her around to face him.

"This has got to stop. The whole town knows. You must stop going about with that man."

She faced him squarely and fought to control her anger. "That man..." she sputtered. "That man has a name. You know what it is, and I will not stop seeing him."

"Roseanne, can't you see? Jason is no better than a gangster is, and Augustus is a complete failure. That farm..."

"I admit that Jason can be nasty, and plenty of our upright citizens despise his boot-legging. I don't much care for it myself. I didn't, however, notice you objecting to his contribution to your wedding. Augustus may not be the best farmer in the valley, but he is an educated and charming man. You sound like Richard Forshay – or his asinine son."

"I don't think like the Forshays. This has more to do with..."

"I'll tell you what it has more to do with..." She hesitated and changed her mind. "No, I won't but for sure what it has nothing to do with are my feelings for Hawk."

"Your feelings!" Damon's voice was like ice. "I will protect this family. I forbid you to continue seeing Hawk Baxter!"

"You what? On a cold day in Hell, you prejudiced bastard. Why don't you have the guts to admit that what you really don't like about Hawk is the fact that his mother's an Indian?"

She turned to leave.

"Roseanne..."

"That will be quite enough."

Neither of them knew how long Everett had been standing in the hall. He stepped into the parlor. He looked hard at Damon.

"I've known this for some time but was too ashamed – or afraid – to face it in a son of mine. I want to talk to you. There's something you need to see."

He turned to Roseanne and smiled.

"And you, young lady, will refrain from the use of certain terminology in reference to family members.

"I've no objection to your seeing Hawk; he seems a level-headed fellow. Jason gets under my skin, and he probably doesn't keep the best company, but that's his lookout – and hardly makes him a gangster.

"Augustus worries about him, but there's precious little he can do. Now please leave us."

A week later, school started on a bright September morning although by late afternoon, storm clouds had formed over the west ridge.

Roseanne arrived at the squat brick building earlier than the other teachers. She had visited her classroom once during the summer. Looking up from her desk, she had stared at the rows of empty desks. She had wandered around the darkened corridors, poking her head into empty classrooms. She had switched on a light here and there and admired the student drawings pinned to the walls. She had seen one stick drawing with a big, smiling face on a man with one arm. Underneath the picture, CLARA L. was written in crude, bold letters. Principal O'Day had arranged for her to get in the building. Buddy Dixon, the custodian, had said, "You've grown up some, but you look the same. I remember you in pigtails fighting with boys twice your size."

Now, on this early September morning, Buddy was turning on lights as she walked down the corridor.

"You're a mite early. We're not open for business quite yet. I guess, seeing as this is your first day, you're a bit anxious. Don't worry. You'll do fine."

When she opened the door to her classroom, she stopped in amazement. Taped to the blackboard behind her desk was a large sign that read: WELCOME BACK, ROSEANNE! Tears sprang to her eyes. She sat down at a desk in the front row and stared at it.

Tommy Locke poked his head in the door, said: "Relax. I'll see you at lunch." and disappeared. Mr. O'Day also stepped in for a minute to wish her good luck.

When the first bell rang, she was watching floating dust motes – her day's plan and several books arranged neatly on her desk. She went to the door and shook hands with each pupil as they entered the classroom. It was unorthodox, but it felt right. She knew many of their families, although a few of them had recently moved to town.

She asked each pupil in turn to stand up, say his or her name clearly, and talk briefly about their summer vacations. Then, as a prelude to their reading lesson, Roseanne began a tradition that she would continue for the rest of her long teaching career. She read aloud to the class. She began with Little Women. After each reading, she would encourage the children to discuss their reactions.

She ate her sandwich sitting with Tommy under a tree in the yard between the high school and the building, which housed grades one through eight. Several teachers stopped to ask how things were going.

"I think this is going to be fun," she said.

The sky was roiled with dark, scudding clouds as she drove home. A sharp, cold wind shook the branches of the maples and bent double the saplings along the edge of the river. She quickly put on a pair of rubber boots and set about cajoling the chickens into the coop by tossing grain on the floor and shooing them from behind. She fed the pigs, helped with the afternoon milking, and gathered a few vegetables for Sally's chicken stew. She sat on the back porch after supper and watched the storm break. The eastern sky was still somewhat light, but a darkening mass approached her across the valley from the west. A huge, jagged lightning bolt rent the sky. For an instant that hung like a fly in a spider web, the whole west ridge was aflame with light. Then thunder and lightning burst over the valley like Fourth of July rockets. She imagined that this is what a cannonade must have looked like from the trenches in the last war. Soon sheets of rain swept across the valley, gathering force as the storm crossed the rolling fields. Like a tidal wave, a wall of water seemed to be headed her way. She was almost frightened.

The first few swollen drops – the advance skirmishers of an approaching army - splashed heavily into the yard, kicking up swirls of dust. Then the rain began crashing down in earnest. The infantry had arrived - with the artillery roaring and spitting flames in the rear. The rain flattened the grass, and the wind rattled the windows. She pushed her chair back until it brushed against the house, but still felt the wetness on her face. Over her head, she heard a rat-a-tat-tat on the roof of the house and porch.

The back door opened. Damon came out and sat next to her. They had not spoken alone since the night of the carnival.

"What a storm," he said. "Beautiful in a way – and frightening."

"Isn't it? Where's Jeannie?"

"Upstairs. She loves to read in bed. How did it go today?"

"I had so much fun. I started reading Little Women to them. They were entranced. I'm going to love teaching here even more than in Burlington."

"Listen, sis. This is not easy for me to say, but I've been a goddamned fool. I've been hanging onto something for a long time - far too long. I hope that I can let it go. Next time Hawk comes by, I'd like to shake his hand."

Roseanne could think of nothing to say so she just threw her arms around Damon and hugged him. Then she thought of the right thing.

"Thank you."

They watched the rain coming down in sheets, pounding the yard, and almost obscuring the barn where she had hung the sheet not so long ago.

She and Hawk made love for the first time a few weeks later on a warm day in late September. They had taken a walk in the woods and, about a mile from the Baxter farm, found a clearing they had never seen before. They were sitting on a log talking when suddenly they were taking off each other's clothes. Later, no matter how hard she tried, she could not remember who had started it.

While it stayed reasonably warm, they returned to the clearing. Hawk snuck a blanket into the knapsack in which he carried the cheese sandwiches that Onatah neatly wrapped in wax paper. They were always ravenous afterwards and sat naked, their backs propped against the log, eating and talking.

"Fall always felt like a beginning to me," said Roseanne. "Now I know why."

One bright Sunday afternoon, with the forest floor looking like an Oriental carpet, they walked through the woods after making love and came upon a brook. It was warmer than usual for October. They scooped some of the clear water into their hands for a drink. They sat on a smooth boulder near the stream, and Hawk started poking in the leafy muck with a stick.

"It's going to be too cold soon, even with a blanket, to go to the clearing," Hawk said as he idly continued to dig in the earth.
"We need to think of something."

"Maybe it's crazy, but I wonder if TJ would let us borrow his shack every once in a while. I trust him to be completely mum, and it's in a secluded spot."

"I don't much like the idea of making love in someone else's bed, but if I brought clean sheets and washed them there..."

"It may be our only choice."

"I know." She leaned over to kiss him.

His stick struck something hard. He scrabbled in the earth and pulled out a round, metal ball.

"Hey, look at this, a musket ball. Wonder how old it is? Before the Civil War, I would guess."

"Probably a hunter," she said.

"Yes. Must have missed his shot."

A cold front moved across the western ridge the following week, and they stopped going to the clearing. TJ agreed to Hawk's request – and refrained from teasing him. He adored Roseanne. They barely managed once a week, however, given the demands of the forge, classes, and farm chores.

Roseanne learned to do more at the forge and helped with the bookkeeping whenever necessary. Hawk came over on the evening of Thanksgiving. Damon was awkward but friendly. Throughout the fall, they went to the movies and Napoli when they felt like splurging. Along with most of the rest of Scudder's Gorge (except Jason who said he had important business), they attended the Christmas pageant at the high school. Claudia had moved to Rutland so TJ escorted Esther, who was working – temporarily she hoped – the cash register at Vermont Clothing.

After going to church separately, they spent time with each family on Christmas Day.

Hawk gave Roseanne a limited edition of Robert Frost's New Hampshire, signed by the author, that he had ordered from a bookseller in Boston. Augustus had helped with the selection. He also gave the Scudder family a set of fire irons that rested on lion's paws clutching a ball. Everett and Damon were particularly admiring. Roseanne hugged him unabashedly as they opened presents in front of the fire.

Rosanne gave Hawk a heavy wool sweater that she had been knitting – with some advice from Jeannie - since late September. She gave Augustus a copy of William Faulkner's As I Lay Dying, which she had asked Miss Crenshaw to find for her. She gave a blue polka dot apron with CHEF printed in bold letters to Onatah, a scarf to Shannon, a linen shirt to Jason, toys to the boys, and a new pair of goggles to TJ.

Onatah fixed a roast haunch of venison with mashed potatoes - pats of butter melting on top - and creamed corn. Jason produced a bottle of French wine. They had baked apples sprinkled with sugar and cinnamon for desert. Roseanne announced that she had never in her life eaten so much – or so well.

They had New Year's dinner with Esther and TJ at Napoli and then – for two dollars a couple - went to a dance in the Elks Lodge on Allen Street. Running parallel to Cedar, Allen boasted two blocks of large homes built late in the past century. Formerly a private residence and, like its neighbors, constructed of local stone and brick, the Lodge sat in the middle of the block. Its two turrets were almost as tall as the First Congregational steeple. The curved staircase with a polished balustrade led to a spacious room on the second floor.

Chester Ames, a descendent of one of the original settlers, was the current Exalted Ruler. He believed in Prohibition and sponsored a family-oriented New Year's Eve function. Tin horns and noisemakers were provided at the door. The First Congregational Ladies Auxiliary placed huge bowls of fruit punch and platters of cookies on a long table. The Creamery sent over a ten-pound cheddar while Vaughan Tyrell brought boxes of crackers.

When the sprit moved them, a few men with flasks braved the frigid, star-filled night. It was well below freezing, and the tips of their noses turned red as they took a slug and hurried back inside.

Several high school students, including two girls, had formed a jazz band; they played Dixieland, Charlestons, fox trots and a steamy tango. TJ tried to teach Roseanne the intricate steps after Esther refused to make "a complete spectacle of herself." Roseanne stumbled and giggled as TJ bent her backwards from the waist.

"Must be what it feels like to do a loop-de-loop in a plane," she said, straightening up.

"Ah, you American girls, *vous dansez comme des…*"

"*…des vaches*, you were going to say? After all, this is dairy country."

"Not what I had in mind at all," TJ laughed and kissed Roseanne lightly on the cheek.

Numerous children chased around the room blowing horns and waving noisemakers. Their parents tried haphazardly to impose some discipline but soon dissolved into laughter along with everyone else. The older children danced along with the adults. Two giggling girls – arms stretched in front of them - glided together across the floor - taking extreme care to get between young couples dancing cheek to cheek.

Pandemonium broke out at midnight as a great din and bits of confetti filled the air. Children and adults threw streamers at one another, and the band valiantly played Auld Lang Syne—gleefully mixing old and new versions.

Rosanne sang with all her might:

> *Should auld acquaintance be forgot,*
> *And never brought to mind?*
>
> *And there's a hand my trusty friend,*
> *And give us a hand of thine.*

With confetti peppering his hair and sticking to his cheeks, Hawk took Rosanne in his arms and kissed her. She laid her head against his shoulder; a teardrop gently trickled down her cheek and carried a bit of colored paper with it.

The dance ended at one, and the long winter began in earnest.

During all but the most benign winters, the road to the Baxter farm was impassable for days at a time. The streets in and around town were now paved, but most of the country roads were dirt. Some were hard and relatively smooth while others were little better than rutted tracks. Joe Yeager (jack-of-all-trades, including school bus driver) managed to plow the better roads within a day or two of a storm. He rolled the rougher roads, but outlying farms could be isolated for several days after a big storm.

Roseanne arrived at school every day anxious to get started. Mrs. Cadogan, who had taught longer than anyone else had, cornered her one morning at recess.

"You're every bit as good as we thought you'd be. Your students adore you."

On snow days, apart from chores, she sat by the fire reading or knitting a long scarf for Hawk. The men repaired farm equipment, and then Brent took a nap while Everett gave Moby Dick a go and Damon caught up on his technical reading in Hoard's Dairyman. Jeannie and Sally knitted and talked - often pulling Roseanne's nose out of Sherwood Anderson or Zane Gray.

"Interesting reading," mused Everett, picking up The Vanishing American. "I can see the appeal. I always liked Riders of the Purple Sage except for the ending—too hopeless and tragic; I like my endings with a ray of hope."

When the roads were clear, she drove up to the Baxter's. She and Hawk hiked up the road or tramped through the woods. With the sky a radiant blue, the sunlight bouncing off the snow made her eyes ache. The ice-coated branches glittered like jewels, and the snow-laden pine boughs bent down as if drawn by a magnet. Hawk plucked mistletoe and held it over her head. They had snowball fights – hiding behind tree trunks. She hit him square in the chest and laughed uproariously until he tackled her, and they rolled over and over in the snow.

They took Rory sledding on an ancient toboggan while Shannon watched from the house or helped Martin with his first steps. Jason was away a good part of the winter. Onatah made them all hot chocolate or tea. Augustus read As I Lay Dying for a second time. They only made it to the shack a couple of times. By the time March rolled around, they were hungry for each other.

Roseanne conceived a plan. They would go to Burlington for Easter weekend. She would arrange for them to stay at Miss Crenshaw's but hint at other accommodations to her father. Miss Crenshaw readily agreed to move in with a friend for the weekend.

School closed early on Good Friday. Just after midday, Hawk picked Roseanne up in the antiquated Chevy. High clouds scudded overhead as they crossed the ridge and headed south and then east. A sharp wind blew swirls of dust and snow across the road. Large patches of snow still clung to the fields. They stopped on a high hill and gazed over a rolling valley. A village of white clapboard houses stood at a crossroads. A church steeple poked into the azure sky. Red barns were tucked in the crooks of hills. She pointed to a Morgan colt kicking up snow sprays as it galloped across a field. It stopped briefly to stick its nose in a drift and shake its head. Its dam watched approvingly.

"I feel like dancing and kicking up my heels like that colt," Rosanne said with a grin. Hawk picked her up by the waist and spun her in a circle. She arched her back, kicked out and shouted, "Yes," at the top of her lungs. The wind caught her hair and spread it like a fan. Hawk set her down.

"That was fun," she said, "if not exactly elegant."

The wind whipped up frothy waves on the lake as they drove into Burlington around four. A smiling Miss Crenshaw opened the front door and pulled Roseanne into her arms. She firmly shook Hawk's hand and gave them a tour of the cottage.

"Help yourselves," she said, pointing to a stack of records next to a phonograph.

In the dining room, Miss Crenshaw ran her finger over the surface of a gleaming mahogany table.

"This belonged to my parents—was ancient when they owned it."

With a breezy, "See you at dinner," Miss Crenshaw picked up a worn, leather valise and walked the few blocks to her friend's house.

The wallpaper in the guest room depicted two workhorses pulling a wagon past a white farmhouse and red barn. Cows and sheep grazed in the meadows. A colt frolicked near its mother.

"Just like in that valley," said Roseanne bouncing on the soft bed in the guest room. "This is going to be such fun."

They met Consuela and Miss Crenshaw for dinner at a Greek restaurant. Roseanne thought the food wonderfully exotic. They had just finished their main courses when a man wearing an embroidered vest began playing a bouzouki. To rhythmic clapping, two men in white shirts, arms draped over each other's shoulders, started a slow, twisting dance. They sidestepped back and forth and then dipped down on one knee only to leap up immediately. Other men joined them, and the clapping grew louder as did the shouts of the audience.

"Do you have any idea what they're saying?" Roseanne, gleefully clapping her hands, asked Miss Crenshaw.

"None whatsoever, but the dancers are ever so graceful."

"I've never seen men dance with each other before," said Consuela.

The line of dancers neared their table, and the last man tugged at Hawk's arm. Looking perplexed, Hawk shrugged and joined them. He tried to follow the steps but was always behind. Laughing, the audience cheered him on.

"Just a minute," said Miss Crenshaw. "This is hardly fair." She got to her feet and pulled Roseanne and Consuela toward the dance floor.

"No," shrieked Roseanne.

"Dios mio," implored Consuela.

Before anyone could react, the three women – hopping and sidestepping – were facing the line of men who froze. The room went silent until a young woman shouted "Opa" and dragged another woman from her chair. Their husbands looked shocked; but the musician struck a chord, and as the women danced, the clapping resumed. The men now increased their tempo, and two more women pushed back their chairs. The two lines danced back and forth facing each other – ever faster with Rosanne, Miss Crenshaw, and Consuela doing their best not to trip over their own feet. The song ended, and wild applause surged through the room like a wave.

"That was such fun," said Consuela collapsing in her seat. "It reminds me of dancing at parties when I was a girl in Cuba."

"I want to dance some more," laughed Miss Crenshaw.

Roseanne and Hawk slept in each other's arms. Roseanne dreamed of a colt galloping across a pasture and tossing its head. The colt stopped and sniffed the fresh morning air. It rubbed its nose in the gauzy, dew-coated grass. She held out some grain, but the colt snorted and ran off. She walked in its direction, hand stretched out. The colt went over a hillock and she was alone in the pasture. She woke with a faint recollection of the dream but couldn't recapture it. Sunlight streamed through the window and warmed her face. She smiled at a line of curly hair running down the middle of Hawk's chest and nudged him awake.

They strolled around the city that afternoon. She showed him the University and they peeked into the Fleming Museum, which had opened the year before. He studied the sculptures, commenting that they gave him some fresh ideas. He had never before visited a museum and realized now that he should have.

She wanted to take him to Gianni's for dinner, but Hawk said that he preferred a quiet place. After some wrong turns, she found the café Miss Crenshaw had taken her to almost a year ago. It was the same waiter.

"We haven't seen you in a long time, but your friend comes in quite frequently."

"I wonder if it's part of his job to remember people or if he just has a photographic memory. I was only here that one time."

"Neither one, it's because you are so stunningly beautiful."

"Flattery will get you anything – well almost anything. Say it again; I liked the way it sounded."

After ordering, he said, "Your Miss Crenshaw is grand, but your description hardly fits."

"She never fails to surprise."

Desert over, Hawk quietly sipped his coffee and then drew in his breath. He took Roseanne's hand.

"I suppose there ought to be some preamble, but I cannot think of any." He kissed her hand. "Will you marry me?"

"Oh my!" Her eyes shone. "Yes! Of course, I will. You know that I will. Yes! Yes! Yes!"

They went to Easter service next morning and told Consuela and Miss Crenshaw over lunch at Gianni's. Consuela jumped up and, to the mild astonishment of the other diners at their long table, hugged Roseanne. She then rushed around the table and hugged Hawk.

"Take good care of her," Miss Crenshaw said softly to no one in particular.

They announced the news to both families the following Saturday, a late summer wedding. Damon clapped Hawk on the back and Everett pumped his hand up and down. Sally wiped her eye with the corner of her apron.

Jason smirked and said, "No surprise." Onatah beamed, and Shannon said, "Sure, and I'm happy for you."

Augustus commented, "I wonder what they're putting in the water over in Burlington these days."

Examining a white hot iron rod, TJ acidly remarked that he would take Roseanne for a ride on the motorcycle to see if that would jolt some sense into her. And not to tell Esther for that would give her ideas.

On a sun-filled morning after church, Everett took a walk with Roseanne and informed her that she had a great-great-great grandfather whom was Abenaki, thereby giving her about three point one per cent Indian blood.

"If I can still figure in my head," he added.

"How disappointing," she said with her toothy grin, "not to be the first Scudder to marry an Indian."

"Did I mention marriage?"

"Oooo," Roseanne mocked, grinning even more broadly, "great-great-great was born out of wedlock, eh?"

"Something like that," Everett remarked and decided to leave it at that.

Hawk laughed uproariously and offered to pass the chip to Roseanne, who could probably carry it better than him anyway.

Augustus said quietly, "It's a story that circulated when my father was young – and earlier – but it probably hasn't been mentioned in sixty years or more. I only heard it because my father told me."

Winter clung to April but lost its iron grip as May carpeted the fields with small yellow flowers. Around the farmhouse, daffodils and irises swayed in the crisp morning breezes. Roseanne woke each morning with a sense of expectation and hurried through her farm work before heading off to school. With Jeannie's help, she made a wedding dress of embroidered white satin. She wrote out invitations by hand and mailed them to about eighty people, including Consuela and Miss Crenshaw. She called a get-together of her friends on a warm Sunday morning in mid-May. Drinking Sally's lemonade, they discussed decorations and food while the children scampered around the yard.

"My," said Sally, "a wedding a year at the farm. I wonder if Howie will be next."

"From what I hear from my friend, Amy, down in Montpelier," said Lizzie, "he might just sneak in ahead of Rosanne."

"Not Howie. He's too much of a lawyer to do anything in a hurry. Poor Elspeth is going to have to be patient. Hawk and I met her when we went to buy the rings. She's very sweet."

Their voices drifted across the yard on a spring breeze. In the fields behind the barn, corn was ripening. Three calves sucked their mother's teats. A robin pulled up a worm and flew off. Roseanne noticed Sally quietly studying the chicken coop.

"Sally, if you're getting any artistic ideas; I want you to be nice to Hawk. He's a sensitive man."

"You didn't seem so concerned last summer," teased Esther. "I recall you admiring Sally's prowess."

"This is different. Damon..."

"Needed a little deflating?" asked Lizzie.

"What man doesn't?" asked Shannon.

"Hear, hear!" said Onatah.

"Not all of them," protested Esther. "TJ is the soul of modesty."

Peals of uncontrollable laughter gushed from the women like a stream tumbling down a mountain ravine.

Spring melted into summer. Hawk and Rosanne took long walks above the Baxter farm and along the river toward the gorge. Gnats and mosquitoes swarmed around their heads unless a breeze blew them off. Their eagerness growing like a wildflower, they could not resist going to the shack, although less concerned now with secrecy.

Coming back from recess on the last day of school, Roseanne found bouquets on her desk and a long sign taped to the blackboard. Above a paper heart were large printed letters:

WE LOVE YOU, MISS SCUDDER

With school out, she took on extra chores and worked on wedding preparations. Hawk and TJ had added new products, and the forge made a small profit each month.

"Better than most today," Hawk said, "and when things get better, watch out."

"I imagine this Roosevelt fellow will do something about the mess," TJ added.

"Fighting words to a Vermonter," said Augustus.

On a hot and humid Sunday in mid-July, Hawk came for lunch after services. The church had been stifling despite the open doors and whirring fans that faced the congregation from the pulpit. Hawk mopped the back of his neck with a handkerchief and held Roseanne's damp hand. At the door, Reverend McHenry asked how the wedding preparations were coming and reminded Roseanne to plan for a rehearsal a day or two before the ceremony.

After lunch, Hawk suggested, "Let's go walk up in the gorge. It will be cooler, and we can swim."

"Grand idea. I haven't been up there in ages."

They parked at the end of North Valley Road. The path hugged the river for a stretch, climbing gradually. They waved to an angler casting in the middle of the current. As they entered the gorge, the trail switched back and forth. It had rained earlier in the week and the stream was running fast, swirling around boulders, and causing pockets of foam to form under the banks. The steepness made her thighs ache. The cascade grew louder. After an hour, they reached the rock-ribbed pool and bathed their faces in the cold water. They climbed further until they reached a ledge partially hidden in a thicket. Roseanne smiled as she remembered the last time she had seen this ledge: when she had happened to see Tommy Locke and Charlotte making love there. They sat for a while, their bodies dripping with sweat.

"Would you like to go all the way to the ridge?" he asked.

"Not today. I'm feeling a bit worn out."

"How about a swim then?"

"You're on. Last one in is a ... something or other."

He held her hand as they scrambled back down to the pool.

"Ah," she said, as she slipped naked into the water. "This is more like it."

They paddled around and splashed each other. He climbed out and stood on the rocky lip of the pool. She admired his lean body, tawny skin, and hard muscles. He dove and surfaced, blowing water into the air. He took her in his arms and kissed her. He pulled himself onto the rock again and shook the water from his head. He called something that she couldn't hear over the cascade. She swam over and steadied herself against the rock.

He laughed and dove over her head. He didn't come up. She noticed for the first time a submerged boulder where he had hit the water. Panicked, she swam toward the boulder and then saw his crumpled body as it drifted, almost lazily, over the edge of the pool. Thumping against sharp rocks, it was sucked into the current and tumbled downstream.

Her scream merged with the roar of the cascade.

When the sheriff found Hawk's body washed up against the bank almost a mile downstream, he had a jagged gash on the top of his head.

At the funeral, Damon walked up to Jason and put an arm around his shoulder. Jason jerked back as if he had been bitten by a snake, but then he extended his hand to Damon. Both men had tears in their eyes.

Roseanne took some comfort in spending time at the Baxter's. On a visit a month after Hawk's death, Augustus asked her to go for a walk. He took her hand as they climbed up the dusty road. The pines looked wilted in the hot sun. A garter snake wriggled out of the tall, dry grass and crossed the road, leaving a faint trail in the dirt. She stopped for a minute to look back over the valley.

"I want to tell you a story," he said.

"And I have something to tell you."

Chapter Nine

August 6, 1945

It promised to be a relatively cool day. A wispy layer of fog settled on the west ridge during the night, and was spilling down toward the valley as the darkness faded. A pair of larks flashed across the rolling fields, ripe with hay. A skunk ambled around the corner of the neatly painted farmhouse, skirted the vegetable garden, and hurried toward its burrow at the edge of the woods. Just south of town, a red fox with a rabbit in its mouth dashed across the Forshay Road and into a meadow carpeted in purple clover.

A lone truck loaded with freshly cut logs sped south along the county road, its headlights growing fainter in the dawn. A housewife pushed open the screen door and stepped onto her back porch. She stretched her back and watched the ridge getting lighter. She saw the truck's dim headlights, yawned, and wriggled her nose at the smell of frying bread that wafted through the screen.

At sunup, two white delivery trucks with Scudder's Gorge Cooperative Creamery painted in green letters above the head of a placid cow circulated through town. Newspaper boys threw papers onto front porches without looking or slowing down on their bikes. Lately, the paper had carried speculation about the need to invade Japan and the probable cost in American lives. A creaky bus with hard seats worked its way along the leafy streets, picking up women and a few veterans (honorably discharged with serious wounds) to carry them forty miles to a munitions plant. A woman looked at her reflection in the streaked glass, but the others tried to sleep – their heads jouncing against the metal rims.

The milking finished (The Scudders had a milking machine, but many

243

in the valley still milked by hand – including several by choice.), Damon attached a mower to his tractor and drove into a hay field. In the adjacent pasture, a cow snorted, turned her rear toward another cow, and awkwardly kicked up a heel. Damon laughed. He cut in long parallel loops, slicing evenly at the base of the tall waving grass and sending little clouds of dust and seeds into the early morning light. He stopped occasionally to take a swig of sharp, black coffee from a thermos that was wedged between an oil-stained toolbox and the base of the hard, concave tractor seat.

Toward noon, Damon was still cutting. All morning, his mind had been on the sick calf he had spent half the night tending. He wiped his forehead with a grease-speckled cloth and rubbed an annoying mosquito bite at the back of his neck. The calf had the scours. Old Doc Colson – although he had force-fed the calf liquids - wasn't sure he could save it. Ned Walker might have had a better chance, but he was somewhere in the Pacific. The older vet was fonder of Kentucky bourbon than keeping up with the latest developments in his field, but when sober, he did have a feel for the business that couldn't be taught at school.

Not that Damon was opposed to an occasional night on the town (meaning the Liberty Tavern) with the boys - friends who were either too old for the service or had draft exemptions like himself. And, of course, Knuckles, who had enlisted in 1942, been blooded in North Africa, landed in the first wave at Normandy, fought across France and was never even scratched (or rose above the rank of private) until he lost a leg at the Battle of the Bulge. His nickname derived from his boyhood delight in schoolyard skirmishes.

Lying on his back on a pallet under a jacked up car, it made no difference if Knuckles had one leg or two. The best – and right now the only - mechanic in town, he would extract a pitted carburetor from a Ford Model A roadster pickup, lean on his sweat-stained crutches, and hold the worn-out part up to the light with a deep sigh of satisfaction before putting in a new one. The farmers fixed their own tractors other than the near terminal cases, which went to Knuckles.

Damon also thought about Roseanne. With school out, she came to the farm almost every day. She loved to work in the vegetable garden – seeming to relish the physical effort. She brought her son, Keith, with her. The boy helped his older cousins with chores. Then the three – two boys and a girl - would traipse off to the woods, sometimes carrying fishing poles. Not that the poles got much use. Far livelier entertainment such as footraces and tree climbing occupied their free time. Keith did catch a large trout in a stream in the spring. Roseanne forbade her son ever to go near the river.

It was a shame she had never married. It had been – what? -thirteen years since Hawk had died. She had gone out with one or two fellows but always squashed their hopes before it went anywhere. Lloyd McHenry had been interested. Despite the fact that the minister was inexperienced in the family department, it might have been a good thing – especially for the boy.

Damon reasoned that he couldn't help in that area. He had enough trouble with his own kids. Sandy was always getting ready to tangle with him, and Genevieve was forever moaning about something - mostly her complexion. Only his youngest seemed relatively placid, but give it time.

Making a looping turn at the end of the field, Damon saw Jeannie running across the lower pasture, waving her arms frantically.

Reverend McHenry left his parsonage on Franklin Street just before eleven, as he did most mornings. He liked to get some exercise and was fond of walking through town and out to the country. It filled him with a sense of order to stroll along the quiet streets and look at the solid, carefully painted clapboard houses. The front lawns were richly green, the hedges neatly trimmed, and the flower beds laid out in respectable patterns. Years ago, he had taken a week's holiday in Jamaica and had been disturbed, even nauseated by the profusion of riotous colored flowers. He had been greatly relieved to return home.

He turned north on Spruce and thereby avoided the center of town. As he passed Greene, he glanced to his left and saw Buddy Dixon hosing down the fire truck. He waved, but Buddy happened to turn away at that moment. He crossed the old bridge and headed west. He checked his watch; he would walk twenty minutes and then turn back - a mile each way. He nodded in satisfaction.

He thought about the sermon he had started for this Sunday - The Coming Peace. He would discuss Christ's sense of forgiveness and argue for installing democratic governments in Germany and Japan that would quickly allow our enemies to rejoin the civilized nations. He breathed in the dry odor of freshly cut hay. He passed an orchard and observed the small apples just starting to ripen. A few had fallen, and yellow jackets were buzzing around their sticky wounds.

A curious thought struck him, why was his church the "First" Congregational? Had the settlers expected a "Second"? If so, the town had disappointed them. The valley was prosperous and friendly even if, as everywhere he supposed, unpleasant elements occasionally rose to the surface of an otherwise tranquil sea.

A tired-looking truck with slatted wooden sides approached; the driver was a thin man with a deeply lined face. Half a dozen baskets filled with tomatoes, squash, green peppers, and corn rested uneasily on the rusting truck bed. A boy of about fifteen with dark auburn hair stood in the rear of the truck facing into the wind and resting his hands on top of the cabin. A black and white mutt sat between his legs. With a grating shift of gears, the driver slowed to a halt and leaned out the open window.

"Morning, pastor," said the driver. "It's a pretty cool day for August."

"Good morning, Jason," replied Reverend McHenry. "How is Shannon? Dr. Gunderson hopes her case has stabilized."

"The pills help her sleep some, but she still coughs half the night. Sounds like a file cutting through a prison bar."

"I am indeed sorry to hear that."

"Gunderson says she smokes too much. Outta' cut back. I never knew a good smoke to hurt anybody."

"If it's cancer, I imagine that smoking is not going to do her a lot of good."

Jason scowled.

"Jesus, give it over and leave us in peace."

"I apologize if you thought I was meddling. I'm just concerned."

Reverend McHenry scuffed his toe in the dirt raising little whirlpools of dust that swirled around his ankles. He squinted as he looked up to watch a hawk circling above the valley. A farmer was cutting hay about a half mile away. Despite twenty-three years as a minister, he was never comfortable cajoling parishioners. The farmers seemed so much more capable than he was. Perhaps if he had married and raised a family, he would feel more their equal. He had tried once.

"There's something else I've been meaning to... uh... mention for some time, Jason. We never see you or your family in church. Especially when life seems most... uh... imponderable, we need to trust in God's mercy."

Jason's tone softened.

"It's hard to get caught up with things, and I can't see what the church can do for Shannon – either yours or St. Agnes. If Rory hadn't run off and joined the navy, things'd be a sight easier."

Glad to change the subject, Reverend McHenry asked,

"Have you heard from Rory?"

"Not in six months."

"I am sure you will. God works in mysterious ways."

The boy leaned over the edge of the truck and spoke up in an eager tone.

"When do you think the Japs are going to quit, Reverend?"

He sounded like he hoped they might not.

"Boy, mind your own business, which is farming," said Jason. "One son lying about his age and running off to fight yellow bastards is enough in one family!"

"I don't know, Martin, but I cannot imagine it will be long. From what you read in the papers, they have taken quite a beating, and yet they fight on. Surrendering just doesn't seem part of their vocabulary."

Jason shifted into first gear.

"Good day, pastor. We'll try to come to church some Sunday."

He spewed dust in his wake as he drove off.

Reverend McHenry walked a little further before turning back. Seeing Jason had made him think of Roseanne. Things had been going so well. Then she just broke it off. It must have been because of Hawk – even after seven years. It had come as a powerful shock. He had let his hopes run ahead of him. Now here it was five years later, and neither of them was married.

He thought back to a June morning in 1940. France seemed on the verge of collapse, and England might be next. He felt ill watching the newsreels of Hitler's soldiers and tanks, but he couldn't always be preoccupied with what was happening in Europe. He was in love for the first time – although at Harvard, during the last war, there had been an Irish girl. They had made love one afternoon. Completely taken aback, he told her not to worry—he would marry her. She had laughed uproariously.

He had worked all that June morning on his sermon, looking occasionally out his study window at the dense maple branches that shaded the parsonage. From one window, he could see the river sparkling in the bright sunshine. A couple of boys running noisily across the churchyard disturbed his concentration. He found it difficult in any case to focus on the sermon. He and Roseanne were going on a picnic in the afternoon, and he planned to ask her to marry him.

He met Roseanne in front of the school. A neighbor had picked up Keith along with her own son. They walked south past the closed sawmill and along a dirt road that followed the river. She never liked to walk north of town, and he didn't press her. Crickets chirped, and cows grazed in a meadow. How peaceful compared to what was happening in France. They turned off onto a path that led to a grassy bank above the river. He took a blanket and a box of crackers and cheese from his worn knapsack. Roseanne took some ham sandwiches wrapped in wax paper from a bag and two bottles of Coke. The sun shone in their eyes. An oriole skimmed low over the river and disappeared across a meadow.

"Look at all that orange," she said. "It's a male."

They ate quietly for a few moments; he listened to a pair of crows in a nearby tree.

"Awful things are happening in Europe, and I'm afraid it's going to get a lot worse. These Nazis are terrible people with their racial laws and persecutions."

"Yes," she said. "You're right, and not enough people in this country see it. Not that we have a clean slate. I shudder when I think of some of the things we've done."

"But mostly in the past, God willing. I don't believe in collective guilt or the sins of one generation being passed onto another like some Greek tragedy. God gives us all a fresh start and we are responsible for what we become – for the mark we leave."

"Maybe, but the Germans will have to answer for a lot and for a long time. I doubt we know the half of it."

His stomach felt upside down and his hand shook as he reached for hers. She accepted his hand, and he thought that maybe this would go well. He had to try. If not now, when?

Roseanne watched the river ripple over half submerged rocks and shivered.

"I think I'm becoming obsessed with the war. It's not what I really wanted to talk about. I had something much more important..." He faltered and couldn't figure how to go on so he pulled her gently closer. She leaned forward. They started to kiss. She shuddered and pulled back. She scrambled to her feet and, without looking at him, said,

"I can't. I'm sorry, but I have to go."

She ran up the path toward the road, leaving her bag behind.

He walked back up Spruce – reliving, as he had done so often, that morning. He noticed that Buddy had finished washing the fire truck and was talking to Dwayne Ingram and Russ Malone, both volunteer firefighters. They seemed excited; he hoped it wasn't an argument. Buddy noticed him and waved him over. He quickened his pace.

Everett set out for town a little after eleven. Jeannie had asked him to pick up two pounds of flour and some sugar at Tyrell's so she could make a spice cake. The walk took over an hour, but Everett considered it unpatriotic to take the Chevy – even if farmers got extra gas coupons. Someone would give him a ride home.

A few older men would be sitting on Tyrell's porch with nothing better to do than complain about Rosie the Riveter or that blackguard Roosevelt. He hadn't much cared for the New Deal, but Roosevelt had done a pretty good job leading the country during the war. Too bad he had not lived to see it finished. Some of the New Deal might not have been so bad; it helped get the country going again. Although he was fairly certain it would have managed on its own.

Everett had helped with the morning milking and would return in time to load hay along with Damon and Brent. At sixty-six, he allowed himself a few hours off now and again, and the conversation on Tyrell's porch entertained him. Rosie the Riveter... he recalled Russ Malone commenting how, when the war was over, the women would go back to their accustomed places. Everett did not think so. The women were used to a little more excitement now. The cat was out of the bag.

He walked along enjoying the sun. He did not like winter so much anymore; his joints ached from the cold. But he still liked to take his grandchildren maple sugaring. They had all gone with Augustus in the early spring.

Augustus could be a curmudgeon, but they had always been friends - best of friends as boys. They still liked to visit each other and talk about books and old times. Augustus had not had an easy go of it. Losing Hawk had nearly finished him. With Prohibition long gone, Jason wasn't good for much, except growing a few scraggly vegetables and making cider, most of it hard. Everett saw nothing wrong with that. He liked a glass of hard cider now and then. Ridiculous that it was illegal. The big liquor concerns putting pressure on Congress and to hell with the small farmers. Everett had no patience for that sort of nonsense.

Jason skirted the law in other, less acceptable, ways – selling chickens and eggs, or his farmer's extra gas coupons, on the black market. Everett believed that every man – and woman – should be given a chance, but only a chance. The rest was up to them. He had been a little old to go to the front in the last war, but he had volunteered anyway. The army recruiter in Montpelier said he could best serve his country by staying on the farm.

Roseanne hadn't gotten over Hawk any more than Augustus had. She spent a lot of time at the Baxter farm – ostensibly, so that Augustus could see his grandson, but Everett knew it had as much to do with keeping alive Hawk's memory. She also felt a need to keep Augustus company now that Onatah was gone. They talked a lot about literature.

Everett wished Roseanne would buy a house of her own – something near the school. It was not good for her to live in a place carved out of someone else's house – even if they were good people like the Samuels. He asked himself how, with that tiny, makeshift kitchen, she could make proper meals for herself and Keith.

"Kitchenette, they call it," he snorted out loud and then looked around surprised.

She didn't even have a real stove. She had been there now for seven years, since Keith was five. He would speak to Damon—should have done so long before. The farm was prospering, and prices – which had started up even before the country entered the war – would stay strong. Surely, they can help her buy a home. It would be sort of a down payment on her inheritance. He paid no attention to the car coming up behind him until the Buick sedan slowed alongside and Logan Forshay called out the window.

"Care for a ride, Everett?"

The Forshays had always maintained a small dairy operation, but their main interest lay in fruit – apples, strawberries and, more recently, raspberries. They also sold apple butter and expensive jams. Logan was currently the mayor while Damon served on the town council, a seat Everett had relinquished in the late Thirties.

"No, thank you. I'm almost to town. I like the exercise even if my neighbors think I'm a fool."

"Your neighbors think you're a fool for sitting on the porch reading Shakespeare or that Hemingway fellow."

"May loved Shakespeare. She died at the end of the last war, and now we're close to the end of another one."

"Closer than you think. They just announced on the radio that we dropped some kind of atomic bomb on Japan. You might want to reconsider that ride."

There was something Everett didn't like as Logan described the broadcast. As they passed a few houses on the outskirts of town, Logan talked about the tremendous power of the bomb – more than twenty thousand tons of TNT and the equivalent of what two thousand super fortresses could deliver. Everett couldn't equate the numbers to anything he knew, but it was clear that this splitting of the atom had released a force hitherto unknown to man. Secretary of War Stimson had stated that the bomb would help tremendously in shortening the war—a bomb that was good for all of us—both American and Japanese lives would be spared.

What he found troubling was a phrase the President had used: "...a harnessing of the basic power of the universe." Augustus had once named a dog "Sophocles" although the poor mutt did not prove worthy of the name – laziest dog he had ever seen. Even though he hadn't read as much of the Greek playwrights as May and Augustus, Everett knew what hubris meant, and this sure sounded like it. He doubted that man would ever understand, much less harness, the "basic power of the universe."

Passing the creamery, he looked through the plate glass windows at the gleaming steel vats. The new plant had been built ten years ago with government assistance – replacing the one he had helped finance back in 1910. The Scudder farm was a leading supplier, and he was still on the Board. Damon had worked on organizing the financing for the new plant, and Howie had provided legal advice. He was proud of all his children—May would have been too.

At the Mobil station, with its bold red Pegasus, Knuckles and the teenage boy who pumped gas part-time were standing in the open bay listening to a blaring radio. Knuckles was leaning on his crutches and staring, open-mouthed, into space.

Further along Mill, he turned to glance at St. Agnes, a ponderous brick building with a white statue of the Virgin Mary in front. Some of the bricks looked worn and the mortar work chipped. Inside, dim light filtered through darkened stained glass windows. Everett had been in St. Agnes only twice– for the baptism of Joseph Trochino's son and the funeral of Joseph's wife, who was killed three years ago in a hunting accident. She was hanging laundry in her back yard (about two miles out of town) when a deer hunter shot her in the chest. The hunter – a dentist from Burlington – said at the inquest that he had been in the woods about seventy-five yards from the house and was aiming at a whitetail buck. The flapping laundry must have confused him. The matter was dropped, and the dentist made a thousand dollar contribution to the St. Agnes orphans' fund.

When he first came to town in 1925, Joseph worked on the Scudder farm for several years. Saving almost every cent, he opened Napoli. A year later, Maria arrived from Boston on a bus. They had known each other since childhood. After the accident, Joseph did not remarry.

They turned onto Cedar. Beyond the school, the blocks surrounding the First Congregational were the plushest in town – decorous white frame houses on Cedar and Spruce and more recent stone and brick Goliaths on Allen. The neighborhood was home to storekeepers, business owners, and professional men. Alan Meyer, who had built the toy factory in the mid-Twenties and had managed somehow to keep going during the Depression, owned a modern-looking brick house on Greene. Most of these houses were set back from the sidewalk and had meticulously maintained front yards.

They continued on Cedar and, just before reaching downtown, passed the cinder block town hall – built in 1936 with WPA assistance. Two statues gazed into the distance, a Civil War soldier in a peaked hat and an Abenaki Indian.

The fourth member of his family to own the store, Vaughan Tyrell only stepped outside during business hours to carry an elderly customer's parcels – and then only if his stock boy was busy shelving. But there he was standing on the porch in the midst of a throng of gesticulating men and women. He broke free when he saw Everett climb the steps.

"You've heard, haven't you, Everett? I imagine the church bells will be ringing soon. Hello, Logan. The war is over – or will be. I don't know what to say."

"Hardly seems so," said Logan. "You're talking as fast as a New Yorker."

Vaughan laughed.

"About as fast as this war should end now."

"It'll be fast all right," said Jason, who was standing behind him. "This is the end for those bastards. They'll quit now or Harry Truman'll blow the whole place to hell."

Everett walked to the edge of the porch and looked down to the river, which seemed to glitter more brightly than usual today.

"What matters," said Everett, "is that a lot of lives will be saved. We've been lucky. We've lost only four, Toby Richards, Steve McGowan, Warren Rawlings, and Samuel Goss. I just want it to end."

He watched Damon drive up in the Chevy. Jeannie, Roseanne, and Genevieve were in the back seat, Keith and Sandy in the front. Jeannie held Farley on her lap. Damon jumped out of the car and looked up at his father.

"It's finished. We've won, and my damn vet can come home. American ingenuity. Think of it, twenty thousand tons of TNT."

"That'll blow a lot of Nips to hell," said Dale Royce.

"Japanese," said Roseanne. She was standing by the Chevy with a hand on Keith's shoulder. "Why can't we call them Japanese – even if they are the enemy?"

"Because of what they did at Bataan," said Vaughan.

"They deserve whatever they get," Dale added. He looked angrily at Roseanne. "You had better stick to teaching third grade."

Everett had been leaning on the railing. He straightened up and started to say something, but Damon spoke first.

"Easy Dale. Roseanne has a point, and even if she didn't, take care how you speak to my sister."

Reverend McHenry arrived with the men from the firehouse in time to hear Damon's remark. He looked at Roseanne who smiled at him. Joseph Trochino had been standing on the side of the porch. He stepped forward.

"Let's just be grateful. It is a red-letter day for America. Our technology has triumphed."

Joseph had introduced several generations in town to the wonders of pizza and spaghetti Bolognese. No one ever mentioned on whose side Italy had fought.

"Joseph is right," said Logan. "This is a time for celebration – and gratitude. Speaking of which, Vaughan said something about church bells. Are you going to ring the bells, Lloyd? And what about the other churches?"

"I think that would be a good idea. I'll see to it right away. It is truly a time to celebrate, and yet I'm also saddened. I imagine that a bomb like this killed many – even thousands – of people, most of whom surely were responsible for neither the war nor Japanese atrocities. The innocent seem to have suffered a lot in this war."

Lloyd walked off in the direction of his church.

"What about the innocent American lives that have been lost – starting with Pearl Harbor?" asked Jeannie. "Were any of them responsible for this war? Did any of them ask to leave their loved ones and die on some God-forsaken Pacific Island?" She was holding Farley by the hand, and her eyes were glittering.

"You tell 'em, Jeannie," said Dale.

"She's got it right," said Vaughan.

"We didn't start this shindig," said Jason, "but we sure as hell ended it."

"You men are right," said Everett, "but Lloyd also made a good point. In our glorious modern era, far too many innocent people are killed in wars. That's the plain, unvarnished truth, stripped bare of any claptrap. I'm fearful atomic weapons are going to make it a whole lot worse." Everett paused to catch his breath. No one said a word. After all, he was Everett Scudder. "All the same," Everett continued, "it's still a time to rejoice. The war may be over in days, and we won't have to invade Japan. That alone is something we could have hardly dreamt of when we got up this morning."

Everyone nodded and murmured assent. Vaughan clapped Everett on the back. Roseanne put an arm around Keith's shoulder. After an instant, he wriggled free.

"You know," said Logan, "there's another side to this. The radio mentioned peacetime uses for atomic energy – powering ships and planes for example. This could turn out to be a great thing for us and the rest of the world too."

"Just be grateful we got there first," said Vaughan. "The Germans were working on one. Maybe even the Japs... Japanese." He glanced at Roseanne who was standing next to the Chevy.

"Maybe if we'd had it to use on Germany some months ago," said Knuckles, who was maneuvering between Damon's Chevy and Jason's truck, "I would still have two legs."

"You're so good with one leg," Roseanne said to him, "that I cannot imagine how anybody could compete if you had two."

He stopped and looked at her. Sweat stains spread from his armpits; he was breathing hard.

"You're the best there is," he grinned and then added so that only Roseanne could hear, "Some people have wounds that aren't so readily seen."

He worked his way up the steps to the porch. Knowing his feelings, no one offered to help. He sat heavily in a chair. Beads of sweat ran down his cheeks.

"I wonder if we would have dropped it on Germany," ventured Russ Malone.

"Why the hell not?" asked Damon. "They're lousy bastards just like the Japanese. Who knows how many they've murdered."

"Hell no," said Dale. "For one thing, they're white."

Silence fell on the crowd. Roseanne gripped Keith's hand. Jason broke the silence.

"At least," he said in a cold voice. "they're white."

"Young man, "said Everett, looking straight at Dale, "your tongue is slipping around more than usual today. Would you care to re-think what you just said?"

Roseanne noticed a small bird chasing an eagle high above the river. The eagle soared upwards ignoring the pesky bird at its tail. The smaller bird gave up and dropped away. She thought of Hawk and wondered if he could be in the vicinity—not that she felt strongly about an afterlife, but wouldn't it be nice?

"I didn't mean Jason and his kind."

"Course, you didn't," said Jason.

"Hell, I apologize if anybody took offense."

"That's a start," said Everett.

"Sure they would've dropped it on Germany," said Jeannie. "Saving American lives is saving American lives."

"If we were only as smart as our women-folk," said Damon. He planted a wet kiss on his wife's cheek.

"I can't for the life of me remember," said Logan, "where we dropped the darn thing."

"Hiroshima," said Roseanne.

"What's that?" asked Jason.

"Hiroshima," repeated Roseanne quietly. "The name of the city was Hiroshima."

At that moment, the bells of St. Agnes and the United Methodist Church started ringing.

Everett put on a sweater that afternoon before going to sit on the back porch. He studied the expanse of the valley – the pastures and cornfields, the line of the curving river, the hillocks rolling like waves and the swaths of forest. He looked north towards the gorge. He had to admit that he had never much liked Jason Baxter. He hated to think that of one of Augustus's boys. Hawk had been an entirely different kettle of fish. Roseanne and he would have been happy together. Hawk's death was so strange – such a rotten trick of fate. Everett didn't really believe in fate; you made your own, but it was uncanny nevertheless.

"Neither Philomena nor Roseanne's sons knew their fathers," he thought, "or mother in Philomena's case. There was also something uncanny about that—one boyfriend her entire life. Oh, a few dates after Hawk, but they didn't count. She never let anything get started. Keith was a fine lad. He would amount to something – like his father, who had worked harder than the rest of his family combined.

"That little canoe I made for him. When was that? Last fall." Everett nodded his head. "Yes, last fall. Two Indians with paddles. It had taken a steady hand to whittle those figures. The canoe was displayed on the small bookcase in her apartment. I really need to talk to Damon about Roseanne. Tomorrow. Damon would agree, and she could start looking. Nothing big, just a nice house with a yard.

"That old .22. Augustus said it had disappeared long ago. When was the last time Augustus and I went hunting? Last fall? No, two seasons ago. We see a bit more of each other since the roads have improved. It's not such a haul. Augustus sure liked that Faulkner fellow. What had Logan said this morning, that Hemingway fellow? I tried Faulkner, but I couldn't follow him. The damn sentences were too long. If God had wanted me to read sentences that long, he wouldn't have invented periods.

"Hell, even Shakespeare is easier," Everett said out loud. He shook his head. He'd been doing a lot of that lately. He had argued more than once with Augustus about Faulkner, whom Augustus considered the greatest living American writer.

He wondered where Thomas was—and also wondered about Tehya. He didn't think about her very often. She had been his first love, but May was the big love in his life. He had thought of her every day for the last twenty-seven years. She had been such a friend – and wonderful in bed. He didn't suppose many people around here thought like that. She was a tigress. She had taught him how much fun there was to be had – in bed and out.

What courage when she knew she was dying. He hoped he would be able to do the same.

"Two big wars in my lifetime," he thought, "and a couple of small ones—more than enough for any man. What makes a war small? It's surely not small to those who die. Does God care if a war is big or small? This atomic bomb isn't going to make wars any smaller. I hope I don't live to see the next one. But if it saves American lives, the bomb's a good thing. Truman seems to know what he's doing. Not afraid to make decisions.

"Wonder what May would have thought of Faulkner. Not much, I suppose.

"Lloyd McHenry. Now there's an odd duck. Been here all these years – never assigned another parish – and never got married. There were women in town that would've jumped at the chance. He courted Roseanne years ago, but he hadn't a prayer. She wouldn't let any man get close to her. Only Hawk."

He knew what that was all about. Look at him. He had tried talking to her about it a couple of times, but she had clammed up. What could he have said that would have made a difference, anyway?

Roseanne had been so difficult after May's death. Tommy had managed a miracle. Everett never knew how, and now their kids were almost grown. Clara and Douglas were both at the university, and Everett – he smiled to himself – was finishing high school. If the war weren't ending, Douglas might have had to go. Tommy went to Canada in the first war and ended up losing an arm. Second battle of the Marne.

"Memory's not so bad," he mumbled. "At least not for the distant past. Don't ask what I had for breakfast. Or if I had breakfast. Hit that damn Cody Murphy right in the forehead with that stone. Nice smooth round one. Fit perfectly in my hand. Wonder if I should've played serious ball. Too late now. I was so scared that night I almost peed in my drawers. She acted so strange when Hawk died – almost normal. But the light in her eyes went out. Only comes back with Keith or talking about her students. Best damned teacher in town."

Everett had prayed to God to help her, but the odds, he knew, were against it.

Howie had taken his own sweet time, but Elspeth was an upstanding woman. Reminded him a little of May, also a librarian. Howie had helped during the tough times. Kept the place going when prices were so low you could have looked in a barrel and not found them.

"Wonder where Richard was today? Stuck up even as a kid. Thinks being a Forshay counts for something other than being a farmer. Not that Richard didn't have his good qualities. Most men did." Everett chuckled. "Both daughters married 'beneath them'. What a hoot!"

"TJ's got a nice business with the forge – two buildings at the farm and employing three men. He and Esther have two nice kids, Marcus, whom Roseanne loves, and Lily. TJ pays Augustus rent. Jason can't be counted on to do much with the farm, except grow a few scrawny vegetables. He's a sour man, and poor Shannon's dying. Why is Jason so bitter?"

Everett figured he just couldn't accept who he was. He sighed and wondered why his thoughts were running in this channel? Like a river, thoughts had a way of making their own channel and there was precious little one could do about it. A bald eagle flew overhead, its white crown plainly visible.

"Don't see as many as you used to. Shame."

Something frightened the chickens, and they dashed across the yard – heads bobbing like yo-yos. "Silly birds, not an ounce of sense among the lot of them." He shifted in his chair. "Augustus didn't do much farming these days. Never did now that I think of it. Only enough to call himself a farmer. He was the leader when we were kids. He loved books and talking about them too much to take farming seriously. He's buried even further in them now that Onatah's gone. A good woman... just what Augustus had needed."

Everett had loved books almost as much as Augustus, but he never let them distract his attention from the main business of life.

"Wonderful the way Damon stuck up for Roseanne this morning. A solid man. Not much of a reader, but dependable and smart about farming. Knows a lot about scientific feeding—set up our mechanized milking system. Straightened himself out, too. Just needed a little shove. Goddamn that fool, Dale Royce, and all that garbage about Germans being white. Can't be sure if Jason was being sarcastic or not. What had Aaron Jenkins said about Thomas? '... acting like he's white.' Fools back then and fools now. Never changes. Aaron's long gone. Oldest boy has the farm. Decent fellow. Contributes to the widow's fund. Rotten father... decent son. Apple doesn't necessarily fall close to the tree. What happened to his brother, Derek?" Everett thought hard. "Yes, left the valley ten, maybe fifteen, years after the shootout. Heard he got killed in a barroom brawl – knifed or shot, can't remember which. No loss. Why the hell does anybody care if you're white or black or any other damn color?"

"What are you thinking so seriously about, Dad?"

Everett started at his daughter's voice. "Oh, not much. I guess this atom bomb thing – and memories. I must be getting old."

Rosanne sat down next to him and took his hand.

"You know it terrifies me," she said. "Just one bomb and a whole city wiped out. I keep thinking of the children. They're not the enemy."

"What scares me is what happens next. How easy is it to build one of these things? I wouldn't like to see the Russians get one. I never trusted them like Roosevelt seems to have."

"The President's statement mentioned a commission. Maybe it can keep things from getting out of hand."

"You know as well as I do," he said briskly, "that we Vermonters aren't in the habit of trusting governments to control much of anything. It seems that, like Icarus, we may have flown a little close to the sun."

Roseanne smiled and stroked her father's hand.

"Ah, the Greeks. Lot of wisdom," she said.

She got up and stepped to the edge of the porch. The ridge across the valley looked like the back of a whale. She noted the dip above Augustus's farm. She turned back.

"It ought to be harder to kill so many people."

"Yes, and what that fool Dale said infuriated me."

Roseanne looked pained. "Don't imagine," she said, "that he's the only one around here who thinks that way." She felt a catch in her throat. "Augustus told me what you two did as boys, protecting your friends. It was shortly after Hawk's funeral. He thought I should know."

"It was a long time ago."

"I'm still proud of you."

She sat down again and put her hand on top of his.

"I got a letter from Lizzie the other day. The divorce is now final, and she still loves working on the paper. She sent a collection of short stories to a publisher in New York and told us to keep our fingers crossed."

"And the boys?"

"Francis is someplace on the west coast. I guess that he won't have to go overseas now. Scott is starting at Columbia in a month. Lizzie is a bit worried about him living in New York."

"I feel sorry for Cyrus," Everett said. "He worked hard to support his family."

"Yes, but Lizzie wasn't happy here, and Cyrus wouldn't do anything about it."

"I imagine there was more to it than that. There always is."

"Dad, do you miss Mom terribly?"

Everett glanced at his daughter in surprise. "Yes, every day. Do you?"

"Not as much as I used to." She looked toward the gorge and saw a bird too high to identify. "And I don't miss Hawk as much as I used to."

"That's good."

She got up. "I'm going to get a glass of lemonade. Would you like some?"

"No, thank you."

Everett rested his head against the back of the chair.

"Good," he thought, "not missing Hawk so much. It's no disrespect, no diminishment of her love." The pain from May's death had lessened over the years, and that was all right. "You can't go on suffering forever. So she knew about the shootout. She'll see the letter sooner or later. Doesn't need it the way Damon did—served its purpose. Set him on the right track."

He felt a severe pain in his chest, and his head began to swim. His vision blurred. He saw May's face in front of him – and Tehya's. The two faces merged together. Then he saw Roseanne's face but it seemed like he was under water looking up at her and she was looking down at him. He heard her voice, but it was very far away and growing dimmer. Her face faded as he sank deeper in the water.

"Daddy," Roseanne screamed as she dropped the glass of lemonade. "Daddy!"

Chapter Ten

Roseanne Scudder

(1909 -)

August 9, 1945

Sally, Consuela, and Miss Crenshaw sat in the fourth row. A frail-looking man with wisps of snowy hair sat next to Miss Crenshaw and held her gloved hand. Consuela had telephoned Miss Crenshaw, now Mrs. Lincoln Grinnell, as soon as she finished speaking to Roseanne. They booked rooms at the Overlook Inn (the only place to stay in town) and caught the bus the next day.

Miss Crenshaw had married Linc three years ago – six months after Dorothy died. Roseanne had gone to the wedding. Miss Crenshaw retired a year later - at seventy.

Fifteen Scudders sat in the first two rows. Roseanne held Keith's hand. Ashen-faced and stiff, Howie and Damon were surrounded by their families.

Howie, a captain in the Judge Advocate General's Corps, was stationed in Washington. Frieda, who taught music and gave recitals in Albany, came with her husband, Roland. Their son, Frank, a lieutenant in the army, was still in France. His wife and two children were living with his in-laws in Kentucky. Frieda's daughter, Karen, worked in a munitions factory in New Jersey. Her husband was a marine sergeant in the Pacific theater. Karen had not seen him in over a year. They had one daughter who had come with her to the funeral.

Augustus – with Jason, Shannon, and Martin – sat behind the Scudders. Augustus was crying softly. Disgruntled, Jason had said he had no time for funerals. Augustus ignored him; Shannon told him to hush up.

The Forshays were across the aisle from the Baxters. TJ and Esther brought their two children while Lizzie had borrowed her editor's car to drive up from Barre with Scott.

The remaining pews were nearly filled: with friends from Scudder's Gorge and a smattering of people from neighboring valleys and towns. The closed oak coffin rested on a bier just below the pulpit. At Roseanne's request, the service began with one of Everett's two favorite hymns: Rock of Ages:

> *Rock of ages, cleft for me.*
> *Let me hide myself in thee;*
> *Let the water and the blood,*
> *From thy wounded side which flowed,*
> *Be of sin the double cure;*
> *Save from wrath and make me pure.*

The Reverend McHenry asked the congregation to bow their heads for a moment of silence; he then read the Twenty-Third Psalm:

> *The LORD is my shepherd; I shall not want...*

> *Yea, though I walk through the valley of the shadow of death,*
> *I will fear no evil: for thou art with me; thy rod and thy staff they*
> *comfort me...*

> *I will dwell in the house of the LORD forever.*

Reverend McHenry spoke at length about Everett's life as devoted husband and father, hard-working farmer, one of the founders of the creamery, town councilor longer than anyone could remember, deacon of the First Congregational Church and generous contributor to local charities. He finished by saying that, as everyone present knew as well or better than he, as a loyal friend, Everett Scudder had no equal.

"Everett Scudder now goes to heaven to join his beloved wife, May. Let us pray:

Our Father, who art in heaven, hallowed be thy name..."

The congregation rose to sing Everett's other favorite hymn: Amazing Grace, written by a slave trader turned clergyman:

Amazing grace! How sweet the sound
That saved a wretch like me!
I once was lost, but now am found;
Was blind, but now I see.

Roseanne walked slowly to the coffin and laid her hand on it. She turned to face the congregation. Tears flowed down her cheeks. Her voice caught as she recited a poem that she had written over the last three days:

The light that led us now is gone;
In sorrow, we tremble at the dawn.
The world feels hollow at its core;
Closed tight now is the oaken door.
My father taught us justice to revere,
Not the calumny of men to fear.
When needed, his deeds were bold;
He had a heart of purest gold.
His mind was calm, his counsels sage.
He bowed not to the tumults of the age.
My eyes are veiled in blood and pain.
Dear God, in thy mercy, keep us sane.
My father gave each man his due;
Never was there a friend more true.
Life, I know, continues to flow;
But Everett Scudder, I miss you so.

Roseanne didn't try to stifle her tears. Consuela took Sally's and Julie's hands. Howie and Damon hugged their wives and children. Augustus wiped his eyes with a handkerchief while Shannon gripped his arm. Roseanne bent over and kissed the coffin.

"Goodbye, Daddy," she whispered.

Keith walked his mother up the center aisle. Tears blurred her vision. The Scudders, followed by most of the congregation, filed down the two side aisles, and touched the coffin. Howie, Damon, and the other pallbearers gathered around the coffin. Reverend McHenry stood to one side. Nearing the last few pews, Augustus saw a slender, handsome woman with graying hair standing next to a tall man. Hands clasped, they stood erect and observed the proceedings. Augustus stopped next to their pew.

"Tehya?" he exclaimed, his voice incredulous.

She looked at him and smiled, "Hello, Augustus."

Followed by Reverend McHenry, the pallbearers carried the coffin to the graveyard. Roseanne walked over and placed a white lily on it. After a prayer, the coffin was lowered into the grave next to May's.

Brent had set up a long table in the yard. Sally insisted on preparing a few dishes, but Joseph Trochino provided most of the food. His two waiters met him at the farm after the service. People talked a little about the announcement that morning of the second atom bomb, but mostly they told stories about Everett. Augustus introduced Roseanne to Tehya and her husband, Lawrence.

"Augustus has told me about you. Thank you so much for coming. How did you know?"

"We live in Burlington; at our age, you start reading obituaries. Thomas wanted to come, but he is having health problems. He still lives on the farm near St. Albans, but he doesn't work nearly as much as he used to."

"It's been, let me see," said Augustus, "forty-seven years and you still look like the young woman that ..." He paused, embarrassed, not sure how to proceed, "...teased you and Everett. Thank you for the lie."

Tehya turned to Roseanne. "I hope it doesn't bother you, especially at a time like this, but your father and I shared a puppy love when we were very young." She smiled at her husband, "As Lawrence knows, Everett was the only other love in my life."

"And you were the only other love in my father's life. I am not at all bothered. I am happy that he loved someone like you. My mother would also have been happy. If he knows, he is pleased that you are here today."

"Carl?" asked Augustus tentatively.

"He died last year. He and Thomas worked the farm together. Now two of Carl's children share the property with one of Thomas's children. We had to build two new houses on the property. Carl's youngest is a career officer in the Navy and fought in the Pacific. Thomas has a son in the army who served in Europe.

"I have two daughters: one in Rochester and the younger in Bennington. One is a teacher like her mother, the other a homemaker. Both are married, and I'm a grandmother thrice over.

"Do you have children?" she asked Roseanne.

"I have one who is twelve. His father – my fiancé – died in an accident before he was born. He was Hawk Baxter, Augustus's youngest."

Tehya was silent for a moment; then she impulsively hugged Roseanne.

"Can you and Lawrence stay the night?" asked Roseanne.

"We tried the Inn," said Lawrence, "but all the rooms were taken. We planned to drive back tonight."

"Oh, you mustn't," said Roseanne. "Between the Scudders and the Baxters, we can find you a place to stay. After all these years, you mustn't leave so soon. Come with me; let me introduce you to my brothers."

"That all sounds lovely. Augustus, is that Richard Forshay standing under the elm tree?"

"Yes and just as stuck up as ever."

One morning three days after the funeral, Howie, Damon, and Roseanne drove into town to see Jonathan Ward, Everett's lawyer, and listen to the will. Roseanne had filled her time with Consuela, Julie, and Linc and getting to know Tehya and Lawrence. She also spent a few hours sorting through her father's possessions. It all kept her from thinking how lonely she felt.

The will divided Everett's assets, including the farm, equally among his three children except for modest bequests to his six grandchildren. Damon would have the management of the farm directly under his control and was entitled to receive compensation for his work prior to any division of farm profits. Howie was named executor and Roseanne directed to dispose of Everett's personal belongings.

That was all except, upon concluding the reading, Jonathan handed them each a large manila envelope.

Roseanne walked behind the barn and sat under a large sugar maple. She opened the manila envelope and found a smaller envelope with her name on it and several sheets of paper, some of which were protected by plastic lamination. She opened the small envelope and took out a handwritten letter:

September 1940

My Dearest Roseanne:

This letter will be given to you upon my death. I want to say first how much I love you, Howie, Damon, and all my wonderful grandchildren. I have been blessed to have such an exuberant, caring, and honest family. You all have been the joy of my life.

I have directed Jonathan Ward to give you the original of Philomena's letter and a handwritten transcription by my father (using modern script and language). I had both these laminated and my father's version typed. You have all three, but your brothers only have the typed versions.

I thought that, as a teacher, the originals would hold the most interest for you.

Until now, only Damon (in your generation) has seen Philomena's letter. I showed it to him the night you and he had the run-in over Hawk. I felt that he needed to be shocked out of his blind feelings of prejudice. It apparently worked, and I am terribly proud of him for vanquishing those feelings.

You, of all people, did not need to see this letter any sooner as you have always been imbued with the sense of responsibility and morality that we Scudders need to pass from generation to generation. When you became engaged to Hawk, I told you of your Indian blood, but thought that the letter could somehow get in the way, like the pea under the Princess's mattress.
I was probably wrong.

In the intervening years, I didn't see how the letter could help you in any way. Again, maybe I was wrong.

I have known for some time that Augustus Baxter told you the story of what we like to call "the shootout." In a sense, Augustus and I were foolish to act independently. Someone might have been hurt – or killed – because of our bravado. Anyway, Wiley Fitzgerald, God rest his soul, did most of the shooting.

I also know that Augustus told you about Tehya. She was a wonderful girl. I loved her – insanely, I thought at the time – but it was a young love. The intense, abiding, passionate love that I felt for your Mother was, in addition to my family and farm, the core of my existence, and will remain so for what is left of my life. Starry-eyed as it may sound, especially from an old man, I loved your Mother from the first moment I saw her in the library. This was over two years after the Zaltanas had moved away.

I hope that you will again allow that kind of love into your life.

Every generation of our family has seen this letter from the time it was written by your ancestor Philomena. She apparently planned to marry her Abenaki come hell or high water. He was your great-great-great grandfather, and the source of your Indian blood.

Show it to Keith at your discretion.

The letter refers to a massacre that occurred in 1799 and that was, apparently, precipitated by Philomena's father, Lucas Scudder. I have done some research. Two letters in the town archives, which you can easily find by looking under the early land grants, sketchily mention a raid on an Indian village in the fall of 1799.

The archives also contain a water-damaged diary of one Owen Harding, one of the town's founders and an Elder in the church, which refers in vague terms to the cause of the raid, the conduct of the settlers and the truth of what happened to "the Scudder girl." I could find nothing else.

Our family has a burden and responsibility that we must always be cognizant of.

I love you and shall hope to watch over you from wherever I am.

Your loving and devoted father,
Everett

Roseanne put her father's letter back in the envelope and sat looking out over the pasture for a moment. Her eyes strayed involuntarily toward the gorge. Then she took a deep breath and removed the sheets of paper. The original letter was in Eighteenth Century script. She started to read the typed, modernized version.

December 4, 1799

To my beloved sister, Carrie,

I now know for sure that I am carrying Susuph's baby and am afraid of what will happen to me. I am afraid also for the baby. You must promise to take care of the baby if something should happen to me.

I also know, from you and others, more of what happened and that Sean Reynolds was following Susuph and me. I don't know how Susuph could have failed to notice; he was so adept in the forest. What Sean said was either a lie or the confused ramblings of a disturbed person. We all know that the poor creature is not right in his mind. I pray that God protect all such as he though, in this instance, a terrible wrong has been committed. The damage can never be repaired. I have lost the man I loved more than life itself.

You and I talked often of the blessings of love and the intimate relations between a man and a woman. Know, my dear Carrie, that I found such love … only to lose it in a cauldron of anger and hatred. Know also that Susuph never attacked me. I made love with him because I wanted to. That fateful and awful day, I tripped and fell down a hill. I don't remember anything after that until I awoke in my bed.

I hope that in your life you will find such a love as blessed Susuph and myself. I so longed to be his wife. I know now that I will never marry.

How could anyone believe a diseased man like Sean? His condition has been known since childhood. What kinds of people massacre an innocent village on the word of an idiot? How could Father have done such a thing? Why did he not wait to hear what I might have said upon my recovery? Help me to understand. No, I shall never understand. Or forgive.

Why does Father hate the Indians so much? What else, other than hate, could have impelled him to act so precipitously, without trying to ascertain the truth? I saw it often enough – that sneer whenever he spoke of the Abenaki – but did not pay enough heed. What have they ever done to him?

I want you to understand very clearly that I was in love with Susuph and planned to marry him. I had hoped for Father's blessing, but I would have married Susuph without it. If necessary, I would have gone to live in his village. I visited the village once and liked it. Everyone, especially his Mother, was hospitable. One old man was not, but he had his reasons, and I would have won him over.I did not know about the baby in September. Had I known, my dear sister, of course I would have told you. We are the closest of sisters… and friends.

I have not spoken sooner because of my fear of what Father might do. He does not want the settlement to know the truth. It must, nevertheless, be known within our family. Father has committed a terrible crime. God's justice is relentless. Father will pay the price for his wickedness. Let my letter be as a trumpet call to the Scudders to follow henceforth the path of righteousness. Let us judge all men for who they are and not by the color of their skin. May future generations of Scudders learn from and never repeat such a crime.

I sound too much like a preacher. You are my loving sister. My memory lingers on the joyous times we have shared. I will cherish your love all my life, whether it be long or short.

I do not know if I want to live without Susuph. Who would take me to wife? Not Seth. Nor do I care. Other than you, I have no one. I do not want to be a burden to you.

Keep this letter and give it to my child when he is old enough to understand. Instruct him to pass it on to his children and so forth down the generations.

If others discover the truth, so be it. If they condemn Father, it will be what he deserves.

I shall give you this letter when the time is right, or I shall hide it so that you find it at my death.

Your loving sister,
Philomena

Roseanne put Philomena's letter back in the manila envelope. She felt a connection across the years with this girl who had suffered as she had – although from different causes. How intense must have been her pain. It might so easily have been avoided. So much pain in this world could be avoided. She sat for a while looking at the valley. She suddenly remembered the musket ball that Hawk had found when they were walking in the woods. It might not have been just some hunter.

She walked along the Forshay Road toward the Farrell place, which had once belonged to the Baxters. Had the family atoned for Lucas Scudder's crime? Only God – assuming one existed – could make that determination. The family had tried; she could say that much. Her father had proved that.

Did God exist?—an open question given recent events. She had read, with growing fury, of the slaughter of Jews and other innocents. How could God permit such atrocities? Was God indifferent to what humanity did? If so, what was the point of God?

This atom bomb was too destructive to comprehend. Yes, the Japanese had started the war, and we had to defeat them. She was clear about that. They, no more than the Germans, could be allowed to ride roughshod over other countries. But wiping out cities with the wave of your hand?

Someone was going to have to put that genie back in its bottle, but she wasn't convinced the politicians would have the courage or the foresight. It might be too tempting, that kind of power. Maybe the religious leaders or this commission the President was proposing? Maybe ordinary citizens?

What if other countries get the bomb, she could hear her brother saying? What about the peaceful uses, Logan Forshay would argue?

She shook her head to clear it. Right now, she had something else she needed to do. She walked back to the house. Sally, who worked a few hours a day now and spent the rest of her time painting, was preparing lunch. Roseanne asked her if she knew where Keith was.

"Down cleaning the barn with Sandy, I think."

"Good. We won't be having lunch. I'm going to make a couple of sandwiches and take him to the river for a picnic."

"That is one of the best ideas you've had in a long time. Take these pears with you as well, and a jug of lemonade."

Roseanne drove across the old bridge and out the North Valley Road. She smiled when she and Keith picked a spot by the stream. Just a few yards away, she had talked to Consuela years ago - hoping to kindle in her an interest marrying Everett. Consuela had been startled by a water snake. She spread out a blanket and opened the wicker basket. They ate in silence for a few minutes. The last time she'd had a picnic by the river was with Lloyd – over five years ago. Germany had just invaded France.

"Keith, I want to tell you about your father and your grandfather, Everett."

"I know who my father was; you've told me lots about him. And I knew Grandfather Everett."

"I realize that, but now I want to tell you some things you don't know - about both of them.

"I want to tell you what kind of man your father was and what kind of man he would hope you would grow up to be. And I'm going to tell you a story about something your two grandfathers did when they were boys about your age."

She began by describing what a wonderful man Hawk was: talented, hard-working, honest, funny, and kind. He had started the forge with TJ and laid the foundations for the successful business it was today. She laughed when she mentioned that TJ had beaten his father at swinging the hammer.

"No one is as strong as Uncle TJ."

"At least not in Scudder's Gorge."

She poured Keith a second glass of lemonade. The stream murmured as it slid over rocks. Two dragonflies hovered in the air, fluttering their diaphanous wings.

"Your father was angry for a time because he had been discriminated against as an Indian. But he conquered his anger, which took courage and determination. You must be just as proud of your heritage from Grandmother Onatah as from the Scudders and Baxters. In fact, you are one sixty-fourth Abenaki on the Scudder side."

She told him about Everett and Augustus's friendship with the Indian family, the Zaltanas, who used to live on the old farm that was now part of the Farrell place.

"Remember the nice lady that came with her husband to Grandfather's funeral. She was Tehya Zaltana. Her brother, Thomas, was best friends with your grandfathers."

She talked about the shootout, and how Everett and Augustus, although a bit foolhardy, had stood up for their friend and his family against prejudice and violence.

"Do you remember old Wiley Fitzgerald? He used to come over for dinner occasionally. He died a few years ago. He kind of saved the day."

Keith vaguely remembered Wiley. Roseanne mentioned that the Zaltanas moved away a couple of years later. She did not mention Everett's love for Tehya nor Philomena's letter. There would be time enough for Keith to learn about the massacre, the little that was known, and the responsibility that the Scudders bore to see that such a thing – or anything remotely like it – never happened again – at least not in this valley.

They sat quietly for a few minutes. It was a warm day with no breeze. Bees were gathering pollen. The valley was at peace. The river flowed gently, rippling and flashing like diamonds. Keith asked if he could go wading. Roseanne flinched but said,

"Yes. But let me go with you. We'll need to stay close to the edge."

They took off their shoes and socks and stepped into the river. The icy water shocked them as it swirled around their ankles and calves. She stopped him from wading out further when the water got to just below his knees. She was careful to stay downstream from him. Keith looked at her slyly, then bent over and suddenly splashed her. She splashed him back, and a fierce water fight was underway. Their clothes soaked, they climbed out and warmed themselves in the sun.

As they drove back through town, Keith spotted Lloyd McHenry walking along Cedar Street.

"There's Reverend McHenry. I think he's a very nice man."

Roseanne glanced at Keith.

"You may just be right."

Epilogue

November 14 – 15, 1969

Lloyd drove Roseanne to the airport in Burlington. She had already flown a number of times (once when she prevailed upon Lloyd to take a spring vacation in Florida), but the idea still excited her. The forecast called for a cold weekend, even in Washington, so she had packed a heavy sweater and was wearing the wool coat that Lloyd had given her for Christmas two years ago.

She didn't like missing a day of classes, but Anita Jennings, who had retired a few years ago, was an excellent substitute. The children were excited about Thanksgiving. They would probably spend a good part of the day decorating the classroom with cutout-paper turkeys, pilgrims, and Native Americans. If Roseanne knew Anita, there would also be drawings of the first Thanksgiving plastered everywhere – and a peace sign drawn on the blackboard, probably by Sandy's daughter Natasha who was clearly the budding artist in this year's third grade.

Natasha was the fifth Scudder – fourth of her generation – to pass through Roseanne's classroom. She counted on one more (Genevieve's youngest) before she retired. Apart from not seeing him and Meg enough, her main regret about Keith living in New York was that she would not be teaching her two exuberant grandchildren.

"Don't smoke any pot," Lloyd whispered in her ear as she lined up to board the plane.

How could she have guessed what an incredible husband Lloyd would turn out to be – not least in bed? They still desired each other after close to twenty-four years. A case of pent-up demand, she liked to say.

"A la the post-war spending boom" was his invariable reply.

She looked out at the tarmac as the turbo prop rolled toward the runway. She chuckled, remembering Lloyd's seventieth birthday party at Napoli last year and all the innuendo and sexual jokes. Her generation was not as prudish as their offspring assumed. At least not in Scudder's Gorge. How could they be, growing up around farm animals?

What had surprised her most was his sense of humor, which grew (and became more ribald) by the year. She loved the one he told at the party about Adam and Eve being expelled from the Garden of Eden. Feeling sorry for the despondent pair, God grants them two consolation prizes. The first, God says, is the ability to pee standing up. Who wants it? Adam jumps up and down,

"I do. I do. Oh please."

"Okay," God replies and turns to Eve,

"You get multiple orgasms."

It brought the house down. Good thing he was already the retired pastor of the First Congregational.

She leaned back in her seat as the engines revved and the plane thrust forward. She loved the moment of takeoff as the nose lifted and she felt herself airborne. The plane banked, and she gazed at the bare trees of Battery Park. How long ago it had been when she walked in that park planning how to tell Forest Tucker that she was pregnant. Life had been good more often than not. They flew down the center of the lake, and she watched in awe as the Adirondacks slid by. Then a mosaic of farms, villages, roads, and lakes slipped past like the slow unveiling of an Egyptian scroll.

Three lovers in her life and two were wonderful men. How lucky can one girl get? She thought of Hawk from time to time but no longer with pain – only a vague sadness for what he had missed. She opened her book, but the plane's motion and the engines' droning made her sleepy. She dozed off. They came in over northern New Jersey and followed the Hudson toward the Statue of Liberty. She was invariably thrilled by the Manhattan skyline and wondered if the mayor paid the airlines to fly this route. How could you not love New York after seeing this? They banked steeply left, crossed Brooklyn and landed at LaGuardia.

Keith met her at Penn Station. They took a late afternoon train. It was growing dark as they emerged from the tunnel and sped across the marshlands toward Newark.

"What did you say to your partners at that high-toned law firm about where you're going?"

"Nothing. What they don't know won't hurt them."

"Just hope you don't appear on television."

"The odds are with us, Mom."

She took a sideways glance at her handsome son who had so much of the Scudders and Baxters in his features and carriage. He had Hawk's prominent nose, high cheekbones, and steady gaze. His skin had a tinge of the Abenaki copper. He delighted in winning the tanning race on family summer vacations.

"I am so proud of you for coming with me to the march," she said and lightly touched his arm.

"Just that never-ending Scudder burden of responsibility. Maybe you should have waited to show me Philomena's letter until either my tennis game improved or I moved on to golf."

She laughed. His humor made her think of Augustus, who had retained his irreverent wit right up to his death six years ago. Keith had played varsity tennis at Dartmouth and abhorred golf.

"I think of it differently," she said. "Lucas Scudder, however unwittingly, bequeathed us a moral compass. Our determination not to be like him and to atone for his crime has served the Scudders well."

"Meaning this little expedition reminds you of the shootout?"

Roseanne chuckled.

"I guess in a way though I shudder at the comparison. Your grandfathers put their lives at risk to stand up for a friend and fight prejudice. We're safely participating in a broadly based protest. It's not as personal, although at least one aspect is the same. I can smell the racial thing in the air. The Vietnamese, like the Japanese, are..."

"Not white."

"Precisely, but even without that, the whole thing sickens me, especially the bombing which has merely shifted from North Vietnam to Laos. I doubt the North Vietnamese or the Viet Cong are angels, but being communists shouldn't make them our implacable enemies. That's so narrow-minded."

"Pretty simplistic, I would agree. There should be more ways of distinguishing between our friends and enemies. The governments we've supported in South Vietnam are hardly models of democracy."

"There's no easy answer," Roseanne said, "but what I want now is for the war to stop and for my voice, no matter how small, to be heard."

The lights of small towns and cities flashed by. They bought sandwiches for dinner. The train swayed gently into Philadelphia, Wilmington, and

Baltimore. In Washington, they took a taxi to a church that Keith's friend said would welcome marchers.

"Funny," said Roseanne as she unrolled a borrowed sleeping bag next to a young woman with long, auburn hair. "I've lived all my life in the country, and this is the first time I've slept in one of these."

"You're going to love it," said the young woman. She was wearing a white tee shirt, faded jeans, and a headband with the Yin Yang symbol in the center. "It's so great to have older people here."

None of the sixty or so people jammed into the church basement seemed ready for sleep. The atmosphere was electric, and the buzz of excited conversations fluttered in the room like hummingbirds. Bowls of chips and a coffee urn stood on a table against the wall.

A young man with wire-rimmed glasses, blond hair, and reddish peach fuzz on his chin and jaw strummed a guitar and sang a well-known Bob Dylan song. A few voices joined in.

Come senators, congressmen
Please heed the call
Don't stand in the doorway
Don't block up the hall
For he that gets hurt
Will be he who has stalled
There's a battle outside
And it is ragin'.
It'll soon shake your windows
And rattle your walls
For the times they are a-changin'.

"Where are you from?" Roseanne asked the young woman.

"Gettysburg College in Pennsylvania. I came down with my boyfriend.

He went for a walk. What about you?"

"I live in northern Vermont in a farming community called Scudder's Gorge. I'm here with my son who lives in New York City. He's also around someplace. I'm Roseanne McHenry."

"Your son? How cool – a family of protesters. My name's Judith, but my friends call me Cherry."

"Why is that?"

"Because I'm so obviously not."

Cherry laughed softly. Roseanne tried to think of a response. Julie Crenshaw would have loved this girl. Hard to believe that Julie had been gone for fifteen years and that Consuela was getting well up there.

"Are you also from a family of protesters?" asked Roseanne.

"Oh no, not me. I'm the black sheep. My brother goes to – ugh – business school and wears skinny ties. My mother is a housewife who doesn't think beyond dinner. My father thinks the only good hippie is a dead one. He would have a fit if he knew I was here. To him, the protestors are all Commies, and the only thing worse is the PLO. He worships Richard Nixon and Golda Meir."

Cherry laughed again, and her eyes lit up.

"Are you starting to get the picture?"

"I think so, but then, it's hard to be in favor of the PLO."

"Oh, that's not what I meant. They're bastards, but the Israelis aren't all so wonderful either. I worked on a kibbutz last summer in a program arranged through my parents' synagogue. You wouldn't believe some of the racism, and the men were such chauvinists. All they wanted to do was get in my pants."

Cherry patted Roseanne on the arm.

"Only one succeeded."

The next morning Roseanne got in line for coffee and drank two cups in quick succession. She hadn't slept more than a few hours. Her back was stiff, and her hips ached.

"Now I know why they invented beds," she said to Keith.

They washed up in the restrooms and stowed their things in a pew. They would stop back on their way to the train. Before leaving, Roseanne sought out Cherry.

"I so enjoyed meeting you. Young people today lead such interesting lives. I've rarely set foot out of Vermont. Good luck – and I have a sneaking suspicion that your family is proud of you."

Keith and Roseanne followed the crowd toward the Capitol. The police were out in force. Roseanne was astounded by the sheer number of people. There were thousands, mostly young; but her generation was not absent. The mood was bright and upbeat. The cold air was redolent with hope.

"I know that we're here for a very serious purpose," she said to Keith, "but this is also such fun."

She admired the myriad banners, signs, and posters. She especially liked two signs being held up by identical twin girls who looked to be college students.

In bold, brightly colored letters, they read:

THE NAKED TRUTH: WAR IS NOT GOOD FOR THE PLANET

and

MAKE LOVE, NOT WAR

Knots of counter demonstrators huddled together. Some silently held signs, others jeered. Roseanne nudged Keith and pointed to one sign that read:

PUT VICTORY BACK INTO OUR VOCABULARY

"They have every right to be here," said Rosanne, "but I think they're missing the point. Vietnam is not about victory; it's about morality and wisdom."

Keith took her arm and bent toward her ear.

"Mom, I've always said this world would be a better place if you were President."

They both laughed. A volunteer marshal wearing a blue and white armband waved them to a place where they could wait their turn to join the march. They inched forward in a sea of people like runners anxious to start a race. Getting to the head of the crowd, they started down Pennsylvania Avenue proudly holding aloft a banner that Roseanne had made with the help of Sandy and Genevieve's kids. Surrounded by a border of entwined flowers was written in bold colors:

STOP THE BOMBING